Once Were Friends

A Novel

Mark Victor Young

Copyright

Once Were Friends by Mark Victor Young

Published by **Hanton House Creative Media** in London, Ontario, Canada.

Second print edition November 2014

ISBN: 978-0-9938558-1-8

Enquiries: HHCreativeMedia@icloud.com

Cover Designed by Christina Young at http://christinalorraineyoung.com/

Acknowledgments

This book could not exist without the help that many people gave me with one or more of the versions of the story. Thanks to Sharon Johnson and Marion Johnson who provided valuable feedback on an early draft, as well as key suggestions which shaped the ending and the beginning, respectively. Thanks to Margaret Sharzer and (posthumously) to Lion Sharzer for their careful reading and shared impressions. Thanks to Robert Chazz Chute and Brian Henry for all their advice and very thorough edits of two different drafts.

Many thanks to my family for their love and support always as well as their help with this novel. Cherry Young and Steve Nayak-Young shared their comments and had multiple discussions on the story with me. Bruce Young and Vic Young spent hours going over all the business and corporate stuff with me as well as Vic's careful proofreading of more than one draft. Christina Young is my constant reader, first impression, reality check, ego booster, and cover artist *extraordinaire,* as well as the love of my life.

I am also grateful to the many teachers, librarians and writers who have inspired and encouraged my writing over the years. You are all guardians and champions of the written word.

"This story shall the good man teach his son;
And Crispin Crispian shall ne'er go by,
From this day to the ending of the world,
But we in it shall be remembered...
And gentlemen in England now abed
Shall think themselves accursed they were not here,
And hold their manhoods cheap, whiles any speaks
That fought with us upon Saint Crispin's day."

Henry V, William Shakespeare, © Penguin Books 1968

"Business is commonly defined as an activity in which individuals, at the risk of loss, seek profit. Shakespeare understood how important it was to take advantage of a business opportunity, to embrace fortune when it presented itself."

Shakespeare on Management, © Jay M. Shafritz, Harper Collins 1962

Once Were Friends

Chapter One

They were pinned down under heavy fire in the empty shell of what had looked like a partially burned-out general store. Hal Mercer crouched below a windowless frame on the second floor, listening for footsteps on the stairs. Damn! Now his mask was fogging up. He tried to wipe it with one finger, hearing shouts in the smoky air as the enemy crawled up their unprotected flank, the heavy *Phut! Phut! Phut!* of sniper fire covering their approach. Where the hell did he go from here?

Hal glanced out the window. Abandoned car wrecks covered with spray paint lined the street in front of the building, stacks of tires lay toppled at the curb, obscure suggestions of movement over there told him that enemy positions were advancing along the tree line to his right, and then the sound of two slugs slamming into the window frame next to his ear made him duck back under the ledge. Raising his gun over the ledge for a moment, he squeezed off a round in the general direction of the trees.

"Archie?" he shouted off into the darkness to his left.

"Yes, mon capitaine?"

"You see those guys coming up by the trees?"

A pause. "Yes, sir."

"Can you create a diversion on your side to draw their fire?"

"I'm on the case, sir."

Archie was playing some kind of game, obviously. He wasn't this good at taking orders and he also hated Hal intensely. He would be more likely to stab Hal in the back than cover it for him.

"Go ahead, then," Hal yelled.

Then a shuffling noise from the next room and several shots followed by a wet *SLAP*, and Archie Bishop's voice shouting, "I'm hit, I'm hit! They got me, captain!"

Hal's heart was pounding in his chest as he reviewed his options. With Archie out, he was likely all alone here on the second floor, with who knew how many of his division gone. Going outside would be suicide, as he could see from the figures advancing on all sides, but staying here only delayed the inevitable.

Then there was a squeak from behind him, and the sound of a careful footstep on the stairs, and Hal, keeping low under the window, crawled to the darkened corner at the far end of the room, his weapon pointed at the top of the stairs. The dark shape of a head bobbed into view, eyes trained along the barrel of a gun that scanned left and right like a periscope on an emerging submarine. Then more of the body came into view: an absurdly tall, hunched-over figure with sticking-out ears and ridiculous fatigues—it was Johnson from Accounting.

"Die, pencil-pusher," said Hal as he squeezed the trigger, firing a single round into Johnson's midsection.

"Ow!" said Johnson. "I'm hit."

The adrenaline rush was amazing! Oh, well. Nothing left to lose. Hal scurried to the window and started firing at anything and everything that moved. "Banzai! This one's for Archie." He caught someone hurrying across the street in front of him and quickly fired a couple of rounds in that direction. A woman's voice called out, "I'm hit," just as he caught sight of the tiny yellow orb coming at him, seemingly growing larger as it descended along its shallow arc, and exploding on contact with his visor.

Shaking his head from the surprising force of the impact, he couldn't quite shake off the darkness of the thick paint obscuring his view.

Hal shouted, "I'm hit," and sank back blindly onto the floor to wait for the whistle. He had been killed yet again, but he couldn't help smiling. Who knows what it was doing for morale, but he was having the most fun he'd had in ages. Why had it taken him so long to discover the joy of paint ball? He felt good about the way the Senior Management team rallied around him, even if they had lost two of their three engagements. What the heck, at worst it was something different for everyone to do on a weekend that was on the company tab.

Okay, sure, he wasn't that "easy come, easy go" about it. He had spent weeks planning this event and was desperately hoping everyone was having fun. And morale simply had to improve; it couldn't get much worse. It was a tough time for the company now and if he was going to achieve what he wanted—no, scratch that—what he had to achieve, then he had to make some changes for the better.

Was he the only one who worried about this stuff?

Right. Sniff, sniff. It's lonely at the top.

* * *

"Okay, troops. Let's bring it in," said Bill Fluellen, the section manager, as they were milling around in the lobby. Pete Malden rolled his eyes. Another management speech. Didn't he get enough of this during the work week? He looked over at Fluellen. His boss was an imposing figure even when he wasn't dressed in military fatigues. His thick red hair and salt and paprika goatee was flecked with sweat and sawdust.

"We did great out there," he was saying. "We worked together and really stuck it to those wallies from the IT crew. Malden and Bardolph, way to cover each other. Where's Bardolph?"

"Right here, sir. Ten-hut!" Randy Bardolph snapped to attention behind his boss in a mock salute.

"At ease. You were quite the drama queen with your little 'death scene' out there."

"Sorry, sir. Next time I give up my life for you in battle, I'll try to go with more dignity."

"Excellent. Bottom line, we came together as a team and defended our position despite overwhelming odds. As your commanding officer, I was damn proud to lead you onto the field. That's the last exercise of the day, so I'll just say enjoy the rest of your weekend, and I'll see you back at the office Monday morning."

Pete sat on a low bench against the wall and covered his nose with his sleeve as the pervasive combined aroma of stale sweat, cigar smoke and something moldy mingled with the fresh body odors filling the room. Randy, Amy, and Arthur sat or stood next to him.

"Pete, I love the blue hair," said Amy, smoothing her own hair behind both ears with her fingertips. "You should really keep it like that." Her dark hair was in a short bob kept away from her face. She had a mostly slim and petite frame, so her navy sweatshirt with the George Brown College logo hung a bit too loosely from her shoulders, but her curvy hips filled out her dark olive army pants so she didn't just look skinny.

He liked being able to see this casual side of her. Even on dress down day she wasn't like this, preferring business casual to jeans and a T-shirt. Those army pants were driving him wild. He wondered if they could somehow make paint ball a weekly thing.

Pete caught her eye and then ran his fingers through the blue patch of hair and looked away. "Yeah, thanks. My version of a battle scar. 'It's a far better thing I do than I have ever done', one life to give for the department and all that."

"So what are we supposed to feel now? A stronger sense of team cohesion?" said Randy. "Or do you find yourself with even more questions about the people you work with?"

"Yeah," said Arthur. "Like what was with those IT geeks who had their own guns?"

"Scary," said Pete. "And some were like automatics or something."

"I have a picture in my mind," said Randy, applying two fingers to his right temple and closing his eyes, his mouth pursed in a little smirk. He was what you might call portly, but with a dignified air and busy hands with long fingers that were animated when he talked and drumming or tapping when he was listening. He cleared his throat. "They are here every weekend, keeping track of their 'kill-shots,' have a full set of military fatigues—no offence, Amy—have no girlfriends, live in their parents' basements which smell exactly like this place, and they're each composing the ultimate online game to ensure their places in history."

Amy put a hand on her hip. "The only reason I have these army pants is because they were in fashion for about 10 minutes when I was in grade 12, and this is the only place I've had a chance to wear them since then, and when's the last time you had a girlfriend, Randy?"

"Touché," said Randy.

"I think you make a cute military chick," said Pete.

"Thank-you, Peter." She smiled at him.

"Yeah, I was going to say that, too, Amy," said Arthur. "I noticed the same thing."

Pete looked at his rival. Shit, that's all he needed. Not that Arthur was much competition. He was tall and thin with a generally hunched posture that looked a bit like he was trying to brace himself for impact. Inexplicably, he was wearing a blue oxford cloth button down and beige cotton chinos, as if he were off to a college mixer of yesteryear, albeit they were now tie-dyed with paint splotches. Did they have college mixers in the Summer of Love?

Amy gave Arthur a suspicious look. "There's no way I'm doing your reconciliation for you next week so you can forget it."

"No, I wouldn't, I just..." said Arthur.

Randy patted Arthur on the shoulder. "Of course you wouldn't, Arthur. Did anybody catch sight of our fearless leader? He was supposed to be here today."

"Hal? No, but I would love to know who shot him," said Pete.

"We'll hear about it Monday, I'm sure," said Amy.

"I'm surprised we didn't get a speech from the little general," said Randy.

"Which unit just squared off with the S&M team?" asked Arthur, using their secret code for the Senior Management group.

"I think it was Marketing, and you know they'd lie down and play dead rather than smoke the big bosses," said Pete, leaning back against the wall and folding his arms across his chest. "They know which side their bread is buttered." He had a slim build and wore black jeans and a long sleeve red t-shirt with a Spider-Man symbol surrounded by webs on the front. His blue eyes and long lashes were the occasional envy of the women in his life, but his normally dark and not blue hair was short and messy-on-purpose.

"They're smart. You've got to learn to play politics with the management types if you ever want to become one." Amy made a nose plugging gesture and craned her neck to see over the crowd. "Geez, it smells. Is that line getting any shorter? I'd really like to get out of here."

"I know," said Pete. "I feel like the smell is in my mouth now. I might just need a cold beer to counteract it."

* * *

"So whose idea was it to do this whole team-building paint ball thing, anyway?" said Arthur as they sat around a table at *The Fletcher's Quiver* Pub. They had a booth to the right of the bar, slightly toward the back. Pete surveyed the room and the various Robin Hood artifacts above their heads.

"Well, what else can you think of that's new around the office?" said Randy.

"Yeah, I know Hal is the new CEO, but do you really think it was his idea?"

"Of course it is. When you're the new guy, you have to come in and piss on the bushes, mark your territory," said Randy. "This is just one of many new things still to come, and not all of them will be good, just wait."

"But it was his father's company," said Arthur. "Why would he want to change things so much? I mean, doesn't that reflect poorly on his dad?"

"More likely he wants it to reflect well on him," said Pete.

"Yes, our boy does have a reputation to live down," said

Randy. "He was the biggest shit disturber of all of us when he worked the floor with Pete and me."

"Wow," said Arthur.

Randy and Pete exchanged an uncomfortable glance, remembering somebody was missing. A year earlier, they would have been here with Hal, talking about the very people he was probably out for drinks with right now.

Thursday nights after work were what Hal had dubbed "group therapy" sessions at the local watering hole. There were always five to ten of them from the office, a revolving door of old pros, new hires who looked promising and the core group of Hal, Pete and Randy. Hal would get Randy going about something and then he would hold court while Hal bought a round of *B-52s* or *Sexes on the Beach* or something and hit on the waitresses. Pete would draw pictures of the senior managers or supervisors and they would end up eating chicken wings for their dinner around 10 o'clock and then close out the bar. Pete and Randy would stumble onto the subway and Hal would grab a taxi going the other way, often with female companionship in tow.

For about the last six months it had been just Pete and Randy. After Arthur had joined their section, he had come out once in a while, but their get-togethers had become less frequent since Hal had ascended the top of the org chart. The dynamic was somewhat flat without him.

"Yeah," said Pete. "And before he surprised everyone and came to work with us, he did the whole life of leisure, rich kid, country club. We heard all the stories, believe me."

Randy nodded agreement while he finished a sip of his martini. "My uncle golfed at his club and knew him well. Hal would spend all day on the golf course. An excellent golfer, I'm told."

14

"I'll bet he was a hit with the ladies," said Amy. "With that rock star hair and those dark eyes… mmm, yummy."

"You have a woody for our CEO?" said Pete. "Ewww. Now I know how you plan to get to the top."

"He can heighten my, um, future prospects any time." Amy smiled at all of them.

"Quite," said Randy. "But you notice the rock star hair was gone before the board meeting when they voted on his coronation? And he actually went out and bought his first suit. Our boy Hal has really grown up."

"I'm sure he had his suit and haircut before the funeral," said Pete. The others all nodded and found it was a good time to have a sip of their drinks and inspect their surroundings. Pete looked down at the Robin Hood caricature he'd been doodling on a spare bar mat, picked it up and shook it to dry the ink. "But I'll give you this: he was the laziest one of any of us on the fifteenth floor."

"Hear, hear," said Randy. He looked at his watch. "Well, I think it's time I moved on. Do you still need a ride?" He touched Arthur's arm.

"Yeah," said Arthur, sucking back the last of his beer.

Randy indicated the half full glasses in front of them. "Are you guys staying on?"

"I'm just going to finish this beer," said Pete.

"Me, too," said Amy.

"Right. See you Monday." Randy waved and walked to the front door and out, followed closely by Arthur.

Pete smiled and had a casual sip of his drink. "Sorry, I didn't mean to break up the party."

"You didn't," said Amy. "It was just one of those pauses in the conversation. And I think Randy was realizing he sounded a little full of himself."

"Doesn't he always?"

"Let's see how you're coming along with Robin Hood.

Hey, pretty good likeness of Hal, there. Is he an anti-Robin? The rich stealing from the poor?"

"Isn't that what the rich always do? No, I just felt like putting his head on a Robin Hood body. Inspired by my surroundings."

Amy nodded. "It's really good."

"Thanks. So what did you think of today, really?"

"I liked it. As corny as it sounds, it does build team spirit. It lets us have a little fun and see a different side of the people we work with, and I would never have tried it otherwise."

"Yeah, I guess so. But requiring us to give up most of our Saturday for a work function kinda bugs me."

"I work plenty of Saturdays as it is."

"Yeah, but that's different. It's voluntary. I don't know, it just rubs me the wrong way. Do I really want to socialize with the people I work with? Don't I see them enough with, what, 45% of my waking hours spent at work already?"

"Should I be offended?"

"I didn't mean you, and you know it."

"Hey, you could've got a doctor's note."

"I know. Ignore me, I'm just lipping off. So what do you have planned for tonight? Any hot date on the horizon?"

"A hot date with my laundry is all."

"What, no boyfriend for the great Amy Quick, after giving Randy a hard time this afternoon over his lack of female companionship?"

"I don't think Randy craves female companionship. And no, neither of us has a boyfriend."

"Whaaat? You think Randy's gay? Just because he doesn't have a girlfriend? Does that make me gay, too?"

"No, with you I can't see it. But Randy has a quality, as

16

they say." She paused and looked towards the door. "He never really talks about his social life, does he?"

"I, let me think… Who did he go on vacation with that time? Down south?"

"My point exactly. A friend is all he said."

"All right, maybe. I don't know. So what if he is?"

"I just like to ride him a little bit. See if I can shake his unflappable reserve."

"But you're not going to cause any embarrassing scenes? I prefer 'don't ask, don't tell,' if we could just keep it at that."

"Oh, I'm not going to out him, don't worry. Now what have you drawn there?"

"Oh, this." He shook the bar mat dry again and showed her the second figure.

She took it and peered at it while holding it to face the light. "What is that? Is that Randy as a cat?"

"That's Randy as a player in Cats."

"Oh, I get it. A Broadway musical." She smiled and put it back down on the table.

"Yes, I guess you've poisoned my mind now, and I will never be able to think of him without thinking that."

"You know what they say about homophobes…"

"No, I don't. And I don't want to know. Not that I think that way. I'm fine with it."

Amy nodded and sipped her drink down to the ice cubes.

"So what happened with, I think his name was Joey, or Joe?"

"What?"

"The old boyfriend? Now no longer."

"Oh, yeah. Well, I guess we were both so busy with work, we were just seeing each other less and less. I'm still doing the night school classes, so it was hard to even get a free night that we could get together. So I said let's quit it and save ourselves a painful break-up."

"Right. That's grounds for a painful break-up right there."

"He was okay. Relieved, almost. We both realized it wasn't going anywhere, I think."

"You think."

"You don't know Joe. He works longer hours than I do."

"Mmm."

"Well, it's getting to be that time." She looked around for a clock. "My dirty clothes beckon."

"Yeah, I guess I'll get going, too. Where are you parked?" He shimmied down to the end of the bench and stood.

"Right out front," she said, standing. "Where are you?"

"Not far." They walked around the front of the bar and out the main door to the sidewalk. Pete pointed back down the road towards the *Paint War!* building. "Back the way we came. About a block back, there. The red one."

"Okay, well, see you Monday." She smiled and squinted into the light.

"See you Monday. Right." He did a sort of wave, and half turned towards his car.

Amy produced a key fob from her purse and aimed it at a car, pressing a button that made the car's lights flash. She walked around to the driver's side and opened the door. "Bye."

He nodded. "Bye."

Pete walked down the sidewalk towards his car, not looking back in case she was watching to see if he looked back. No more boyfriend. This was fantastic. He hadn't lied about her military outfit—he was hot for her in those clothes. He had, of course, always noticed her tight little body and always felt a bit of the tease in the way she looked at him and talked to him. Now that there was no boyfriend in the picture, it was all about strategy. Time to make his move. He would have to deal with Arthur, of course, but that would wait until Monday.

It was a cool fall day, slightly overcast. He drove home with the windows down and his music turned up, smiling at nothing. Home was a one-bedroom apartment in the Danforth, Toronto's Greektown area. It was sparsely furnished, had a cabinet full of movies, and everywhere boxes and boxes of comics. Various framed superhero posters by his favorite artists decorated the walls.

The kitchen table was also his drawing board for his own drawings, most of which were of the superhero or heroine variety. His Saturday night consisted of a heated can of ravioli eaten at the table while working on a large-scale Batman scene, with the original Batman movie, the one with Jack Nicholson as The Joker, playing in the background for atmosphere.

There used to be more furniture, and some throw pillows, and tasteful decorative prints on the walls, and no room for any of his things in the bathroom, but that stuff had been gone for some time now. Now there was more room for his comics, and he could leave the boxes all over the place and no one complained.

At the same time, he missed the other stuff.

Chapter Two

"Suppose within the girdle of these walls
Are now confined two mighty monarchies,
Whose high upreared and abutting fronts
The perilous narrow ocean parts asunder."

- Prologue, Henry V - William Shakespeare

Hal Mercer walked into the Monday meeting certain of
one thing: he wasn't going to let his father's company fail.
Not on his watch. These people could either jump in the
trenches with him and start helping him shoot the enemy
or they could get the hell out of his way. He opened his
portfolio and set out his agenda and notes for the meeting.
He cleared his throat and began.

"Okay, everyone. Why don't we get started?"

Hal waited while people began sitting down and
looking his way.

"Good morning. Today I want to talk about the
prospects for our merger with D'Arville." *That really
quieted them down. Good. They were all listening.* "The main
question before us is what to do if they reject our merger
offer. Do we then pursue a hostile takeover? As you all
know, our competitors are showing signs of weakness.
Their president is rumored to be ill and poised to retire.
Although they have a larger market share than we do,
their stock value is down lately. Where do we stand, and

is everybody on side with this? Archie, why don't you start?"

Hal sat down and gave him a big smile of encouragement. Archie Bishop, the VP of Finance, was just as pleasant as he stood up to have his say. He was wearing a charcoal gray suit and a white shirt with a burgundy tie, his balding scalp ringed by a neat fringe of white hair. He adjusted his glasses and smiled back at Hal. Just a couple of old buddies working together for the greater good. You'd never know the man was still feeling the sting of the board's rejection. Too bad, baldy, they went with the younger model CEO.

"Thank-you, Hal. I want to start by saying I support the move. Pursuing these value-creating acquisitions that fit into the company's current business line is one of the key strategies behind achieving our goals. I also believe that through our distribution model and product refinements we have some key components that allow us to accelerate growth.

"There has never been a better time for us, financially, to contemplate this kind of acquisition. The Bay Street buzz on our differentiators favors our side. But we absolutely have to consense on this going forward. And it goes without saying that buy-in from all departments will be mission-critical, because this will require 110% commitment at every level of the organization."

"Hear, hear," said Hal, sighing to himself. *What a grandstander.* "But how about the finances?"

Archie chuckled. "Sorry. I tend to digress when I enthuse. The finances are rock solid. We have created a very strong balance sheet with no leverage and excess capital. So we are in a strong equity position right now, and are achieving optimum cash flow. Our share value is at a 26 week high as of yesterday, and, as they say, fortune favors the bold. This is the optimal method of growing our market share and operational leverage. If you'll turn your attention to the spreadsheet I've created showing our quarterly figures for the last 4 quarters, you'll see the positive trending I've identified."

They all squinted at the myriad tiny figures splashed all over the screen in rows and columns, nodding and hmmfing. Jimenez from R&D remained oblivious, displaying an almost preternatural donut focus. Archie explained the calculations that went into the ROE and NIAT columns, and a set of assumptions that Hal hadn't noticed, off to one side. More nodding, occasional sips of coffee, and one stifled yawn.

"So, without question," said Archie. "The finances are onside."

"And what about competing bids?" said Hal.

"None that I can foresee. They're not far away from a cash flow crunch, so wouldn't be attractive to anyone outside the industry. I can't say for sure about other competitors, but I don't think anyone is in the same position we are. But it won't be long. Industry consolidation is bound to occur."

"Thank-you, Archie. Excellent work." Hal steepled his fingers and looked out the window for a moment, slightly nodding his head. Archie was really laying it on thick here, making it seem like this was all his concept. The company he had taken over from his father was financially sound, but their industry was very competitive, and it was all about market share. There was no room for small players anymore. The prospect of merging with D'Arville brought up some old ghosts for him as well, in particular a beautiful brown-haired ghost from his university days who slipped through his fingers like the elusive spectral presence she was at that moment, but he tried to push her from his mind. He sat straighter and looked over at Archie. "Having a strong balance sheet with no leverage and excess capital is not an ideal position to be in long-term, but if we can use the capital to make acquisitions, then we can bring about a balance sheet that will help the company perform at the ROE level in the future, which should make the shareholders happy."

"Yes," said Archie, still smiling. "I couldn't agree more."

Hal sat back and continued. "What concerns me is how this will affect our internal stability, if all our efforts are focused elsewhere. I don't want to jeopardize all this success Archie describes by taking our eyes off the ball. And the front lines always get nervous when there is talk of a merger or takeover. It usually means layoffs. Can someone speak to that?"

"I think Owen will back me up when I say that any resource attrition will be on their side, not ours," said Archie.

"Owen?" said Hal, looking to the chair immediately to his right.

Owen Percy—Senior VP of Operations, Corporate Secretary, stalwart of the old guard, still a suit-and-tie guy, Harvard MBA and matching look of Ivy League pedigree, and Hal's uncle to boot—sat forward in his chair. "We would definitely look to trim costs on their end, with minimal right-sizing on ours."

"Hal, let me assure you," said Archie. "Our people are best of breed, and we will let them know just how valuable they are. We have nothing to worry about internally. We are as organized as a colony of bees. Just because some of us will be out, say, gathering the buds, and others venturing trade elsewhere, doesn't mean we won't have plenty of soldiers here on the front lines, and workers backing them up, and our king bee overseeing it all."

"Isn't it a queen bee?" said Hal, frowning. "I'm not sure I like that analogy."

"Yeah, and who are the drones in this picture?" said Fisher, laughing.

In the middle of much similar joking, Hal's secretary opened the door and walked over to whisper something in his ear. He listened, nodded, and said, "Thanks, Margaret. Wait a few beats and then send them in. All right, everybody. We have important guests waiting outside from D'Arville Industries."

Some confused looks went around as Hal surveyed the room. "I asked them here for a little back and forth about a possible merger offer. I don't expect a positive response, knowing them, but it never hurts to be clear on where your competition stands."

"Who are they sending?" said Owen.

"I don't know. That in itself will tell us a lot, I think," said Hal. Just then the door opened, and two men were shown in. The two were dressed in similar navy suits with buttoned down shirts and conservative ties. Hal stood up and walked over to greet them.

"Welcome, gentlemen. Thanks so much for coming. I'm Hal."

"Hello," said the first man, shaking his hand. "I'm Orlando Bretagne and this is Wilfred Parker. We're both in the, uh, Marketing Department over at D'Arville."

"Nice to meet you both," said Hal.

"Hello," said Wilfred, also shaking Hal's hand.

"Have a seat, over here is fine," said Hal, ushering them to the near side of the table, facing the windows. Always have your adversaries dazzled by backlighting and looking at their enemies in silhouette, his father had told him. "Can we offer you some coffee?"

"No, thanks, we're fine," said Orlando. Wilfred nodded.

"So, what news from Chuck? Too busy to make it, today, I guess," said Hal.

"Yes, Mr. D'Arville sends his apologies," said Orlando, taking a deep breath. "He sent us to say that he has considered your proposal regarding the merger and that it does not meet our present needs and respectfully that we decline and he sends this gift as a token of his esteem and regret, as I said, that he couldn't be here himself to speak to you, but also that he will talk to you soon. Here's the gift." He produced a small box from within his briefcase and handed it down to Owen Percy who looked it over and set it on the table.

"What is it?" asked Hal, without breaking his eye contact with Orlando.

"A dozen golf balls," said Owen, also looking down the table at the gift-bearer, who was fidgeting with the latch on his briefcase.

"Ah. A reference, of course, to my younger days," said Hal. "It's true I did enjoy pounding it around on the links. A very kind gesture. Tell the younger Mr. D'Arville that I understand his meaning perfectly and that I thank him for the golf balls. Let him know, however, that the match we're going to play won't take place on the golf course. And win or lose, it's his company that's at stake." He paused to see if they would make some reply and then raised his eyebrows and stood up, motioning a hand towards the door. "Thank-you for your time, gentlemen. We won't detain you any further."

Orlando and Wilfred stood up and walked to the door in silence as everyone watched them. The door closed behind them, and everyone turned to look at Hal. He turned to his executive team and waited a beat before he began.

"So I think we're clear now. The merger is off; the takeover is on. I want readiness reports from all department heads by the end of the day, including your best current SWOT analysis." Everybody began to scribble notes as he was talking. "I'm counting on all of you for the kind of leadership I know you're capable of. You're the ones who have to motivate and inspire our people. Now more than ever, we must project confidence in everything we do. I want us to meet every Monday morning at this time from now until the press conference where we announce the takeover is complete, and we're putting up our signs outside their elevators. Anyone who isn't 100% committed to this thing, now is the time to get out. I have no time for anyone who isn't going to throw in with both hands." Everyone was quiet as he looked around the table. "All right, then. Let's get at it. Owen, I'm going to need to go over a few things with you if you've got time right now."

"Certainly," said Owen.

They all gathered up their things and filed out, Archie shooting him some raised eyebrows and his patented little smirk. *Oh, he was really enjoying this.*

Owen followed Hal to the doorway and down the hall to his office. Owen entered first, and Hal closed the door behind them. Hal's calm face broke down and he threw his portfolio across the room. It crashed into the blinds and then hit the floor. "Goddammit, I'd like to kill that little shit."

"Take it easy, Hal." Owen sat on the leather couch and set his folder on the coffee table as Hal paced back and forth.

"Oh, it's on, now. This means war. I kept thinking *this is just business*, but now it's fucking war."

"It was war before. We just called it business." Owen crossed his legs and pinched the crease in his pants above the knee.

"He humiliated me in front of my senior staff."

"He tried to, but you didn't let him. You handled yourself beautifully."

Hal shook his head. "Fucking golf balls. And I can just imagine him yucking it up, telling the story at their next meeting."

"Believe me, everyone was looking at you to see how you'd react. There were some in that room who would've loved to see you lose your cool, but you didn't."

"Was my face as red as it felt?"

"Best damn poker face I ever saw."

Hal picked up his portfolio, pushing the loose papers back inside, and set it on his desk. He sat down. "Oh, we have to win this thing now. We can't afford to lose. I can't afford it. Did you see Archie grandstanding today?"

"He's a pompous ass."

"But he wants my job. He thinks I'm going to fail and then he'll be there to clean up my mess. He wants this takeover to fail."

"True, but he's still an accountant at heart," said Owen. "He wouldn't make the numbers lie."

"But he thinks I'll fail despite having the financial wherewithal."

"Probably."

"We have to get this thing done. You're going to mobilize the troops, right? I need you to provide the internal stability while I'm on the attack."

"You can count on me." Owen nodded and looked at his watch.

"I know," said Hal.

"Well, I'd better get started on all those reports you

want. Slave driver." He stood up, and walked towards the door.

"Yeah, thanks a lot, Owen. Talk to you later."

"Right," he said as he walked out the door.

Hal looked around the office. At the couch, the two chairs, and the old desk, none of it changed since his father...

He fired up his laptop and opened his portfolio to review the reports again. He made a mental note to send an e-mail around to everyone to keep a tight lid on their budgets for the next little while. He typed his password, and Bill Gates's software jingled to life. The clock in the lower right hand corner of the screen said 8:40 am. Most of the staff probably hadn't arrived yet, and he had already begun a takeover bid that morning.

Later, he would remember that this was how things started, with acrimony and bad feelings, so it was little wonder that they would lead where they led and end as they did.

Chapter Three

"Sir Thomas Grey, knight, of Northumberland -
[Has] for the gilt of France - O guilt indeed! -
Confirmed conspiracy with fearful France…"

- Act 1, Scene 2, Henry V

Tom Grey looked over his shoulder as if an alarm were about to go off and an IT SWAT team come bursting out of the supply room. He watched as the progress bar on his monitor worked its way slowly from left to right. The office was filled with light. The sunshine streaming in through the blinds made him feel conspicuous. He drummed his fingers on his desk and looked around him for something to straighten up or put away, but his desk was neat and tidy, as always.

It didn't feel 100% right to be doing this, but what were they going to do, fire him? He'd helped to build Mercer Incorporated, so what he was taking was partly his anyway. But it wasn't the company he and Henry Mercer had built; it was now in the hands of his goof-off son, Hal. The company started dying the day Henry found out he had cancer. Now that his friend was gone, Tom Grey was just helping things along towards a quick demise, which was like an act of mercy with a sick animal.

Retirement wasn't that far away for him. He couldn't afford for the company to go sideways and end up in a middle management purge after some other big firm comes in on a bailout or a forced merger. He was going to get a new job on his terms, with a company that would be there in the long term. To be unemployed at his age was a terrifying thought. What would that mean for his family?

The pictures on his desk of his happy clan featured a younger him, without so much gray hair. There was one of him with his wife on the beach, which reminded him that he had to start getting out to the gym again, and then a portrait of the whole family, the two kids' faces echoes of his face, with his strong nose and big ears. God, how could he have worn those Coke bottle glasses for so long? His new ones were more fashionable and had the compressed lenses with the anti-reflective coating. He brushed his hand across the surface of the plate glass to remove the dust that had built up there. Marilyn and the kids meant everything to him. He was doing this for them.

The files finished downloading and he pulled his flash drive out of the USB port and slipped it into his pocket. No alarms so far. Tom Grey grabbed his coat and headed for the elevator. With any luck Kenny had talked to his contact and they would already be waiting for him. It was the beginning of the end for Mercer.

* * *

"Ladies and Gentlemen, 'Pistol' Pete Malden..." Randy clapped his hands, and Arthur quickly joined in as Pete made his way over to his desk, spot on nine. Yet another Monday had begun. "Protector of the smelly building, scourge of the IT Group — laying waste to their ranks in a hail of colorful bullets."

"Thank-you, thank-you," said Pete, grinning as he sat down. Their cubicle contained their four desks, one at each corner, and four people, including Amy.

"They weren't exactly pistols, though, were they? Weren't they more like little sub-machine guns?" said Arthur.

"It was a reference to a basketball player nickname," said Randy. "Pistol Pete Maravich. One of the best of a bygone era."

"Oh," said Arthur, pushing his glasses up the bridge of his nose. "I don't watch basketball."

"Where's Fluellen?" said Pete.

"All the section managers were called into a meeting at about 8:30," said Randy. "This after Hal had the S&M team in for an early meeting."

"That can't be good," said Pete.

"No," said Arthur. "Randy thinks they're talkin' merger."

"So the rumors are coming true, we think?" said Pete.

"The indications are there," said Randy. "First a big crowd-pleasing trick at the paint ball, then pull a rabbit out of a hat with a big merger. Presto, a hero appears out of nowhere. Then let the right-sizing begin."

"Right-sizing?" said Arthur. He looked from Randy to Pete and then back.

"The backwards resourcing, the synergizing, the paradigming, the expense optimizing," said Randy. "Stop me when you hear one you like."

"The lopping off of heads," said Pete.

"You think that's going to happen?" said Arthur.

"Dear, naive Arthur," said Randy. "It always happens. That's the whole reason for the merger, or the takeover, or the stock swap, or whatever they want to call it. It's all about the redundancies. Just keep your head down and try not to be noticed. It makes no difference to us who's CEO."

Arthur just sat staring over towards the windows, and Pete switched on his computer and took his phone off the busy setting. Amy and Randy's computers were by the front of the cube, and Pete and Arthur's were at the back, visible to passersby. Computers made it very easy to appear busy, but they had to actually be on to accomplish this. Randy had the Internet up and was checking his gmail.

"Where's Amy?" said Pete.

"She went to talk to Jill in Finance about the TR-50s, some new idea she has about them," said Randy.

Pete craned his neck to see down the corridor. *No time like the present,* he guessed. *Might as well just lay it on him.*

"Good, because I just wanted to let you guys know that I'm going to ask her out," said Pete.

"What?" said Arthur, looking away from the windows as if startled. "Uh, no way. I've been working on her for, uh, for months. You know I have a thing for her."

"What working?" said Pete. "You mean acting like a lovesick puppy and hoping she'll ask you out? I haven't seen you make the slightest move."

"She had a boyfriend."

"Had? So you knew about that and still haven't done anything."

"That's none of your business. No fucking way you're asking her out now."

"You have got zero chance with her. Why don't you just give it up and face reality?"

"Oh, and you have a chance? Mr. Comics Geek, with your pansy little drawings."

Pete stood and so did Arthur.

"Gentlemen," said Randy, standing between them and

putting a hand on each of their shoulders. "Let's not have a ruckus, as entertaining as all this has been. If you carry on in this medieval fashion, jobs will be lost."

Pete stood glaring at Arthur, saying nothing.

"All right, then," said Randy. "Arthur, it does seem that if something were going to happen between you and Amy, it would have by now. Why don't you try Judy in IT? She has the hots for you, or do you prefer unattainable goals?"

Arthur said nothing.

"And Peter," said Randy. "It's not very polite to come in and rub Arthur's nose in this the first thing on a Monday morning. Can't you both just do whatever you're going to do without making it personal with each other?"

"What did I miss?" said Amy. She stood in the cubicle's entrance, looking at the three of them standing there. Randy looked at Arthur, who shrugged his shoulders, and then at Pete, who nodded.

"Nothing," said Randy, putting his arms around his two podmates. "We had just decided to go down for some coffee to celebrate the absence of management. Would you like to come along?"

"Sure," said Amy. "I could go for a coffee."

"I have to be back by 10:00, however," said Randy. "I have an online game of *Unreal Tournament* scheduled with a friend across town. If I'm late, he gains the upper hand."

Pete walked out of the cubicle towards the elevator without saying anything further, and Amy followed after him. Arthur and Randy brought up the rear.

That went pretty well, thought Pete, *all things considered.*

"Judy has the hots for me?" he heard Arthur saying.

"Yes," said Randy over his shoulder. "Don't you remember at the Christmas party last year? She was talking to you all night, and you never even asked her to dance."

"Shit."

Pete looked back in time to see Arthur push his glasses up his nose, which made him grin.

"Come on," said Amy. "The elevator is here."

They walked into the elevator and then descended fourteen floors to the café at ground level. They all picked their usual latté or juice, and wandered over to have a seat at the table by the window. Pete picked the chair beside Amy's and gave Arthur a look.

"So what do you hear over in Accounting?" said Randy as he took his first sip of foam.

"Everyone figures merger," said Amy.

"Shit," said Arthur.

"Yeah, that's what we figured. Cheers." Randy raised his paper cup. "To better bosses." They laughed.

"Would they lay off managers?" said Arthur.

"Middle management generally takes the hardest hits," said Amy. "But still, we've got to try our best to look good between now and when it happens. They'll be thinking, 'who do we cut?' and 'who do we keep?' all the time now."

"No," said Randy. "You're better off not being noticed at all than to stick out as good or bad. Best to just keep your head down altogether."

"No, I think you're better to look good," said Pete. "Like Amy said, they're going to be thinking about who to keep." He looked over at Amy for agreement. He really didn't give a crap one way or the other, but he figured he should try to come down on her side of the argument.

"But the problem is, those who look too good start to look like management prospects who can replace the ones doing the thinking," said Randy. "Then they see you as a threat."

"I thought you could always tell the management prospects from the lobotomy scars," said Pete.

"Ah, yes. I stand corrected," said Randy.

"So is it better to look good, or keep your head down?" said Arthur. He was systematically picking the label off his half-finished bottle of orange juice.

"My night school teacher says, 'There's always room for the best,'" said Amy.

"Older generation… same rules no longer apply," said Randy. "Keep your head down and you won't go far wrong."

"Thanks," said Arthur, balling up his torn label and throwing it onto the table. "It's all clear to me now."

"As soon as this rumor goes around, everyone in the company will be on a major suck-up campaign," said Randy. "With that much brown-nosing going on, it'll be hard to stand out, anyway. Maybe they'll appreciate you for not trying too hard."

"Randy just likes that idea because it's less work," said Pete. "Heaven forbid that this merger should limit our coffee breaks, right?"

Amy laughed, and Randy shrugged his shoulders. "When you're capable of working twice as fast as everyone around you, it leaves you with lots of free time while they're catching up."

"Maybe we should get back up there," said Amy. "They're probably going to be finished the meeting soon." They all looked at her.

She looked sharp in her conservative business attire, dressing for the job she wanted, not the one she had, Inside Sales Groupie, less than a year of sales floor experience, a year before that as an Assistant Manager in retail, for god's sake, college diploma in communications and halfway towards a night school Marketing certificate, serious hair and good teeth, no-nonsense handshake betraying her ambition, HR file thick with interview results, but CV sorely lacking in substance.

"Yeah," said Pete. "Let's head up."

They gathered their "to go" cups and bottles and made their way to the elevator and up to the fifteenth floor to actually begin work, nigh on ten in the morning. Randy settled in for his game of *Unreal Tournament*, ready with the quick Alt-Tab switch to the accounts database if a higher-up should happen past. Pete made some phone calls, doodling as he spoke. Arthur kept his head down, but Pete thought he could still see steam coming out of his ears, no matter what he said to Randy about Judy plans. Amy just worked hard, as always.

About ten minutes before noon, with his neck stiff from cradling the phone handset between his shoulder and ear, Pete noticed the time, had a quick look around, and then rolled his chair over to Amy's desk. "How about some lunch?"

Amy looked at her watch. "Sure. Sounds good. Are you guys coming?" she said to Randy and Arthur.

"I can't," said Randy. "I have a prior engagement."

Everyone looked at Arthur, who looked at Randy for a second, then said, "Yeah, I, um. I brought my lunch. Thanks, anyway." Then he turned back to his computer and continued typing.

"Okay, then," said Pete. "You ready?"

"I guess so," said Amy, grabbing her purse from under her desk and getting up.

"See you guys later," said Pete. Arthur continued staring at his computer screen but stopped typing, as Pete cast a glance his way and then followed Amy over to the elevators.

* * *

"So how goes the night course? Any exams coming up?" said Pete as they waited for their noodle soups. They had a table by the wall farthest from the door. The smell of cooking oil and garlic mixed with a smoky smell of seared meats really got the saliva going. Waiters clattered plates and glasses onto trays, many soups were slurped, low conversations carried on around them, the open kitchen hissed and sizzled, and the street noise provided a muted wall of sound as a backdrop to all this.

"Oh, it's going well. There's an exam, um, yeah, when is it? Sometime soon."

"But you're enjoying it?"

"Yeah. I really like the marketing stuff. It's the most fun. Oh, Thanks." The waiter set down their big noodle soup bowls in front of them, and they set about breaking apart their chopsticks and positioning their napkins.

"Considering a career change?"

"Oh, yeah. In a second. I've applied for a couple of postings, but haven't got the right fit, yet. I think it will make a big difference when I'm finished the certificate. Having no experience and no credentials has been a pretty deadly combination."

"Well, you know the company, and soon you'll have the certificate, so I'm sure that will help."

"Mmm."

"Mmm yes, or mmm good soup?"

"Both. How's yours?"

"Tasty." He pinched a fold of noodles and gathered it into his mouth with the chopsticks.

"I wonder who Randy's meeting for lunch. Some

mystery date?"

He chewed and then swallowed, wincing as the too hot noodles slid down his throat. "He didn't say."

"All very mysterious, though, if you know what I mean."

"Are you trying to get a rise out of me or him on this?"

"Whoever. I just think it's funny that someone could still be in the closet. This is the 21st century, for god's sake."

"So, maybe he's not," said Pete.

They slurped their soups and Amy looked at the pictures of famous people over Pete's shoulder.

"Who's caught your eye up there?" he said.

"Nobody. You got any vacation planned for this year?"

"No, not really. I might go and stay with my sister in Vancouver if I can get a cheap flight, I guess. How about you?"

"I might take a week off and do one of those one-week courses. Get a head start on my cert."

"Do you have any activities that don't involve your career?"

"I eat, breathe, and sleep. What do you think?"

"I think it sounds like you don't have any free time when you just do things for fun. Some call it a personal life."

She sighed. "I do fun things."

"Like what? Do you go to movies?"

"Yeah, I go to movies."

"Do you want to go to a movie with me?"

She paused with her spoon in mid-air. "With you?"

"Yeah. A fun one, of course."

"On a date?"

"Yeah, I guess. If you have to put a label on it."

"It would be very weird to be on a date with you."

"Thanks so much."

"Just because you're a... friend."

"So few people recommend dating your enemies that I just wouldn't try it if I were you."

"When?"

"You say. I'm more flexible than you."

"Well, it can't be this weekend, because I have to study."

He looked out the window as if considering the matter. "What about tonight?"

"No, I have my night class."

"Tomorrow is no good for me, so how about Wednesday?"

"I usually study for my Thursday class."

"Tell you what. We'll skip dinner and I'll pick you up at 8:00 Wednesday. That'll give you a couple of hours."

"All right, then. What do you want to see?"

"Doesn't bother me. I'll let you choose since you apparently don't get out much."

"I don't even know what's playing."

"Let's roll up to the theater and choose based on which one has the best poster."

"Okay. Wow. I'm going on a date with Pete Malden."

"Don't worry, these office romances never work out."

"Ah. Nothing like a little optimism."

"Just kidding."

They finished their soups and went back to the office. It was a little awkward in the elevator, not knowing where to look. They were in some limbo phase now, not just co-workers, or friends, but nothing more, yet, either. They watched the little circular lights above the door, and then he let her off first when they reached fifteen. They went back to work and Pete wondered what he was going to do with his eyes until Wednesday night.

Chapter Four

"Why, how now, gentlemen?
What see you in those papers, that you lose
So much complexion? Look ye, how they change!
Their cheeks are paper."

- Act 2, Scene 2, Henry V

First thing Wednesday morning, Hal called a meeting of the Senior Management Team for 10:00 am, but didn't say why. Most of the group was already in the boardroom waiting for him when that time arrived. Owen Percy had a file in front of him of a new flow chart he was working on and he was wondering where the small efficiency was hiding. There was always one in there that he hadn't seen before, one corner that hadn't been smoothed or cut. Hal's younger brother David, who worked in R&D, sat next to him and worked on something of his own. As Owen shuffled his papers back into the file folder, he saw David glance up at him and do likewise.

"So, you have no idea what this is about?" said David.

"No, he never mentioned anything to me. Maybe it's just a pep talk for the takeover," said Owen, wondering why he didn't know. Hal usually told him everything.

"Maybe. But if that's the case, I'm pretty busy right now, and don't need much extra pep."

"I wish I'd had a chance to talk to him this morning. I

just heard some disturbing news."

"What?" said David, turning in his chair.

"I was talking to Ernie from Office Services, and he apparently saw Tom Grey and Ken Walker having drinks with somebody from D'Arville over at The Rosewater."

"Wait a second, Ernie was at the Rosewater? We're obviously paying him too much. How did he know it was someone from D'Arville?" said David.

"Ernie wasn't sure of his name, but he saw him at an industry function last year."

"So maybe they just know him. Or ran into him there. Grey and Walker have both been with us for a long time. I can't imagine they'd be thinking of jumping ship."

Owen nodded. "I might have thought that, too. But I heard from my buddy on their board of directors that they are trying to recruit from our side."

"Oh."

"I just got off the phone with him a half hour ago and I couldn't find Hal."

"The last thing we need is for them to be gathering information while we're in the planning stages, and then take it with them. What about the new product specs we've been working on? I'm going to have to lock…"

The door opened, and Hal walked in with Tom Grey and Ken Walker.

"Shit," said Owen and David at the same time. Owen tried to catch Hal's eye, but he wasn't looking his way. He had to warn him, but not with those two jackals by his side.

"Yeah, I'm really excited about it," Hal said to the two of them. "You'll be hearing more about it at this very meeting, in fact."

"That's great," said Walker.

"Excellent," said Grey, as they both took their seats.

"Good morning, everyone," said Hal. "Thanks for gathering so quickly. This won't take long." He produced a handful of envelopes from his briefcase and began to distribute them to each person around the table. "I just wanted to let you know that I am aware that the people in this room are the keys to our success, and that I take care of my people. Because I know this is going to be a lot of extra work and stress, I am giving you the rewards you merit in advance. I have no problem doing this because I am confident that our efforts will be successful. There, you all have your envelopes now; you can go ahead and open them."

There was much rustling and tearing of paper as everybody opened their packages, and then many smiles and eyebrows raised around the table as people mentally recalculated their take home. Someone said, "Wow." Tom Grey's face had turned bright red and he was now staring at Hal. Walker, by contrast, had gone so pale he looked sick, and just kept looking down at the piece of paper he held in his hands.

"Our friends Mr. Grey and Mr. Walker don't look so happy with the rewards they have merited," said Hal, returning Grey's stare, and everyone else went quiet and turned to look at them. "Well, they haven't shown that they're capable of the same loyalty and team spirit as everyone else, so their packages contained something quite different from everybody else's. I'm sure they are disappointed. Perhaps they'll be happier with their new friends over at D'Arville."

There were a couple of sharp intakes of breath, and one or two whispers around the room. Grey looked around, but no one would meet his eye. "Fine. If that's the way you want it," he said, standing up. "Well, I guess this is goodbye. It's been a pleasure working with most of you."

He smiled until he turned to look at Hal. "Hal, you're not your father and you never will be. This never would have happened under his lead."

Hal returned his hard stare.

Don't, thought Owen. *Never swing at a pitch in the dirt.*

Hal seemed to consider it for a moment, then walked over and opened the door, and two security guys walked in and positioned themselves behind the guilty parties. "These gentlemen will help you clean out your desks," Hal said flatly. "Then they will escort you down to street level. Goodbye."

"Yeah, fine," said Grey, sneering at Hal. "If anybody else is worried about the iceberg that Hal is steering towards, give me a call. I'll throw you a life preserver."

Ken Walker stood up. Grey walked directly to the door, but Walker walked over to Owen Percy and put a hand on his shoulder as if he was going to say something, but then he shook his head and followed Grey out of the room, trailed by the two escorts. Hal looked around the room with his arms crossed. David looked at Owen. Owen could see he was thinking the same thing: *there goes a lot of history; there go two big names from their team.* The door closed and it seemed even quieter. Hal drew out the silence for another moment before speaking.

"Now that we have the housekeeping out of the way, I can now say that I am confident that everyone in this room is 100% loyal and 100% dedicated to this task. Our competitors have taken their first shot, and it just tells you this thing is going to get nasty. They are going to come at us from all angles, and we can't afford any leaks. But we move ahead without bitterness. Our friends made decisions that have taken them in another direction, that's all.

"Going forward, we've got the big trade show coming

up in Windsor on the 25th, which is critically important to what we have to get done. It's our key to increasing our U.S. sales, as there are always a lot of American buyers at that show. We have got to *own – the – floor* at that show. I'd like to hear any ideas you have for making this thing a huge success. There is no such thing as a stupid idea. Whatever you can think of that will help us maximize our sales, I would be interested in hearing it.

"That's all I have for you for now. Thank-you for your time, and most importantly, your loyalty."

Everybody got up, picked up their envelopes, pushed in their chairs, and walked past Hal on their way out. Some thanked him, and all shook his hand before leaving by one door or the other.

Owen glanced over as he was leaving and saw Hal staring out the window. *There may be some of his father in him after all,* he thought.

* * *

After a late dinner at his favorite Indian restaurant, Hal sat in front of the gas fireplace in his penthouse condo, staring into the blue flames. The events of the day were still occupying his mind, scenes repeating like slow flashes of a very deliberate strobe. Grey and Walker had been old guard hires of his father's day. It was him that they had betrayed, not Hal.

What hurt was that he thought they had been in his camp. Who else did he trust now that would turn on him? At least with Archie he knew where he stood. Oh, well. It was all about the money, at the end of the day. How much had D'Arville offered them? They wouldn't have come cheap. And what exactly had they taken with them? He had Julie and her people looking into it—maybe they left some kind of digital intrusion footprint at the scene of their crime.

He thought of the e-mail he had sent to everyone: *Tom Grey and Ken Walker have moved on to pursue other opportunities. We thank them for their past service, and wish them luck in their new endeavors.* Rumors would be flying. He couldn't afford to lose any more of his senior officers. The rank and file would be getting nervous enough with the merger talk. How was he going to take over another company if his own started falling apart? But he couldn't afford to fail. He had to accomplish the takeover to secure the company's long term future. The market was going to gobble up the small players or leave them in the dust.

He wondered what impression he had made on his team so far. Tall with blondish brownish hair and gray-green eyes was obvious; still a bit tanned from the summer; a couple of years of sales floor experience and six months as a Special VP when his father was sick; then the ascendancy, based entirely on having the right last name the whispers said; an undergrad BA in Commerce many years in the past; a so-called "Executive" MBA after his name now, acquired within the last several years (some said flat-out paid for by his father, which was a lie, but you can't worry about things like that); and now, at 33, the youngest CEO in the history of their industry. That was the talk. But his actions would create the deepest impression.

According to the clock on the mantle it was just after eleven. He was exhausted, but still had several hours of reports to go over and memos to compose. He closed his eyes, smoothing his eyelids down with his fingertips, and then massaged his temples. Was it all worth it? Why was he knocking himself out? It was Dad that talked him into coming to work for him, into "challenging" himself. And now he was running the company, which just meant that he worked harder than everyone else. When had he become a hard worker?

It wasn't just the working hard, which was bad enough. Another thing he had noticed since he had become CEO was that he didn't really have any friends at work anymore. There is a certain distance that comes between the boss and everyone else. This was something he hadn't really noticed as much when he was on the other side, working the sales floor and goofing off most of the time with Randy and Pete. Probably because the boss was his dad. He had been busy enough that he didn't really notice it at first, but lately he had started to feel really isolated from the energy and flow of the company. If he didn't have Owen to talk to, he'd be going crazy by now.

And what was with these headaches? And feeling lonely all the time? When he had time to think about it, he realized that his life was now all about work, sleep, repeat. He didn't have time to meet a woman, and if he did, he wouldn't have any time to spend with her. Maybe this was making up for all the times when he'd done no work at all and went out with lots of women. Good times. Often right here in this sunken living room, in fact. Feeling like he had all the time in the world, and no worries. Now he had seemingly nothing but things to worry about. Maybe he would eventually reach a state of balance. Sure, that was as good a theory as any.

The thought of another lonely person, probably also sitting by herself right now, made him pick up the phone. He dialed the familiar number and waited only two rings.

"Hello?"

"Hi, Mom."

"Oh, hello, Hal. What are you doing up so late?"

"Mom, it's quarter past eleven. If I were in bed right now, it would be a record."

"That's not good for you."

"No, I'm sure it's not. How are you?"

"Oh, I'm fine."

"What did you do tonight?"

"Oh, tonight was our theater night. At the Alex."

"You renewed the subscriptions?"

"Yes, of course. We had excellent seats, and I didn't want to lose them."

"Who do you go with?"

"Well, I usually find someone for the other ticket. Tonight I had to go alone."

"You should have called me."

"I didn't want to bother you. I know how busy you are."

"Tell me the date of the next one, and I'll put it in my calendar right now."

"Okay, but I don't have the package handy. Let me, hmm. I'll send you an e-mail tomorrow. I don't want to go all the way downstairs. It's so quiet in the house at night."

"Maybe you should get a dog."

"Oh, perfect. The Widow Mercer resorts to canine companionship to ward off the heebie-jeebies."

"What do you care what other people think?"

"It's not just that. They get hair everywhere, and I can't stand the smell."

"Okay, whatever. Where did you go for dinner?"

"I ate in. I made a lasagna."

"You made a lasagna? Mom, you're going to be eating it for weeks."

"I realized that afterward. I can't seem to get the hang of cooking for one person. Old habits are hard to break, you know."

"I miss him, too."

"Yes, dear. Would you like some of the lasagna?"

"No, thanks. Why don't you invite David and Pam and the kids over? They'll take care of it in a hurry."

"That's a good idea."

"I gotta go, Mom. A few things to do before I go to bed."

"All right, dear. But don't work so hard. You know that's what killed your father."

"It was cancer, Mom."

"That's what they say, but we know better. Just promise me you'll take it easy."

"I promise. G'night."

"Good night, love."

Hang up the phone, stare at the wall, and pick at the stitching on the cushion. Man, it was quiet. Maybe he should be the one to get a dog. Taking in a deep lungful of air, Hal stood up and walked over to the study. Now to fire up his laptop and press on with the night's work. He looked out his windows at the dark sky and wondered if this momentum he was building was a thing he could control or if it was something inevitable that would happen to him whether he pushed against it or not.

Chapter Five

"PISTOL: Come, let's away. My love, give me thy lips."

- Act 2, Scene 3, Henry V

Randy was late on Thursday. Everyone looked up as he walked in at about ten after with a latté and the *Financial Journal*, and took his place in the cubicle. "Good news, ladies and gents. The Dow is up, my stocks are bouncing back nicely, and all is right with the world."

Neither tall nor fat, but enough of each to be a substantial presence, more casual than business casual, cowlick brown hair no fast track to success, perpetual ironic smile belying any attempt to appear serious, Masters in History and aborted PhD, seven "satisfactory" P.A.'s, one for each year on the floor, too long now for promotion in the chain of command, stuck where he was and not seeming to be troubled about it.

"So lunch is on you, then?" said Pete. He put his phone on Do Not Disturb to stop it from ringing, and the others did the same. They deserved a quick break for a chat. He looked at Randy and wondered if these stocks of his were what kept him going. Did they keep him getting up in the a.m. and schlepping down here every day?

"Not a chance," said Randy, turning on his computer. "I'm just letting you fine people know that one day soon

I'm going to be riding the bull out that door."

"Oh, yeah?" said Amy. "I heard the bear was guarding the door."

"Very possible, mi'lady," said Randy. He stroked his chin and looked at the ceiling. "But Warren Buffet tells me the bull is stronger than the bear. Warren is wise. Warren knows all."

"But does a bear shit in the woods? Or is that too much bullshit for this early in the morning?" said Pete.

"Ohhhh," said his chorus of co-workers.

"Sorry," he said.

"For that you should be flogged," said Randy.

"Yeah," said Arthur. "I'll help."

"I'm willing if you are, sweetie," said Pete. He made a kissy face in Arthur's direction. Arthur looked away.

"Get a room, you two," said Randy. "So, have I missed anything this morning? What's the latest gossip?"

"Um, not much," said Amy. "Fluellen asked us for our TR-50s from last year's trade show. Didn't say why he needed them."

"Hmm. Interesting," said Randy. "Well, we know that Captain Fluellen never ventures out of his office without good reason."

"Um, look out, it comes this way now," said Pete.

They all snapped into action, switching their phones back on, which started to ring right away, and slipping back into busy workplace mode as their manager made his way across the office. He first stopped in two cubes down, then at the next-door cube, rumbling something at their neighbors Williams, Bates, Kravitz and Court for a moment. Then he came into their area.

"At ease, troops. We're going to have a unit meeting this afternoon, so make sure you're up to date before you go to lunch. I also need you to bring your best ideas for increasing sales. Meeting's at 1400 hours. See you there."

With a vague, dismissive wave, he was away, back across the floor to his office, closing the door behind him. They all looked at each other and laughed silently.

Randy covered the mouthpiece of his phone. "Sir, yes, sir!"

"Aye, aye, captain," said Arthur.

Randy turned to his computer and Pete saw the words *Historiography Chat Room* pop up on his screen. Amy and Arthur turned back to their work. Pete pulled out a sheet of paper that he had shoved under his keyboard, and continued his drawing of Bill Fluellen as Sgt. Fury, then moved on to cast the rest of them as the Howling Commandos.

A little while later, he took a quick look at Fluellen's door and fired up an interoffice e-mail to Amy. *Hey, there, hot stuff. I had a fantastic time last night. If I were Superman, you'd be kryptonite, because you make me weak. Let's do it again soon. Kisses, Pete.* She turned to look over her shoulder at him, and he was already looking her way. She smiled at his goofy grin, had a silent giggle, and turned back to her computer.

He had picked her up at quarter to eight the night before, too impatient to wait the extra fifteen minutes. She lived in a high-rise just north of Bayview and Sheppard, and he had even tried to sit still in the parking lot and wait it out before walking up to the door to buzz, so as not to appear too eager.

"Hello?"

"Hey, it's me. Are you ready?"

"Oh, hi. Just give me two seconds. I'll be right down."

"No problem." He stood reading the names on the buzz board. Nice and neat, alphabetical order, separated by letter, *Quick, A.* the only Q, but a *Malden, D.* in the M's, perhaps even a distant relative. Cousin Dave? The lobby was sparse furnishings, mirrored walls and fake plants. Big couch in the middle of the floor to the left. It would have been nice if she'd buzzed him in to sit in the lobby. Then the elevator door opened and she was walking towards him.

It was only a white tank top and jeans with a black leather jacket, but on her it was the hottest outfit he'd ever seen. That little patch of exposed skin where her neckline scooped was nice, obviously not a turtleneck, off limits situation. He felt his face flush as she looked at him, and he couldn't help smiling as she opened the door, despite his best efforts to appear cool.

"Hi, there." He smelled her perfume as she walked by.

"Hi, yourself. You're early."

"Oh, was I? Sorry about that. Did you want to go back up and cram in another 10 minutes?"

"Funny. So where are we going?" She pushed open the outer door and he followed her out.

"I like the theater at Yonge and Sheppard because they've got the stadium seating and all big screens."

"All right, then."

"This is me," he said as they reached the parking lot, and he opened and held the passenger door for her. "You look gorgeous, by the way."

"Thanks."

They pulled out of the parking lot and kept on with the light banter, trying to calm their nerves at this new way of relating. Pete watched the road, but his eyes were full of her on quick glances and peripheral vision. He could hardly believe she was in his car in hot, non-work clothes.

When they reached the theater, they lingered in the lobby, looking over the movie posters and trying to decide which offered the most common ground.

"So, we've got *Rock the Bleachers, Trip to the Zoo, All in one Day...*"

Amy shook her head at the first one. "No thanks to a movie about cheerleaders. What about the other two?"

"Do you like animation?"

"No thanks to that."

"Okay, this one's a romantic comedy about a dweeb who falls for his woman boss. It's by the same director as *Kitten Love*."

"And what was that about?"

"Okay, moving on. What about *It Stays Inside*?"

"It looks scary."

"Yeah, it's a kind of a ghost story, I think."

"That sounds like such a first date movie. I'll be all screaming and grabbing your arm for protection and whatnot."

"Works for me."

Pete paid for their tickets and as they were a bit early, they decided to have a coffee at the little theater café. It was a semi-circular counter coming out from the wall, with an espresso machine, gourmet coffees, muffins, pastries, and various other snacks. He paid for their drinks and they proceeded to one of the empty tables off to one side.

"Are you going to want popcorn or a drink during the movie?" he said, setting his mug down on an empty table.

"No, I'm fine with the latté," she said, sitting down.

"Okay, then."

"This is a nice theater. I haven't been to this one before."

"No?" he said.

"I don't come down here at all, to tell you the truth, because the roads are such a mess right now."

"Yeah, but it's worth it for a great theater like this. Wait till you see the seats and the big screen, and hear the Dolby Digital sound."

She nodded. "You go to a lot of movies, then."

"Pretty much all of them."

"I see. A very big fan."

"Oh, yeah," he said, mock toasting her with his coffee.

"So a typical date with you would be a movie."

"No, not always. My former girlfriend—"

"This was Rose?"

"Yeah. The one I was living with. We went to movies, but we also liked to eat out a lot. There are so many choices down where we live. Where I live." He looked down at his hands on the table, and traced the pattern with his finger.

She bailed him out of his uncomfortable moment. "And you're near the Danforth, right?"

"One street south. It's a great area."

"How long were you guys cohabiting?"

Pete squinted as he tried to recall. "Almost three years."

"Wow, I had no idea. You must have been… it must have been hard. Breaking up after all that time."

"Yeah."

"Do you still talk to her?"

"No."

"Oh. That's too bad, I guess." She sipped her latté, nodding. "What about your first girlfriend?"

"My first ever?"

"Yeah. Way back when."

He laughed. "My first girlfriend ever was one Kelly McFadden."

"And how old were you?"

"Ten."

"You got an early start, then. And are you still in touch with her?"

"No, I don't even think she went to the same high school I did. We only went out in public school. And it was totally innocent. I don't even think I kissed her. We used to climb trees and just talk for hours. I remember she would often say to me, 'Make me laugh.' Out of the blue. And I would have to try whatever way I could to make her laugh."

"And was tickling the obvious choice?"

"Oh, god, no. That would have involved physical contact and embarrassment. No, I used to make all kinds of faces, talk in weird voices, roll around like a dog, whatever it took. And she would try not to laugh. It was bizarre, but absolutely the only thing in the world I wanted to be doing whenever I was with her."

"And were you able to make her laugh?"

"Always."

"I can see that happening." Amy looked at her watch and indicated it was time.

As soon as they were settled in their seats, he just reached out for her hand as naturally as if they had been dating for years. All through the movie they held hands, which was a nice feeling. It was warm and familiar at the same time as it was strange. During the scary parts, she would squeeze his hand, and then she would look over at him and smile or laugh, and he couldn't tell if she was being facetious or if she was really scared.

When he pulled into her parking lot later, he couldn't tell if he was going up with her or not. He parked the car in the same spot he had vacated earlier, switched off the ignition and got out, moving to open her door. But she got out unaided and they walked across the yard to the front door.

"So, it wasn't the greatest movie. But it had a few good scares." She got out her keys, opened the door, and they went in.

"And great special effects," he said, as if this were self-evident.

"Sure, if you're into that sort of thing."

"Oh, I am." They were standing by the elevators now, but Amy hadn't pressed the button. She turned around to look at him, and he looked back without saying anything.

"Thanks for a great evening," she said. "I had fun."

"Me, too." He paused and looked again at the elevator button. "Aren't you going to press the button?"

"No, we should say goodbye here."

"Oh, come on. Aren't you at least going to let me see your apartment?"

"Not tonight."

He grinned. "So there'll be another night?"

"Sure."

"All right, then. I wouldn't want to keep you up late when you've got work and a class tomorrow." He moved a little closer to her and she smiled and leaned back against the wall, but kept looking at him, her eyes flicking down to his lips. He reached behind her, his hand at the small of her back, and kissed her. Her lips were open and inviting—not just a little goodnight peck. She put her arms around him and he brought his other hand up to the back of her neck, brushing her temple with his thumb. She felt so good in his arms.

They kissed like that for a while and then she said goodnight and he was out the door. But the memory of the kiss was still warming him the next day as he read her reply e-mail: *Superman, eh? Can you draw that for me? I had fun, too. My lips are still tingling. How about lunch today?* He smiled, nodded his head slightly, and clicked Reply.

As Pete was typing his reply, Billy Wilkins came by with the mail cart and began to distribute their mail.

"Good day, William," said Randy. "And how are things in the mailroom?"

"Busy." He dropped a package on Randy's desk.

Amy leaned over to his cart and picked up a book. "Oh, what are you reading? Ah, *The 24-hour MBA*. This is a good one."

"What's this?" said Randy. "Ambitions above your station?"

"You know it. I'm not going to be in the mailroom forever."

"That's for sure," said Arthur. "After the merger, we're all going to be fired."

"Nah," said Billy, shaking his head. "Won't happen."

"Oh, yeah?" said Arthur. "And what do you see happening, mail boy?"

"Well, let's see. The whole thrust of business today is in realizing economies of scale. The merger is an opportunity for us to get stronger, which means more job security for us."

Randy turned in his chair, warming to the subject. "The whole 'thrust,' as you inelegantly put it, of realizing economies of scale is in cutting expenses. And whenever you hear an executive say the word 'expenses,' you can substitute the word 'people.' Because they want to replace us all with computers someday, anyway. That way the ruling class oligarchy can guarantee the continuance of the social order."

"But the basis of the free market system is consumer spending," said Billy. "For consumers to have lots of money to spend, they have to have jobs."

"Yeah, and besides," said Amy. "All the trends over the last number of years show the middle class is shrinking, and this has tanked the economy. They, if there is an organized 'they,' wouldn't want to jeopardize that."

"'Middle class and proud,'" said Pete. "Good slogan for a t-shirt."

"Don't let them get you down, Billy," said Amy. "I believe you can get ahead in the world if you try."

"Yeah. Plus, I'm in the ideal starting place," he said. "Whenever you read those articles about the most powerful men on Wall Street, where do you think they got their start?"

"Uh-huh," said Pete. "What makes you think you'll survive the merger?"

"Since I'm paid the least of all of you and do the most work, I'm sure I'll be just fine," said Billy, and he wheeled his cart away to the next cube without even trying to hide his smile.

Chapter Six

"FRENCH KING: Think we King Harry strong;
And, Princes, look you strongly arm to meet him."

- Act 2, Scene 4, Henry V

Kate D'Arville entered the building just before 9:00
a.m., and proceeded up to the 26th floor to visit her father.
Despite the cool fall weather she was wearing a skirt, and
a light cardigan over her blouse for some warmth. Her
face was flushed from the cold air and her long, sandy-
brown hair was looking wind-blown.

She got off the elevator and walked past the reception
area and along the corridor to her father's office. His
secretary stood as she approached.

"Hi, Kate. He's busy right now, it's probably best if you
come back."

She kept on walking. "Don't worry about it, Soraya. I'll
just poke my head in and say I muscled past you."

The blinds were closed and the office was dark, but she
could still make out most of the room. Her father was
sleeping on the leather couch, his suit jacket hung on the
coat rack by the door. She walked over and looked at him
for a moment. She put her purse on the coffee table and
knelt down beside him. He had missed a few patches here
and there when he was shaving. He still wore his tie,
although it was loosened at his neck and his top button

was undone. She smoothed his white hair where it was sticking up. He didn't wake up.

She stood and walked to his desk, sitting in his plush chair. The surface of the desk was clean. There were no papers of any kind, and no folders, pens, or calendars. The phone sitting at the far right corner was the only thing on the desk. She opened the top drawer, where she found a pen and pencil and some paper clips. All the other drawers were full of old files.

The room had a vacant look to it, despite the pictures and degrees on the walls. She swiveled around to face the window, pushing open one of the blind slats with her foot. It was a bright and sunny day, and the sunlight coming in illuminated a volley of dust particles. She eased it closed with her foot and it went dark again.

She closed the door behind her on the way out, and Soraya didn't look up. She sat looking at the telephone, tapping a pen on the desktop. The phone remained quiet.

"I'm heading out," said Kate. "Can you let him know that I stopped by, and that I'll try to call him later?"

"Sure," she said, catching Kate's eye for a second and giving her a quick smile.

Kate walked off down the hall, past the elevators and over to the north side of the building, where she stopped outside her brother's door. C. J. D'Arville III. She knocked and opened the door.

"Just a minute," said Chuck, hunched over his laptop. "Oh, it's you, Katey."

"Don't call me that," said Kate. "Trying to hide the porn?"

"How did you know?" He grinned at her and finished whatever it was he was doing on the computer. Chuck was still dressing for prep school: crisp white button down and dark tie with black pants, jacket over the back of his chair. Old habits die hard. He was slight of build, about 5′10″, with small features and a thin, dry mouth. She had told him that the slicked back hair wasn't working for him, but he insisted on keeping it that way. Probably thought it made him look like a real player. It just looked greasy.

"What else could you be getting up to in here all day?" she asked. She sat in one of the chairs opposite his desk and set her purse on the other chair.

"Oh, I'm a busy man these days."

"I'll bet."

"So, what brings you into the city today? Doing a little shopping? Anything for me?"

"No. I won't be visiting any toy stores. I came in to see Daddy, actually."

"Oh, yeah. We have a big meeting this morning on the Mercer situation."

Kate looked quickly at her brother to see if he was winding her up, but he seemed oblivious. She felt the name stir within her as she digested it. She shook it off and tried to look as though she were brushing the hair out of her eyes. "Well, give him awhile. He's asleep in his office."

"Way to go, Dad. I've got to get one of those big sofas for my office." He made a note on his desktop with an imaginary pen.

"He shouldn't even be here. He's not well and you know it."

"What're you talking about? He's fine."

"Mom talked to his doctor today, and he couldn't believe he's still coming in to work."

"Dad's strong as an ox. It's going to take more than this to slow him down."

She gave him a look. "Dying would really slow him down."

"Get outta here."

"I'm serious."

"So am I. Get out of here." He laughed at his own joke.

"Hilarious. I'm asking if you'll talk to him. Tell him to take it easy. Maybe you could start taking more responsibility around here so he wouldn't feel he had to come in so much."

"Now you're starting to make sense. Move him along slowly to early retirement."

"He's 66 years old. It's a bit late for early retirement."

"You know what I mean. Maybe I could have a new title." He looked off into the distance. "Like 'Acting President' or 'Chief Operating Officer' or something. Put some things in place here that I've been waiting a long time for."

"Great. Whatever. Just so he's not coming in every day."

"Sure. I'll talk to him this afternoon."

"Thanks. So what's the 'Mercer' situation? You mean Hal Mercer?" She tried to look nonchalant.

"Yeah. Mercer Incorporated."

"Yes, I heard he'd taken over after his father died." She smiled and looked down at her hands. "That should be interesting to watch."

"You're telling me. And the little runt offered a merger, if you can believe it."

She looked up at him. "What?"

"Yeah, I had to laugh. And so get this. I send—"

"You mean he's actively pursuing this?"

"Yeah, whatever. So listen to this, it's brilliant. I send Orlando and one of his boys over to respond to the offer at their big meeting, and I send along a little gift for Hal."

"And?"

"I sent him a box of golf balls." He laughed and slapped

the desk. "I would've paid money to see his face."

"I'm sure he wasn't thrilled." She smiled. "But he did play a lot of golf."

"Yeah, and played a lot of women, too." Chuck locked eyes with her.

Kate looked away. "Don't go there."

"Hey, you were lucky to be rid of that guy. I knew he was trouble from the word go."

"Yes, you made that more than clear."

"Well, I was right, wasn't I?"

"Can we just forget about ancient history? I want to know what's happening today with my family's company."

"Nothing at all. Everything is fine. Mostly."

"Mostly?"

"We're seeking a little bit of expansion capital to get us over a hump. He probably caught wind of that and thought we were in trouble. End of story." Chuck looked over at his laptop at the sound of an incoming e-mail.

"There were a lot of people who thought he would never work a day in his life." Kate looked out the window towards the building across the street as if Hal might be framed in one of the thousand windows there. "I'm surprised that he's playing this much of an active role in the company."

"You and me both. But it doesn't matter. He's going to fail either way."

"What if he doesn't fail?"

"What, and he, yikes, takes us over? A company that has thrived through two generations and just about to embark upon a third? A company that is, what, three times as big as his? Well, I guess I know I'll be out of work for sure."

"No question of that. I'd fire you myself if you pulled a

stunt like that on me."

"I know. Brilliant, wasn't it?" He grinned.

"Let's wait and see."

"Sure. It's a classic." He pointed his finger at her and winked. "It'll stand the test of time."

"Mmm. Well, when's this meeting?" She stood.

"Why?" said Chuck, also standing.

"Because I want to be there."

"What, Suzie Shopsalot is going to prick up her ears because her old flame is in town?" He laughed and really seemed to enjoy her reaction.

"Fuck you, Chuckles," she said. She grabbed her purse, walked out the door and turned down the hall toward her father's office.

Chuck stood in his doorway and yelled after her. "Hey! Don't call me that!"

* * *

Kate watched her father, Charles D'Arville, *de facto* president and CEO of D'Arville Industries, as he called the meeting of his senior staff to order later that morning. He was sitting at the head of the boardroom table in a room full of black, silver metallic, white, modern art and glass. It was all very nice, but he looked like an antique in the middle of it all. The way he was sitting uncomfortably in his chair, with his dark suit jacket bunching up at the shoulders, gave him a kind of propped-up look, as if he could tip forward at any time. His jowly, wrinkled face was shiny in patches, and his thinning white hair had a slightly damp look about it. Chuck sat on his left, and Edward Mortimer, the VP of Operations sat to his right as they waited for everybody to arrive.

"It was a stupid stunt to pull. I don't know why you insist on provoking him," Mortimer told Chuck. Kate was sitting quietly a couple of chairs down from her father, taking it all in.

"Because it's fun," said Chuck. "It'll make a great story for my interview in the *Financial Journal* when all this is over."

"It won't look so good if you're explaining how you lost your grandfather's company," said Mortimer, his dark eyes framed by neat, almost white eyebrows to match his short, almost white hair. His choice of attire favored the traditional: three-button tweed jacket with a herringbone pattern, gray slacks, crisp white shirt with a severe-looking tie knot. The more uncomfortable the garment, the more comfortable he looked.

"Yes," said Charles, as Orlando Bretagne entered the room. "That wouldn't be good."

"What are you talking about?" said Chuck. "You honestly think golf boy is going to make a successful takeover bid? Please. Their company is tiny compared to ours, and they've got this lame duck country club president at the helm. Yeah, I'm really scared." He nodded slowly with wide eyes and a tight grimace as if he were terrified.

He really is a prick, thought Kate.

"That's true, Edward," said Charles. "They are smaller."

"I think you're underestimating him. He's an excellent speaker and a bright kid. He worked side by side with his father for the last six months until the old man got too sick, and he has excellent people under him, including Owen Percy. Orlando, what was your read on him?"

"He didn't bat an eye at the golf balls. He took it right

in stride, although I could see it pissed him off. He kept his cool. He had this look of real… determination. And I told you what he said."

"Yes, let me see if I remember," said Mortimer. "He said, 'win or lose this game, it's your company that's at stake.' He doesn't sound like he's scared, either."

"Mmm, mmm," said Charles. He wiped sweat off his forehead with a handkerchief and put it back in his pocket.

"Let him try what he likes," said Chuck. "Our shareholders know that the best thing for this company is to have a D'Arville at the helm. We've always made them money in the past and we have years of tradition on our side."

"Yes, I'm sure tradition means a lot to them," said Mortimer. "Our sliding return on equity is nothing next to that."

"Ah, but we're going to change all that, aren't we?" said Chuck. "With our new additions and certain information they're going to provide us."

"What additions?" said Charles as Brenda Whitney, the VP HR came in and sat down, placing her portfolio and a stack of papers in front of her.

"We stole a couple of their people from right under their noses," said Chuck. "Tommy Grey and Kenny Walker. They both have a ton of experience, and a lot of their marketing strategy and product info comes with them."

"Oh, well. That's good, then. What about that, Edward?" said Charles.

"We'll never really be able to use any information they might give us."

"What's stopping us?" said Chuck.

"Well, patent law, for a start," said Mortimer. "And probably iron-clad non-compete clauses. But the time to market lag would also be prohibitive. Any takeover would be long over by the time we were geared up and ready to bring a reconfigured product to market."

"That's okay, because there isn't going to be a takeover," said Chuck.

"I hope you're right," said Mortimer. The steady, serious look he was giving Chuck worried Kate more than her brother's confidence could win her over. She longed to ask a question, but kept biting her tongue. It wasn't her place.

"Okay," said Charles. "What other items do we have for today?"

Chuck sat back in his chair. "I want to talk about why we have such horrible staff. They're lazy and rude."

Mortimer also sat back in his chair, sighed, and folded his arms across his chest. Brenda Whitney leaned forward to look down the table at Chuck.

"Do you have any specific people in mind?" she said.

"A few. They're getting too cozy around here. I think we should fire somebody just to make everybody sit up and take notice. Remember that we're providing a living for them."

Brenda looked at Mortimer, who shook his head.

"We can't just fire somebody without cause," she said. "That might even have the opposite effect on morale to the one I think you intend."

"Hey, if you want to make an omelet," said Chuck. "You've gotta break a few legs." He laughed at his own joke and poked Orlando Bretagne, who jumped.

"We also have to be wary of wrongful dismissal suits," said Brenda. "The courts have been willing to hand down significant awards."

"I just want to walk up to someone, and say, 'How long have you been with us, not including tomorrow?'" Chuck laughed even harder. Orlando forced a sick chuckle.

Mortimer tried a smile and sat forward. "Yes, well. That's funny. But what we really came here to discuss is the... situation, shall we say, facing us this Fall. Frank and I met with the bank yesterday, and they are getting nervous about our working capital situation. Frank?"

Frank Stokes, the VP Finance nodded. "We have two problems right now. We have the trade show coming up on the 25th, and we're going to have to ship a lot of product in a short amount of time. This is always expensive, and right now it looks like we'll have to, uh... we're going to need an additional infusion of cash to cover those costs. And the next issue is hitting our sales targets at the show—our aggressive sales targets, I should add, having looked at the numbers—and, uh, staying on top of our payments into the New Year."

Mortimer turned to look at Charles, who was nodding and staring at a faraway place as if in deep thought. Chuck took the opportunity to jump in. "What do you mean, 'aggressive?' I set those targets myself, and we should have no trouble hitting them."

"That's good to hear," said Frank, consulting his papers. "Because a 44% increase in sales over last year would really help." He looked across the table at Chuck with no hint of a smile on his face.

"You got it," said Chuck, returning the look. Kate knew her brother was an ace at sales, but also tended towards lofty goals and had a tendency to explain away his failures by finding faults in others.

"So, okay, problem two solved," said Mortimer. "But in the meantime, we are going to need funds to ship 44% more product. Who wants to go shopping for money with me in this climate?"

Charles took a sip of his water and continued to give the

matter thought.

Mortimer continued. "I don't want to bring up a touchy subject, but we just turned down a merger offer which would have meant an infusion of working capital as well as, I'm told, some solid finance backing from some very heavy hitters."

"Mercer?" said Chuck. He snorted. "Don't make me laugh. He may be able to line up a putt, but not financing. He just can't talk the language."

Mortimer looked at Frank, then back at Chuck. "Okay. But we're going to need—"

"I've got a few accounts lined up that I can close in the next couple of weeks," said Chuck. "We obviously need to kick ass in sales. Leave that to me. I'm on it."

"That's good news, of course," said Frank. "But given the fact that any company you close will stretch their payables for 60 days minimum, probably 90, and we're into January before we see that money. We need it now."

"Well," said Chuck. "What if we offered them favorable terms if they gave us a chunk up front?"

"That's a maybe, but it would be a drop in the bucket, even if you could." Frank put down his pen. "Bottom line —we need cash."

"All right," said Mortimer. "So Frank and I have our work cut out for us. But continue to, um, be aggressive on the sales front, because we're going to need it no matter when it rolls in."

Chuck pointed his finger at Mortimer like a gun and cocked the thumb at him. "You got it."

"So, are we finished here, then, Charles?" said Mortimer. "It looks like I have some meetings to set up."

"What?" said Charles. "Oh, yes. Yes, by all means. That's all, everyone." Everybody started leaving. "Thank-you for your input into this, ah, matter. Keep me posted.

With any information about, ah, well, yes."

Kate looked around the room, empty now except for her father and brother.

"Good work, Chuck," said her father. He winced as he tried to lift himself out of the chair. "I think we have the situation well in hand."

"Nothing to worry about," said Chuck.

Kate was sitting there with the opposite impression and resolved that she had to do something about it. But what? What could she do to make a difference?

Chapter Seven

"Suppose th'ambassador from the French comes back;
Tells Harry that the King doth offer him
Katherine his daughter, and with her, to dowry,
Some petty and unprofitable dukedoms."

- Act 3, Chorus, Henry V

Hal was working hard on Friday afternoon, trying to finish his agenda for the Monday meeting so he wouldn't have to take it home with him. He felt like he needed a weekend to himself. Play thirty-six holes and get into that new Harry Bosch novel. That would be just the thing. Margaret buzzed him at about 2:00.

"There's someone here to see you."

"I don't have anything scheduled. Who is it?"

"Someone you knew from university."

"I'm busy right now. Tell them to make an appointment."

"Her name is Kate."

Hal smiled immediately.

"Send her in."

He saved the file he was working on and stood just as the door was opening. "Hi, Kate. This is a surprise." He walked over to meet her, unsure if he should hug her or just shake hands. She looked down at his hand as if trying to gauge the same thing.

"Thank-you. It's good to see you again." She extended a hand and they shook without really making eye contact. Hal showed her to the couch.

"You, too." He turned one of the chairs in front of his desk around to face the couch. "Can I get you a coffee or something?"

"No, I'm fine, thanks."

"So. This is a surprise. I said that already. I mean, it's been a while."

"Yes, I know. And I just feel terrible that I didn't send you a card or anything. I was so sorry to hear about your father."

"Thank-you."

"How's your mother doing?"

"She's fine, health wise. Still a little lost, I think."

"I can only imagine."

"Yeah."

"And how have you been?"

"Great, now. Never better."

"I hear they've got you doing an honest day's work around here. What's that all about?"

"I can hardly believe it myself. It certainly wasn't part of the plan."

"Weren't you voted 'most likely never to work a day in his life?'"

"I was one of the people who voted for me." They laughed.

"Best laid plans, eh?"

"Yeah, tell me about it."

She looked down at his hands. "So, are you married?"

"Nope, not yet." He offered his left hand as evidence.

"Seeing someone, then?"

"No. I don't seem to have time these days."

She raised her eyebrows in mock disbelief. "The great

Hal Mercer? Not dating?"

"I know. It's hard to believe."

"You must really be loving this stuff."

"Yeah, I guess I am."

"It must be hard work, running a company this big." She looked around the office. "But apparently it doesn't give you enough to do."

"Why is that?"

She looked back at him. "Well, I hear you're out looking for new companies to muscle in on. To add to your workload and ensure you never have another date in your life."

"I was wondering when we were going to get to that."

"Well, we're there now. What do you think you're doing, coming after a company that's been in my family for three generations?"

"It's nothing personal. It's just a good business opportunity."

"Aren't there any other business opportunities out there that you could, um, look into?"

"Of course, but D'Arville Industries is a key competitor, and frankly not quite as healthy as it used to be."

"All the more reason to leave us alone."

"No, that's what makes it attractive for us to acquire. And keep in mind that I offered a merger."

"What good does a merger do us if you're in charge?"

"It would make us bulletproof. If we got together, we could be a dynamite combination, take the industry by storm."

"Yeah, well. I'm here to tell you it's not going to happen."

He raised his eyebrows and smiled. "Oh, and do you have any golf balls for me?"

"Now that was just a stupid prank. You said this wasn't personal, so don't make this a you and Chuck thing."

"It's not. That's just a sideline, not the main event."

"What is all this about? Are you sure you're not just lonely, or something?"

"How do you figure?"

"This isn't like you."

He smiled at this. "Why, what am I like?"

"I just think that if you had a girlfriend, this probably wouldn't be such a focus in your life."

"I agree I would probably be the better for some dinner companionship." He had a sudden thought. "How about tonight?"

"What? Me have dinner with you?"

"Yeah, why not?"

She forced a laugh. "You must be pretty full of yourself to think that I would go out with you, given the current situation."

"Oh, come on. It's just dinner. What if it turned out to be fun?"

"That's not the point. This is personal for me. It's my father and my brother."

"What if we didn't talk about business at all?"

"That's the only thing I would want to talk to you about. And I think we're finished now. I know where we stand." She stood.

Hal stood also and walked with her to the door. "Thanks for coming by. It was really great seeing you. I hope you'll reconsider and we can get together again sometime. Talk about—"

"Let's just leave it there." She turned and stalked off down the hall before he could even open the door for her.

"Good-bye." Hal watched her until she got to the elevators. She had that kind of light brown hair that you could tell used to be blond, and for some reason, he liked the idea that she didn't bleach it back. It had smelled nice as she walked by him. Some kind of nice-smelling shampoo, he imagined. The elevator dinged. She looked back and smiled at him as she walked in and out of his sight. It was a nice smile, which surprised him, considering the situation. She was pretty, there was no denying it. And she had felt so good in his arms back when that smile was all his.

Kate had been a natural fit with him at university. They hung around with some of the same people, attended the same parties, occasionally she had been in one of his classes. He remembered her sharp wit and sense of humor most of all. Well, except for that trim little figure that first turned his head. They were friends before they were lovers and that was unusual for him. It had felt good, comfortable. But then it seemed to hurt more when they split up. It felt so good to see her again. Too good.

Ugh. Why this? Why now? The game was afoot and now the rules were shifting. But then… was it conceivable he had this possibility in the back of his mind all along and that was something that spurred him on? He decided to go refresh his coffee and clear his head.

The best coffee he'd ever had was from that little diner near the university back in the day. It was just that sort of ordinary, low-key type of restaurant that moved at a very slow pace. This made it a great place to hang out instead of going to class. There was a whole group of them that used to get together there, including Kate. The Kate that used to be "his Kate." They would drink coffee and share a newspaper. What a difference a decade makes.

"Thanks for putting that coffee on," said Pete as he came in. "I'm going to need a couple of cups to make it till five."

"Who said you could have some of my coffee?" said Hal.

"This is staff coffee, buddy. Aren't you supposed to be getting yours from the executive lounge?"

"I wish."

"Well, what are you waiting for? Call a meeting, start the ball rolling. I'm seeing plush leather chairs, espresso makers, European chef, the works."

"Not in the budget, I'm afraid." He laughed and clapped him on the shoulder. "Still have the Spider-Man mug, I see."

Pete looked down at his left hand. "Oh, yeah. Not gonna retire Spidey anytime soon."

"So, how are things?"

"Boring as ever. How about you?"

"Same. I can't seem to convince anybody to have a good elastic fight in the boardroom."

"Just come on down our way. We'll teach you a thing or too."

"I bet. How's Randy doing these days?"

"Same." Pete made a bug-eyed face and they laughed.

Hal moved over to the counter and picked up the coffee pot. "Can I pour you a cup?"

"Sure thing."

Hal poured them each a cup and replaced the pot. "What's the word down on the floor these days?"

"Full-on panic mode."

"That's what I thought. The merger?"

"Yeah. Everyone figures they'll be out of a job. For me, of course, that would be the best thing ever, so I know it ain't going to happen."

"Of course it isn't. Seriously, I would never allow that." Hal opened the refrigerator and found the milk.

"Sure you wouldn't. What about your golden

parachute?"

"Not going to happen, and you can take that to the bank."

"All right. You say it and I believe it."

Hal had a flash of memory. "We've got to get together some Thursday and grab a few beers. Just like the old days."

"This is the first time I've seen you inside the office in about three months. I'm not counting on seeing you outside of it."

"I have been busy, but I'll make some time. I've gotta get caught up with you and Randy. Sometime soon."

"Absolutely. Just name the date." Pete looked at his watch. "Well, better get back at it. I think I can make it through till five now."

Hal nodded. "Good luck. I'll check my calendar and let you know about that beer."

They turned and walked in opposite directions, Pete back to the sales floor, and Hal down towards the executive wing.

When he got back to his office, he sat back in his chair and stared out the window. The morale problem was obviously worse than he had thought. Of course people would be thinking about their jobs. He had to make it clear to them that it was their company that was going to come out on top, not D'Arville. And more than ever make them feel they were a part of the company. *The profit sharing plan.* Archie said it was nearly ready, so maybe move it up in the schedule where it would do the most good.

Kate, Pete, Archie... trying to clear his head this afternoon was proving difficult. He looked at the half-finished meeting agenda and the numerous reports scattered around his desktop. It looked more like he was going to have to take them home. So much for his work-free weekend. Maybe he could work Saturday and get in eighteen holes on Sunday. He'd have to see how it went.

But what would he do with his time if he were free and easy? He'd lost his simple knack for leisure pursuits. All his friends had coupled up, making him a third or fifth wheel. Could he actually go to a movie by himself and enjoy it? He wondered what Kate was doing this weekend? It would have been nice even just to have a friend to talk to. If not for his stupidity all those years ago, how would things have worked out for them? And how much stupider that the "other woman" was just a drunken grope-fest at a party—no sex, no big affair. Never mind that he could still conjure in his memory the lip gloss and cigarettes taste of her kisses, although not her name now he came to think of it, but could still imagine the feel of her breasts, his hands struggling in her too-tight bra, not yet accustomed to the idea that girls were willing to let him do this stuff, never thinking for a second that Kate would appear there in the doorway of the fraternity living room, of all the shit luck.

For all that it cost him with Kate, the tonsil hockey with the girl… Sandra? Their fooling around never even progressed into a formal meeting of their sober selves. Just one in a long line of girls that followed whom he would pass in the hallways of the UC and look the other way. To lose Kate over such a small indiscretion seemed so unfair at the time and gave him some anger to keep him company after the break-up. But as the anger faded, it was replaced by embarrassment. How could he have screwed up his first serious relationship? A chance at love. Just because some drunk chick came on to him at a party? What a typical *guy* thing to do.

It still stung, seeing her all these years later. Was she

going to be a part of all this? She knew about the golf ball thing with Chuck, so she was obviously somewhat in the loop. Maybe she was more involved in the business than he thought. And what would that mean if she were? Just business. The rules of engagement and the art of war. Would he be able to pull out the "just business" card if Kate was at the helm?

Whatever the case, they must be getting a little nervous if they were sending her over here to talk to him. A little blood in the water, perhaps. He looked at his calendar. It was Friday the 13th. Less than two weeks to the trade show. Her visit had been excellent timing, as it turned out. As soon as she walked in the door, he had already decided two things: he was going to the trade show in person, and it was time to finalize the financing and begin the process of closing the deal. Find a way to close the deal with Kate, too.

Chapter Eight

"Once more unto the breach, dear friends, once more,
Or close the wall up with our English dead!"

- Act 3, Scene 1, Henry V

Pete had to remain standing on the train Monday morning as usual. All the early morning commuters coming in from Scarborough got the seats. He hung on to the pole near the doors as they all rocked from side to side and their droopy eyelids bobbed up and down. Mondays were the worst. It was like reaffirming your commitment to a job you hated once a week, the drudgery of your workaday life an unbearable thought after two days of freedom.

Looking around at all the people in suits and ties, jackets and uniforms, all the different faces, black, white, Asian and more, he thought about all the poor slobs like him on the subway every day, keeping the machinery of commerce grinding in one way or another. They all looked as tired as he felt, but he knew that this very subway car was full of go-getters, bright people full of enthusiasm, and probably even some who enjoyed their jobs. Unlike him.

He got off at the Yonge stop with most of the rest of the train to transfer onto the southbound line that would take him farther downtown. A huge swarm of them moved in unison to the escalator and then across to the southbound platform. There were people working on their Blackberries or laptops, reading accounting textbooks or e-readers, and many sipping their morning java, waiting for that good jolt to jump start their working week. The train rattled and screeched in the tunnel to their left and then burst into the station in a gust of wind, slowing to a stop and letting off hundreds of people. He and the transfer crowd pushed and jostled their way in and the doors closed behind them.

His problem was that he didn't understand corporate ambition. These people like Amy, how could they care about sales reports and customers and office politics? What on earth moved them to work as hard as they did and strive for meaningless promotions and work overtime for no pay? It was just a job—a gotta—which they had to do to pay their rent and buy food and go to the movies. Where did the enthusiasm come from?

Didn't they always fantasize about getting out of the rat race like he did? Ever since he had started working, he had had an almost daily fantasy that he would win the lottery and be able to quit his job and draw full time. He imagined how he would tell his boss, the looks on his co-workers' faces, what he would do first with the money: pay off his credit cards, buy a small place where he could live rent free, get a good investment guy to help make the money last, fly to New York City to shop his portfolio around to all the big comics publishers, or start his own comic book company, even better, and then he would be free.

The smell of burnt coffee and nervous ambition greeted him when he entered the office and walked to his desk to begin another day as a drone.

* * *

First thing Monday morning, Hal joined the Senior Management team in the boardroom for their weekly meeting. He noticed that even the senior executives were less enthusiastic on a Monday, so he kept the agenda loose and informal, and opened the floor to discussion of sales ideas. Owen Percy came back with the first contribution.

"We received a suggestion from Amy Quick on Bill's team," said Owen, inspecting his notes. "Something about the TR-50s being online and connected to the inventory system. We're just process mapping the idea right now to get a feeling for how it would impact workflow. This would mean that we no longer have to scan and batch file the TR-50s. And of course we would save on storage and time moving paper copies around. Julie, who did you put on this project?"

"I have Martha Sykes looking into it," said the VP IT. "We're looking at both the online system and the intranet."

"Okay," said Hal. He looked up at the ceiling as if the answer were written there. "So, the TR-50s are already on the computer, but we currently fill in the screens and then print them off."

"Right," said Owen. "But if they were online and connected to inventory, we would be able to confirm the order on the spot."

Julie Hamilton said, "I understand this will be a real-time solution, so we could even put the initiation of the delivery in the hands of the sales teams. Get the message to the warehouse the instant the order is taken."

"So why hasn't this come up before?" said Hal, looking

to Julie for the answer.

Owen sat forward to catch the VP IT's eye. "There was a preliminary exploration of something like this in the '09 Process Improvements Project, if I'm not mistaken."

Julie nodded. "Yes, at the time it was a speed issue. Our network couldn't handle the traffic. But since the Fall upgrade, we might be able to handle it."

"Excellent," said Hal, again looking at the ceiling. He folded his hands into a steeple. "So what if we could get this done before the trade show, and then we brought laptops to connect to the wifi on the sales floor. Wouldn't our customers be just blown away by this?"

There was an uncomfortable silence as Owen and Julie exchanged glances. Hal looked at them both. Owen cleared his throat. "That would give us only nine days."

Hal turned to Julie. "And does that mean it's going to be impossible?"

"Well..." said Julie, looking down at her notes.

"Don't answer that," said Hal. "I'll give you till the end of the day to give me an answer. If it's impossible, then that's one thing. If not, if it could be done, just tell me what you'd need to make it happen."

"Okay," said Julie.

Hal nodded. "Good. Whatever happens, though, I want everyone to remind their section leaders of the value of listening to new employees. Amy Quick has been with us a little less than a year, if I'm not mistaken. New people look at the way we do things and ask, 'Why?' People who've been around longer look at the way we do things and say, 'Because.' You've always got to be attuned to those whys.

"On a completely different note, I just wanted to let you all know that I've decided that I'm going to attend the trade show in person this year. Just to give our customers that extra boost of confidence and our people that extra support." Everyone nodded and looked at Hal. "And speaking of supporting our people, I am also working on a memo to all staff to be sent out in the next couple of days, just letting them know of some of the initiatives we are working on. This will be a 'rally the troops,' 'once more into the breach' kind of thing. The profit-sharing program developed by Archie and his team will be the centerpiece. Which, by the way, is excellent work, and I think it deserves a round of applause from all of us." Hal began clapping and everyone else joined in.

Archie sat up. "Thank-you, Hal. I hope it will be as well received by the front lines." He sat back with a look of great humility, which was, of course, pure bullshit and turned right away to a calculating look that he trained on Hal. But Hal was unafraid of subordinates making contributions. One thing Dad had taught him was that a great leader brings out the best in the people around him.

"I'm sure it will," said Hal. "All right, I think that concludes the meeting. Just a reminder to everybody to meet with section heads ASAP to get things ready and rolling for the trade show. We're going to need our best people for this show, because making it a big success is critical to our takeover efforts with D'Arville. Keep Owen in the loop on your progress. Thank you all."

Then they all picked up their papers and mugs and wandered off to their corners of the office, the IT people in particular looking more worried than others.

* * *

Typical of my luck for a Monday, thought Pete. *Not even*

84

10:00 and I find out Fluellen thinks of me as his bitch.

Fisher had called a meeting of his Sales and Marketing Team, one member of which was Fluellen, who was dragging Pete in as "Meeting Timer and Scribe." This was Amy's thing, not his.

"The trade show, as you know, is October 25th in Windsor," said Fisher. "Which is about a four hour-drive. We'll need to arrange for car pooling and hotel rooms for the teams you designate." He handed them all some information forms. "We'll need your best, most experienced people for this, because Hal wants to really shoot the moon on this one. He thinks this is the battle that could win the war."

"How many will we need?" said Sarah McMorris.

"From your team, I imagine we will need 2 or 3. From Bill's team, we will probably need 7 or 8, I'm guessing."

"Why do we need any marketing people at all?" said Bill Fluellen.

"Because there will be national accounts there and distributors from overseas," said Fisher. "They'll want to talk about more than just writing up an order. Your team will handle all the straight wholesale buyers."

"But that will be the majority of the action, am I right?" said Fluellen.

"Yes, probably."

"So why do you have McMorris down as point person on this project?"

"Because you'll be too busy with your people taking orders." Fisher looked at both of them. "Don't think of it as who's in charge… think of it as a team, and everybody has a role to play."

"That's fine," said Fluellen, sitting forward in his chair. "I'm all for teamwork. But the team leader should be from the largest section."

"Bill just can't handle the thought of a woman leader," said Sarah.

"It's not that at all," said Fluellen, turning his eyes and those bushy eyebrows towards her. "Why does it always have to be about some kind of male-female thing?"

"You tell me," said Sarah.

Pete had to stifle a giggle. *Man, Fluellen was getting owned.*

"I would be saying the same exact thing if you were a man," said Fluellen.

"That's true," said John Gower. "You haven't been to the Sales meetings."

"All right, people," said Fisher. "Let's not let this… let's not get into name calling. I need you to be focused. The true leader will lead by example, and that's what we need you to do. Sarah will keep track of the details, and Bill will keep track of his people, and you will both show leadership in doing so."

"So, let me get this straight," said Jennifer Jamy. "You'll be going down a day early to set up, you'll be there all day on the 25th, and then back the next day. That's a long time to be without the bulk of our inside sales team."

"Well," said Fisher. "John and Jennifer, that's why I wanted your teams to pitch in on the phones for those two days."

"That shouldn't be a problem," said John.

"I can work something out," said Jennifer.

"Good," said Fisher. "We're all doing our part. As a team." He looked at Fluellen, who said nothing.

"Who's booking the hotel and organizing the booth and all that?" said Sarah.

"I'm leaving hotel and travel arrangements to you. Owen has arranged for our booth and we will probably be in charge of setup and breakdown, etc. One other thing I should tell you is that we are currently looking into an online sales system that will connect the sales team to inventory and delivery systems, and we might be rolling this out for the trade show."

"In nine days?" said Fluellen, blinking. "And just when are we going to train people on the new system?"

Fisher tapped his finger on a TR-50. "I'm told it will be based on existing forms and procedures, but it will link them through the network. This is based on what you and Amy Quick came up with. It might not happen in time, I'm just letting you know it's a possibility, that's all. And Hal will be attending this event, just so you all know."

They all exchanged glances, and there were several slow nods. Pete was still processing the Amy Quick information. She would most definitely be pleased with that.

"Okay," said Fisher. "So everybody got it?" He gathered up his papers. "Good. Now it just remains to inform the troops, which I will leave in your capable hands."

* * *

By the time Fluellen called their team into the meeting room, Pete noticed that his face was no longer red and puffy-looking. By then, he just looked like his usual grouchy self. He herded them into an empty meeting room and said he'd be right back and buggered off to find a pen or something.

"So, what kind of bad news do you think it will be?" said Rick Williams.

"Who cares?" said Jeremy Bates.

87

"It could be about the merger," said Arthur. "In which case, I care."

"I'm with Artie," said Williams. "If it's about the merger, it'll be pink slips all around."

"Do you think they would let Fluellen deliver that message?" asked Randy. "We'd more likely be hearing about his pink slip at a meeting of all staff."

"Yeah," said Bates. "Merger shmerger."

"So why are we having a meeting now," said Amy. "When we just had one on Thursday?"

"Well," said Pete. "I could tell you, but then Fluellen would have to kill me. But it's just another meeting. Nothing to worry about."

"Perfect," said Marla Court. "Let's play buzzword bingo. I've got synergize and paradigm."

"Oh, come on. We are now post-*post*-Dilbert," said Randy. "And besides, Fluellen is not exactly a buzzword kind of guy."

"Yeah," said Pete. "But we could play curse word bingo. I've got *fuck*."

Just then, Fluellen walked in the door. "You've got *fuck all* is what you've got, Malden. And now you're getting *shut the fuck up*." Everyone laughed, including Pete.

"All right, lads and lasses," he said as he sat and put his folder on the table. "Let the meeting come to order. The main item on the agenda today is the trade show. Everybody but Kravitz and Davidson is going. You guys are going to hold the fort here while we're gone. You'll have some reinforcements from some of the other divisions. Everybody else, it's on the 25th and we're going down a day early for setup. Someone from marketing will be sending you your hotel information and arranging for the car-pooling. Anybody who could drive a few people should send an e-mail to McMorris. Yes, Bardolph?"

"Do we get matching t-shirts or anything?" said Randy.

"I don't know. Maybe," said Fluellen.

Randy laughed. "I was just kidding. Are you saying we might actually have to wear some kind of goofy uniform down there? I don't suppose you'd catch Hal in one of them."

"Well, he'll be there. So if you're wearing one, he'll be wearing one."

"Oh," said Randy, looking at Pete and then Amy, and shrugging his shoulders.

"And you'll be using your principles of *Extraordinary Selling*," said Fluellen. He gathered up his papers. "So, are we clear? Good, thanks, back to your desks, then, and let's all try to get ahead in our work so that we are in good shape by the time of the show. If anybody has any questions or ideas for the show, just e-mail them to Quick, here,"—he indicated Amy—"and she'll keep me in the loop. And, Malden…"

"Yes?" said Pete.

"I think you were the clear winner at bingo today."

"Yes, thanks," Pete laughed. "I couldn't have done it without you." What do you know? Manager Man had a sense of humor somewhere in the sub-crust area of his personality.

* * *

When they returned to their desks, the Inside Sales Group, third cube from the elevators, put their phones on "Do Not Disturb" to discuss the situation at hand.

"This sucks," said Arthur, pushing his glasses up his nose. "First they're going to make us work our asses off and then they're going to fire us."

"Welcome to the modern corporate world," said Randy.

Pete sat down, shaking his head. "I can't even begin to imagine how busy we're going to be when all these orders from the trade show start rolling in, added to what we normally get in a week, plus we're going to be away from our desks for two days. Work sucks."

"But think how exciting it will be to go to the trade show," said Amy. "This will be great experience for us."

"Yes," said Randy. "It will look great on our resumés..."

"Ohhh," said Arthur, groaning and covering his eyes with the heels of his hands. "I forgot about that. I haven't even looked at my resumé in years."

"And job interviews," said Pete. "Remember how much they suck."

"Oh, they suck all right," said Arthur. "Suckity suck suck SUCK!"

"Kinda makes you think, what's the point?" said Randy. "If we're going to be fired, anyway, then why bother working at all?"

"So you don't guarantee it," said Pete, picking up paper and pen.

"Yeah," said Amy. "You're all talking like it's a sure thing. They're going to need sales staff even if we do merge with D'Arville."

"But they're so much bigger than we are," said Arthur. "They'll keep mostly their people and turf us out like yesterday's garbage."

"I'm afraid I must concur with young Arthur, here," said Randy. "It does seem likely that they will get the lion's share of the job retention."

Arthur nodded. Pete started drawing Owen Percy with a black cape and scythe.

"Think of the bad PR," said Amy. "They wouldn't just come in here and clean house. They'd make a few small cuts maybe and then just trim by attrition."

Pete tried to look for a positive to support her argument. "So what if we get off at a different subway stop? That's about the worst that will happen."

"I have a picture in my mind," said Randy, applying two fingers to his right temple and closing his eyes. "You will be visited by three ghosts. The first is the ghost of corporate past, where your thinking comes from. The second is the ghost of corporate present..."

"Where they're getting a false sense of security?" said Arthur.

"Right," said Randy. "And the third is the ghost of corporate future, where our jobs are outsourced to a third-party call center in India and we are serving non-fat, decaf, vanilla lattés at Starbucks."

"I think I've heard this one," said Pete. "Are we loudly protesting our parents' value system and writing communist poetry on our breaks?"

"Something like that," said Randy, opening his eyes again, grinning proudly.

"May I remind you that we're also post-Gen-X," said Pete. "So I'm afraid that can't be it."

"And besides," said Amy. "There will always be changes to the way corporations do things, but they will always need people."

"Yeah," said Arthur. "To lube, oil, and filter the robots doing all the real jobs."

Amy ignored him. "Our generation will retrain more often and change jobs and even careers between five and ten times in our working lives."

"That is the party line," said Randy. "I hear that all over the place. And as with all conventional wisdom, I am forced to conclude that it is flawed."

"Randy," said Amy. "Whether you think it's half empty or half full, we're both drinking out of the same glass."

"Fair enough," said Randy. "I will endeavor to think the best. As long as my stocks are doing well, I will wear a happy face."

"I know, I know," said Amy. "One day you're going to ride the bull out that door."

"Indeed I am, mi'lady," said Randy.

"How big a bull is it?" said Pete. "Because that's not a very big elevator."

"Speaking of elevators," said Arthur. "Isn't it lunchtime? I'm starving. All this talk of unemployment is making me appreciate the meals I'm getting right now."

"Funny, all the talk of bulls was making me think of beef fried rice," said Pete.

"Let's all go to the Chinese place," said Amy. "I could go for some of that Moo Shu pork. Yummy."

"Why not?" said Randy. "It's almost noon. And we deserve a long lunch after all the extra worry they've been putting us through.

Pete hid his drawing of Owen Percy as Death under his keyboard, grabbed his jacket and followed the other three out to the elevator. He watched Amy smiling and talking and got a warm feeling remembering the feeling of her lips on his. So nice to know that secret side of her, he thought with a quiet smile as the elevator closed and the chitchat happened around him.

Chapter Nine

"Where is Montjoy the Herald? Speed him hence,
Let him greet England with our sharp defiance.
Up, Princes, and with spirit of honour edged,
More sharper than your swords, hie to the field!"

- Act 3, Scene 5, Henry V

Chuck was feelin' it. Doing what he did best: closing the prospect, making the sale. This was a new customer, a fairly large account that would represent some big dollars in monthly orders. He loved the closing, loved the reticence, the weighing of options, the humming and hawing, and then him with the gentle pressure, the reassuring voice, the product features, blah, blah, blah. And all the time playing a cat and mouse game in his head, circling, ready to pounce, but timing it right so he didn't scare them away.

He had been selling since he got out of college. College was the University of Pennsylvania down in the States, a school with beautiful old buildings in the Ivy League tradition. The jump to an American college hadn't been much of a stretch, as he had attended a private high school in Massachusetts called the Brooks School, the same alma mater as his father. After finishing grade twelve, he spent four years at the Wharton School on campus working on his undergraduate business degree. As he wasn't much of a joiner, he had avoided the fraternity life, but was a highly ranked squash player, loving the intensity of the one-on-one competition. When he graduated at 21, he went back to Toronto and started in the family business right away, taking to sales immediately.

"Yeah," said the prospect, Ken Banks of Banks & Co. They were in his office in a glass tower up in North York. The office décor was Spartan to non-existent, and there were still files in boxes, much to Chuck's distaste. Chuck sat across from his desk in an uncomfortable wooden chair, but refused to squirm. Ken sat back in his faux leather reclining chair. "But what about delivery? Would that be third party freight, or do you do your own?"

Gotcha. Once they started talking delivery, he was already sold. Just had to close. Chuck leaned forward and folded his hands on the desk in front of him. "If I could guarantee you on time delivery through our own network, would that seal the deal?"

On the way back to the office with the signed papers in his briefcase, Chuck shuddered at the necessity of having to deal with hicks like Banks. The only pleasure he got was in the kill. Ink on paper, his ass out the door. Take the pink carbon carcass back to the office and dump it on some sales slug's desk to handle the details. On to the next sucker. He checked his phone messages with one hand and negotiated the traffic with the other, the cabs and delivery trucks no match for the many German-engineered horses at his command.

Off the elevator, he stopped in the sales wing to drop off the initial order before heading down the hall to the executive wing and his office. Mortimer was just coming out of his office as Chuck approached.

"Hey, Eddie," said Chuck. "I closed the Banks deal. A few more shekels for the coffers, eh?"

"What?" said Mortimer, blinking. "Oh, good. But I need to talk to you right now."

Chuck looked at his expression. "Who died?"

"Nobody. Your office or mine?"

"Mine," said Chuck. "Follow me."

Mortimer followed him down the hall and Chuck entered his office and put his briefcase on the credenza behind his desk. Mortimer sat in a chair and let out his breath in one long blow.

"What's the problem?" said Chuck, sitting down.

"The problem?" said Mortimer, rubbing one eye with the heel of his hand, and then letting his arm flop into his lap. "The problem is that the bank has called our line of credit."

"Son of a bitch." Chuck slapped his desk. "Those fuckers." He looked up at Mortimer. "And how'd you do today?"

"Nothing. Which makes it official: I've been turned down by every I-Banker on Bay Street this week."

Chuck shook his head. "You have got to be kidding me. Don't they know that we are the shit? We're going to get shit done around here, and then really kill them at the trade show and, shit… things will turn around."

"At this point, we couldn't even ship product." They locked eyes. "Another few weeks and payroll will be iffy."

"I don't have time for this," said Chuck, breaking the stare to stand up. "Don't doubt a D'Arville, baby. They're messing with my money, now, and I have a long memory." He walked over to the window and folded his arms across his chest.

Mortimer leaned forward in the chair. "We're going to have to call an emergency board meeting to discuss our options."

Chuck nodded. "What we need is some kind of silver

bullet. Like a game-changing acquisition or something."

Mortimer continued as if he hadn't spoken. "The return on equity hasn't been there lately, and they aren't going to be in a great mood. We're going to have to find enough working capital to float us until after the trade show, and we're running out of options."

Chuck turned around. "Don't say it."

"They brought it up."

"No way." He sat back down in his chair. "I'm not having him talking to our board."

Mortimer cleared his throat and just looked at him without saying anything.

"No way," said Chuck, shaking his head.

"They are responsible for upholding the shareholders' interests. They want to hear the Mercer offer. Just as one of the options."

"It's not an option," said Chuck.

"Well," said Mortimer. "I guess if your family is willing to float some additional funds that would be different."

Chuck looked across the desk at him, chewing on his lower lip. He nodded. "I'll talk to my dad."

"If you can pull off something like that, that would probably be enough to hold them off for now. But in either case, Brian Meyer from the bank is contacting Hal Mercer today to invite him to a board meeting tomorrow."

"What the fuck? Tomorrow?"

"They're not messing around, Chuck. We're going to have to be able to show everybody some numbers they like, or Hal's offer is going to look pretty good."

Chuck sighed. "Where are we meeting?"

"They've got a room down at the Convention Center. A small one. With us, the board and the bank, there won't be too many to contact today."

"Why the Convention Center? That's kind of bush

league."

"Neutral territory. Because the bank called for the meeting."

"Oh. Have you got anything put together yet?"

"No, I wanted to talk to you first. And we'd better go down to Finance and talk to Frank before we put together any scenarios."

"Yeah," said Chuck. "That sounds like fun."

"Yes. Fun." Mortimer stood up and Chuck pushed himself up out of the chair to follow him out the door.

"Jesus Christ, Eddie. Did you have any idea that it could get this bad?"

Mortimer shook his head. "No."

Chapter Ten

"Prithee, honey-sweet husband, let me bring thee to
Staines."

- Act 2, Scene 3, Henry V

Pete woke up at blue neon 2:08 a.m. in Amy's bed and
lay awake for about half an hour before getting up and
slipping out of the bedroom. He wandered down the hall,
passing by their clothes on the floor by the entranceway
and collecting his boxers, and continued on to the living
room, which was barely illuminated by the city light
coming in from outside. Her neat and space-efficient
furniture was grouped around the sliding doors to the
patio, and he inched his way over there, not wanting to
find an invisible low table with his shin.

After pulling on his boxers and a moment of peering
out at the nondescript parking lot below, he turned away.
She had a small TV on her shelving unit, which was also
full to overflowing with all manner of books. Despite the
chaotic arrangement, the spines were all neatly aligned
with the edge of each shelf, and he imagined that if the
light were better, he'd be seeing a slew of guru books:
*Good to Great, Who Moved My Cheese, The 7 Habits of
Highly Effective People,* and many more like them. The
kind of self-betterment tomes she always had with her at
work as pleasure reading between textbooks.

Moving on into the kitchen, he opened the fridge and had a look inside. He loved looking inside other people's fridges. With bathroom cabinets, he couldn't care less, but a fridge could be fascinating. He wasn't sure what it meant that Amy had every kind of sauce he'd ever heard of in her fridge door, including most of the President's Choice ones. This made him think of the term "saucy wench," which made him smile. Wherever the President went, Amy went also. There were a few leftovers, milk and juice, eggs… as he was still pretty full from the late dinner noodles, he decided to pass on a snack.

Walking through the dining room, picking up several pictures and squinting at posed, smiling faces, Amy's often among them, running his finger along the smooth surface of her table—he finally ended up back in the living room. He sat down in a small wingback chair and looked out at another apartment building, and up at a small patch of night sky.

They had left work together, and he had asked her out to dinner, but as it was Monday, she had her night class. So he had a snack with her in the food court, and then went with her over to George Brown College for her class. While the teacher lectured away about the five P's or something like that, Pete sat beside her and drew funny pictures of the teacher and the other students. Amy was all serious and concentrating for the most part, but she would look over at his book occasionally and he'd catch a glimpse of her pretty smile.

After her class, he convinced her to have some real dinner with him, and they ended up around the corner at his favorite Thai place for hot noodles.

"So, that's a heck of an interesting class you have there," said Pete, after they had ordered.

"Yeah, well, maybe not to you," said Amy. "But I find it

interesting, and I've got to have it for my certificate, so it's got to be done.

"So many gottas, so few wannas."

"I guess so. But I think of it as short-term pain for long-term gain."

"Long-term career gain."

"Yeah."

"What about you, personally? What do you want out of life besides a meteoric climb to the top of your chosen career ladder?"

"Well, um, just a good life, I guess. Plenty of friends, a family someday, and not having to worry about… things."

"What kind of things?"

"Oh, just, well, money is what I meant. I don't want to have to worry about money."

"Right. Well, nobody wants to, really."

"But I have my, I have better reasons than most, I think."

"Oh, okay."

"It's not a big secret or anything, I just—"

The waiter leaned over and set a big bowl of noodles in front of each of them, gave a polite bow, and then went away again without saying anything.

Pete put his napkin in his lap and gathered his chopsticks. "Not a big secret…"

"Yeah, but I'd prefer if you didn't mention anything to the other guys."

"I won't."

"The thing is, my mother had, well, she was a single mom raising my brother and me, and things were always tight. Very tight. We, um, would occasionally take… well, I guess be on welfare, when she wasn't working." She looked at him and waited.

"There's nothing wrong with that."

"I know." She looked down at her noodles and poked at a shrimp with her chopsticks.

"Lots of people, you know… I'm just glad that at least some of the money was going to people who deserved it. That's what it's there for." He thought about taking her hand, but didn't.

"I know. So that's why I think I'm a little… driven, to succeed."

"I understand."

They ate their noodles and Pete watched her eyes scan the room. He thought about how her eyes looked by movie light, how they looked when he had kissed her at the elevator, and how they looked when she was laughing.

"What?"

He smiled. "What what?"

"You're looking at me."

"Does it bother you?"

"Yeah, cut it out." She stuck her tongue out at him, and he laughed.

"I was just thinking how beautiful you look."

"Oh. You didn't always think that."

"I did so."

"Well, why did it take you almost a year to ask me out, then?"

"I believe his name was Joe. Or was it Ugly Kid Joe?"

"Oh, yeah. Him. Well, I'm glad I finally dumped him and you finally asked."

"Me, too."

They finished their noodles, passed on dessert and walked back towards Yonge Street and the subway, Pete with his arm around her, but only partly for warmth.

He got up from the wingback chair and walked down the hall to her bathroom, which, unlike his own, had a feeling of careful decoration, pictures in just the right places. He took a leak, washed his hands and dried them on a very soft towel, and then went back to the bedroom and got under the covers again. Amy stirred and rolled over a bit, but didn't seem to wake up. He could just barely make out her features in the dark.

Pulling the covers up, he felt her body heat warming him and he noticed a hint of their combined scents wafting out, which brought back delicious memories.

He hadn't even been thinking of coming over, but when they were approaching the Bloor subway stop and he kissed her goodbye and stood to leave, Amy put a hand on his arm and said, "Don't get off."

"This is my stop." He laughed. "You want me to come home with you?"

"Yes," she said. She looked into his eyes without blinking, and he returned the look. As the doors opened, he sat back down.

"Okay," he said. "Anything for a few extra moments with you."

"Okay."

And he had ridden all the way up to Sheppard with her, and they had taken the transfer bus to her place, neither of them saying much, just sitting there and exchanging occasional looks, which would produce a kind of half smile, and then she would look out the window. They got off the bus and walked up the hill, cutting across the grass to get to her building, and they were inside the front door and waiting for the elevator.

"This is as far as I got the last time," Pete said, leaning in to kiss her neck.

"Uh-huh."

"I seem to be getting the green light to come on up this time."

"So far," she said as the elevator doors opened and they

got on.

"I'll be on my best behavior," he said as the doors closed. He wrapped his arms around her waist and kissed her then, holding the warm part of the small of her back, his hands caressing in slow, circular motions, letting just the tips of his fingers travel down the inside of the back of her pants, as his tongue parted her lips, touching her teeth, and then the tip of her tongue.

"Bad boy," she whispered when she took a breath. He smiled and she put a finger to his lips, as if to say shhh. They got off the elevator and he followed her down the hall to her front door. She felt around inside her purse for her keys for a second and let them both in.

She dropped the purse on a hall table to her left, pushed the door closed with one hand and grabbed him by the belt with the other, pulling him over to her and kissing him, her tongue pushing into his. Pete's hands were tugging at the top of her pants, fumbling with the button, all the while kissing her, finally getting the button open, and pulling the zipper teeth apart. She pulled her sweater over her head as he was pulling off her pants and kissing her belly. He knelt down in front of her and began tugging the panties down as she stepped out of the legs of her pants. She was pulling up the back of his shirt as he paused to kiss the fronts of her thighs, holding her from behind, and he put his hands up in the air as she tugged his shirt straight up and off him. She pulled him up and kissed his chest, squeezing his ass in both hands.

"Shouldn't we light some candles?" he said as she unzipped his pants and yanked them straight down.

"Fuck it," she said, stepping on his pants in between his feet so he could pull his legs out, kick off his shoes, her hand up inside his boxers, his cupping her small breast in the curve of his palm as he kissed the bottom of her neck

103

near her collarbone and then reached around to undo her
bra as she pushed his boxers down.

They walked each other down the hall, Amy walking
backwards while kissing him, Pete clutching her to him,
his erection poking in her stomach. The door was open,
and she guided him to the bed, where she sat down and
took him in her mouth, driving him wild with her tongue
as he stroked her hair. After a few minutes of that, she lay
back on the bed, pulling herself up to the pillows and he
slipped between her legs and lay on top of her. He could
feel that she was ready, but he didn't enter her, only
pressed against her, kissing for a while and then leaving a
trail with his tongue all the way down her chest and belly
to her legs, where he nuzzled the soft skin of her inner
thighs and threaded his arms under her upraised knees to
grasp her to him and press his face into her, kissing her
deeply.

Lying in her bed with her sleeping beside him, he still
couldn't believe his luck. He remembered the first time
Fluellen had introduced her around the department and,
looking her over, he had imagined doing energetic things
with her, but at the same time never imagined it would
really happen. He shook her hand and smiled, and then
turned back to his computer. And here he was in her bed,
all this time later. Was he going to wake up and discover it
was all a dream, or would he fall asleep and dream they
were back at work that same day?

He thought about the furniture in her living room and
then of his own couch, which wouldn't match. She had a
nicer dining room table than his, but would all her stuff fit
at his place or would she want him to move his stuff in
here? And what would she think of all the comic boxes?
Of course, he could rent a storage garage, which would
mean that he could finally have his whole collection in one

place, gathering the stuff from his parents' basement as well. But then he'd just be visiting it on weekends.

Or maybe they'd get a bigger place with an extra room for a study slash library. That would be cool. Get those shelves with the pullout clear plastic drawers like the ones at the comic stores. And have a nice balcony—do his drawing out in the open air. Even with the price of a small storage garage, if it was necessary, and a larger place, they would both be paying less rent in the long run. How perfect was that?

But he shouldn't get ahead of himself. Just having a good time, it's all casual, no pressure.

It had all happened so fast with Rose. One minute his lease was coming due, the next he met her at a friend's party and they were living together. That hadn't been a recipe for success. But that was in the past now. She could keep his coffee maker for all he cared; he wasn't going to be the one to call first.

Had he ever been in love with her? If so, he certainly wasn't now, so does that mean that love comes and goes? That it isn't a permanent thing? If it isn't, then is it really worth the risk? And worse, was it something you were able to agree to or decide upon, like a magazine subscription, or was it involuntary, coming along unannounced? He didn't like the idea that he was helpless to prevent love from coming over him in cases where the outcome was still uncertain, the risk of the pain assumed despite the wisdom of his experience. The whole idea of love was a little bit frightening, but maybe that was a good thing. It didn't pay to take love too lightly.

He shook his head and rolled over. He had to get some sleep or he would be a zombie tomorrow. Just the thought of all the work they had coming up with the stupid trade show made him tired. Then he thought of the merger and his stomach did a little flop. Why was he thinking about work now? That was no lullaby. Had to think about spending the whole weekend with Amy. Sleep in, read the paper together, go to brunch, maybe catch a matinee, dinner out... heaven.

The clock was insisting that it was three-thirty. It was only a few hours now until they would have to get up and get ready for work. Maybe shower together. He realized that he would be wearing the same clothes two days in a row. This made him smile, as everybody would know what that meant, and he could flash Arthur just the right look and really rub his nose in it. Things just kept getting better and better.

Chapter Twelve

"Bardolph, a soldier firm and sound of heart,
And of buxom valour, hath, by cruel fate,
And giddy Fortune's furious fickle wheel,
That goddess blind,
That stands upon the rolling restless stone..."

- Act 3, Scene 6, Henry V

Randy came in on Tuesday morning looking like he had twenty-pound bags of shit suspended from both shoulders, dragging him down into a slumped posture. He sat in his chair, crumpled a small take-out espresso cup and threw it into his garbage. He sat staring at his blank computer screen. By this time, everyone had turned to look at him.

"What's up, Randy?" said Pete.

"Hmm?"

"I said, what's up with you?"

"Oh," said Randy, taking a deep breath. "It's not what's up with me. I wish it were what's up. It's what's down that's got me, um, down."

"Okay," said Pete. "What's down?"

"The Dow, my stocks, everything."

Pete looked at Amy and raised his eyebrows.

"How bad is it?" said Amy.

"Oh, it was bad," said Randy.

"Does this mean you won't be riding the bull out the door anytime soon?" said Amy. Pete smiled and looked back at Randy.

"Oh, the bull will rise again," said Randy, sitting up straight. "He will rise phoenix-like from the ashes and gore the damn bear through his soft and ugly midsection. And then we'll ride."

"It's not like you have to retire tomorrow," said Arthur. "Why do you care so much about the stupid Dow?"

"How could I not?" said Randy. "The Dow is everything. It's the key indicator in our lives. In its rise and fall we can track the paths of all our fortunes."

"Or the loss of your fortune in some cases," said Amy.

"Quite right," said Randy. "But that's exactly what I mean. It can, uh… it's like a horoscope, telling you exactly what to expect from your day. What to do, what to watch for, even what to wear."

"Say what?" said Pete. "An exchange indicator told you to wear that wrinkled shirt?"

"Yes, of course it did. This is a perfect example. When my stupid, asinine, under-performing American Eagle stock is down, I'm not going to wear any AE clothing under any circumstances. So today I wore Eddie Bauer casuals." He smoothed out a few wrinkles on his chest. "The wrinkles are more due to my mood this morning."

"What about if all your stocks are down?" said Arthur, choking down a giggle. "Are you going to come to work naked?"

"No, but another few days like yesterday and I might come in wearing a potato sack."

Pete laughed. "No, a barrel with shoulder straps."

"Yes," said Randy. "Just like in the comics. But the various stock indices are the heartbeat of our capitalist society, so, in a way, all our days depend on them. All our fortunes are hung on what is, basically, a gamble… a gamble of monumental proportions. When I say the Dow, I am speaking metaphorically."

"It sounds more like you're speaking metaphysically," said Pete. "That could be your religion: the Tao of the Dow."

"The Tao of the Dow," said Randy. "Or Dowism. Oh, I like it. Can I use it?"

"Sure," said Pete. "Knock yourself out."

"Thank-you," said Randy. "It will be a comfort in dark times such as these."

"So I guess you're not much for the buy and hold philosophy," said Amy. "You're like a day trader, huh?"

"A bit of both," said Randy. "Just an honest speculator trying to raise his station in life through careful investment. But, alas, the odds are stacked against us at this casino, and the house always wins."

"Your metaphors are starting to make my brain hurt," said Pete, gripping his head in mock pain.

"Mine, too," said Amy. "If the stock market crashes, how does that mean that the house wins?"

"Oh, it doesn't." He sighed. "I just mean that we're stuck in our place as the modern-day equivalent of plebes, or peasants. With no chance of getting ahead."

"Nice ambition," said Amy, turning back to her desk.

"Yes, well," said Randy, turning on his computer. "You don't see me quitting my day job, do you?"

They all got back to work. Many orders were coming in, and if their desks were piled too deep, Fluellen would be on the warpath. The phones rang, so that made it difficult to make a lot of headway. For a while, they were uniformly productive and focused, keeping themselves to themselves. In fact, the whole office had the quiet hum of an active beehive. All the troops formed a phalanx of busy heads arranged in the pod formation of the cubicle rows and columns, bent low over their electronic pursuits, individual efforts constituting group purpose.

Then the simultaneous *bee-boo* of a hundred or so e-mail programs announced the arrival of a message for the masses.

Pete looked at his screen, and had a look around to confirm that everybody was reading the same thing. It was a memo from Hal addressed to the entire company. They sat for a few moments of silence until Randy snorted with laughter.

"Oh, he's really outdone himself this time," he said. "A Strategic Plan, Core Values, a Mission Statement… he was probably up all night with this stuff. He must've gotten wind that the front lines were getting restless and fearing for their lives."

"Yeah," said Pete, turning around. "He asked me about it on Friday when I saw him in the break room getting coffee."

"So you're responsible for this," said Randy. "Well done. Give them all something to worry about. Now if we all just leave our resumes sitting out overnight 'accidentally on purpose,' maybe we'll start hearing about some pay rises."

"There's a lot of good stuff here," said Amy, still reading from her computer. "Did you actually read the whole thing? Listen to this: blah-blah-blah, um, yeah, 'I am aware of everyone's hard work over the last weeks and months, and to recognize the integral part that we all play in this company's future, the Senior Management Team has developed a Profit-Sharing program for all employees so that everyone who is part of our success will share in it.' Yada-yada-yada, 'details will follow from your manager.' That's something new."

"Cool," said Arthur, who had turned to face the others. "I stopped reading way before that. What else did I miss?"

"The Mission Statement is quite a piece of work," said Randy, peering at his computer screen. "Quality quality quality, excellence excellence, satisfaction, more customers, we win."

"That is good," said Pete, laughing.

"What is so wrong about having a Mission Statement?" said Amy. "It came up in my course on Best Practices, and most of the gurus endorse it."

"Well, it's a load of horse, isn't it?" said Randy, turning to face inward. "It's a lie we can all believe in."

"It's just something to give us all clarity about the big picture," said Amy. "I like it."

"What does it do for you?" said Randy.

"It's something you can be proud of at the end of the day."

"I see. I admire your ability to think positively," said Randy.

"Thank-you," said Amy. She looked around to find everyone looking at her, and cast her eyes downward at her shoes.

"So what do we think of this?" said Arthur. "Are our jobs safe now?"

"Jobs are never safe," said Randy.

"Well, Hal told me on Friday that there was no way he would let anyone lose their jobs over the merger," said Pete.

"Really?" said Arthur. "What about that, Randy?"

"You've got to remember," said Randy. "Hal is no longer just Hal. He's now *Management Hal*. He has to lie every day of his life just to survive. If management says no jobs will be lost, then start worrying. It's when they're ignoring you and not talking about jobs at all that you can feel better."

"So no matter what he says," said Amy. "You think he's lying."

"I think if management tells the truth, it's by accident." Randy leaned back in his chair and crossed his arms. "This whole memo thing is just to shut us up, make us do the work they need us to do to make this merger happen."

"So why aren't you looking for another job?" said Arthur.

"This job, another job, what's the difference? They're all the same."

"So I still need to be worried, then," said Arthur, sighing.

"What have you got to worry about?" said Fluellen, coming around the cubicle door. Everyone swiveled in their chairs to face their computers. "You've got a job where you apparently don't have to do any work, and you can sit around chatting all day."

"We were just discussing the corporate memo," said Randy over his shoulder. "Lovely piece of writing, didn't you think?"

"Fantastic. Now, if you're finished with that, may I remind you that the trade show is only a week away, and you are all very busy people. Let's stay focused and get ourselves in good shape before then." He turned back the way he came and walked back across the floor to his office.

Randy jumped up out of his chair and stood at attention in the middle of the cubicle, saluting their departing boss. Everyone stifled a laugh. Pete popped his head over the wall of the cubicle to make sure Fluellen was out of sight.

"Man, everyone has got their knickers in a knot over this trade show, eh?" he said.

"Yeah," said Arthur. "You'd think it was do or die for

the company the way they're acting."

"My point exactly," said Randy, slumping back in his chair. "It's probably a key to the merger plan. And me with my portfolio in the dumps... what timing." He stood with a visible shrugging of the shoulders. "Anyway, who needs a coffee? I could go for another espresso. The effects of the last one are starting to wear off."

"What about Fluellen?" said Amy.

"He's made his rounds for the morning, don't you think, Pete?" said Randy.

"Yeah, I think he's probably holed up in there for the duration. At least till lunch."

"Good enough for me," said Randy. "Shall we?"

Amy looked at Pete, and shook her head. "You guys go ahead. I still have loads of orders to put through."

Pete looked at her. "I guess I could clean up my desk a little, too. You go ahead."

"I definitely need a coffee," said Arthur, following Randy out of the cubicle. "This whole situation is stressing me out, and the coffee is the only thing keeping me going."

Pete watched them wander over towards the elevator, heads tilting downward, gloom settling around their shoulders like fog coming in off the Waterfront to cling to the skyscrapers. Pete smiled at Amy and let her get back to her work, turning to his own computer to finish what he was working on before the memo arrived. He inhaled the scent of Amy's deodorant coming from his armpits and grinned to himself all over again.

Chapter Thirteen

"Go bid thy master well advise himself:
If we may pass, we will; if we be hindered,
We shall your tawny ground with your red blood
Discolour..."

- Act 3, Scene 6, Henry V

"Thanks for coming with me," said Hal as he drove down University toward the Convention Center.

"Of course," said Owen Percy. "I think it will look better if you're not out there all by yourself making all those promises."

"It never hurts to have someone who looks as experienced as you by my side, right?"

"You mean old. But yes, I agree with you. Their first impression of you will probably be how young you look. I can certainly help balance that out. When you start to speak, you'll wow them, and I can just head back at that point."

"No, you don't. You're staying with me."

"If you insist."

"I do." Hal turned onto Front Street and moved into the left lane. "Listen, off topic, but have you talked to Mom recently?"

"Yes, of course. Janey and I had her out to the house on the weekend."

"I took her out for dinner at Rosewater. She still seems pretty out of it to me. Thanks for calling her."

"She's my sister… I knew her before you did."

"True. I'm just glad everyone's making sure she gets out and gets a phone call most days. She still seems pretty lonely."

"Which is to be expected."

"I guess."

Hal turned into the parking garage of the convention center, took a ticket at the gate and proceeded down a couple of levels till he found a spot. They got out of the car and gathered their briefcases, snapped on BlackBerries and picked up their favorite pens and laser pointers. They each retrieved their dark suit jackets from the back seat and pulled them on, fastening a single button at the front of each. They brushed down their shoulders and arms in unison and snapped on small magnetic metal-stamped brass nameplates with the Mercer logo. Hal nodded at Owen and they climbed the stairs.

"So, to confirm, Parker and Flesherton are on side?" said Hal.

"Yes, I spoke to both of them yesterday."

"So I'm on Teschke and you'll take Green?"

"Right."

"So let's get together at 9:45 by the front table or wherever they have us."

"Right. Good luck."

"You, too," said Hal. Owen split off and walked into the conference room, shaking hands almost right away with someone he knew from the D'Arville board, working his way across the room, his face radiant with the energy of doing what he did best. His gray hair showed the years, but they were successful years. The whole room seemed to become aware of his presence at once though not everyone was happy to see him.

Hal smiled and looked around the lobby for Simon Teschke, but instead he saw Kate sitting in an armchair over by the wall. She stood as he approached.

"Well, Ms. D'Arville," he said. "This is a surprise."

"Hello, Hal." She didn't offer her hand this time.

"You're here for the meeting?" he said.

"Of course."

So beautiful. Ouch. "Sure you are. So I hope I can count on your support."

"You can always hope."

"This is a win for both sides. Part cash, part shares, and everybody is part of a stronger company going forward."

"With your name on it."

"So if I kept both names you'd go along with it?"

"No way."

"Look at it this way, a strategic alliance now will strengthen the long-term picture for all of us and make us unbeatable."

"Is this a preview of your speech?"

"Maybe."

She crossed her arms. "I've heard better."

"Well, never mind the delivery. What do you think of what I'm saying?"

"First of all," she said, looking down at his brass nameplate. "Your company is way smaller than ours."

"But we've got the financing all lined up, believe me."

"Don't interrupt me."

"Sorry, go on."

"Second," she said. "I like how you refer to a hostile takeover as a 'strategic alliance.' Very smooth. What, you think we don't know the difference?"

"We're not into hostile territory, yet."

"Yet."

"Look, it doesn't have to be that way. This is going to be good for everybody."

"But mostly for you. Excuse me." She walked around him and headed for the door to the conference room.

Hal caught up to her. "Hold on, hold on. Just for a second."

She stopped and crossed her arms again.

Out of the corner of his eye, Hal saw Simon Teschke walk across the lobby and into the room.

"What?" Kate said, sighing.

"Why don't we discuss it over lunch today?"

"If I have lunch with you, will you forget about this takeover?"

Hal laughed. "Steep price for lunch."

"I'm worth it."

"You know I can't do that. But it would be really great to go out with you again. We used to have something."

"That was before, and we both know how that ended."

"Seeing you again has stirred something up. I know you've forgiven me."

"You think so?"

"Oh, come on. We're different people now. We could start fresh."

She just looked at him.

"Think about it. It's just one date."

"So, is that it?" She moved towards the doors.

"For now." He smiled at her.

She smiled in spite of herself, but kept on walking, through the doors and into the large conference room, mingling with the crowd until he could no longer see her.

He looked at his watch. 9:30. He had missed Teschke, who could be anywhere in there by now. He scanned the many faces turned this way and that, engaged in conversation or looking at him, sometimes with unreadable expressions, sometimes antipathy. There was an unwelcome feeling growing in him, which seemed to be located in his stomach.

Was this all going to go wrong? Would he falter now, before the end game? If he did, was it the beginning of the end for his company?

Then he saw Teschke break out of the crowd and walk to the coffee table by himself, and the thought came to him, the idea he'd tried to impart to the staff with his memo, something to give himself a shake: *Once more into the breach.* Eyes locked on his target, smile forming as he shot his cuffs, he pursued his prey.

"Simon, are you ready for some fireworks?"

"Sure." Teschke shook his offered hand. He wore a two-piece taupe suit with an Icelandic blue shirt and matching tie. His high forehead eventually encountered hair that swooped back and to each side, with long curls down the back of his neck. "Good to see you, Hal."

"You had a look at the proposal I sent you?"

"Yep."

"And you liked what you saw?"

He looked around. "I think I left something out in the lobby."

Hal nodded. "I got you. Lead on."

Teschke picked up his coffee and walked towards the door and out to where Hal had seen him earlier, with Hal following.

"So you liked it?" Hal said.

"Um, yeah. It's a start."

"A start. Okay, that's good."

"I think it had a lot going for it, but too much was implied, not enough said straight out."

"So what'll it take?"

"A seat at the table."

118

"Well, Simon, you don't have anything to worry about there. We'd consider you an asset."

"Term?"

"Three years guaranteed, and an option for another three."

"Only three up front?"

"That's our board charter, but I'll tell you right now that we don't have a lot of turnover."

He nodded and sipped his coffee. He looked out the window. "Who else do you have?"

"Simon, you're the first person we came to."

"Uh-huh. Who?"

"We have high hopes for Parker and Flesherton, and Owen is talking to Green right now."

"And you're expecting me to talk to a few."

"Well, actually, that's a great idea, now that you come to mention it."

"Uh-huh."

"So are we on?"

Teschke drank down the rest of his coffee and wiped his lips with a napkin. "We are."

"You've made the right decision, Simon. We'll be in touch."

He nodded and walked back the way he'd come, setting his cup and saucer on a table by the door. Hal walked over to the window with an entirely different feeling in the pit of his stomach, and had to force himself to wait a few minutes before going back to the room. Even though most people probably saw him leave the room with Teschke, he didn't want to leave them without a shadow of a doubt that they'd been talking. A little buzz in the room would be good, though.

When he went back, Owen was already waiting for him by the guest chairs at the front. People were beginning to take their seats while the chairman of the board arranged his notes at the head table.

Hal undid his jacket button and smoothed out his pants. "All went well?"

"Yes. You?"

"Yep."

"Excellent." Owen likewise undid his suit jacket and crossed his arms in front of him. "I think we're making some progress here."

The board chair then stood up and called the meeting to order. Hal half listened while going over his speech in his mind, mentally checking off the points he wanted to hit, section by section.

"Ladies and gentlemen, as you know, we have a guest speaker with us today. Hal Mercer from Mercer Incorporated. The board recognizes Mr. Mercer."

Hal got up from his chair and walked to the lectern amid scattered applause. He produced his notes from the inside pocket of his jacket, set them down on the platform and adjusted the small microphone upwards. He looked around the room at all of the expectant faces, his eyes settling on Kate in the third row. To his surprise, he saw just a hint of a smile there, almost a challenge.

He smiled, leaned forward, and began.

Chapter Fourteen

"FRENCH KING: 'Tis certain he hath passed the
River Somme."

- Act 3, Scene 5, Henry V

After Hal finished speaking, all Kate could think was,
Damn, he's good. We're in trouble here.

Burke Foster, the Board Chair, stood and thanked Hal
and asked him to leave so they could discuss the proposal
and allow the board a chance to vote on whether or not to
present it to the shareholders. Kate watched as the men
from Mercer walked out of the room and damned if Hal
didn't shoot her a little grin as he walked through the
door. *Cocky bastard.*

Kate tried to coax her throbbing temple out of a
headache with a two-finger massage. She knew that the
spreadsheets Chuck and Mortimer had been working on
were no match for a really good speaker. Someone had to
stand up and counter Hal's impact with a speech that
would restore everybody's belief in the company.

It was clear that the bank was going to support the
Mercer offer and that her family would oppose it. The
board would likely be divided, depending on which
members Mercer had gotten to and which they hadn't.
This left Mortimer as the likely swing vote. Would he
vote their way or had he already cut a deal with Hal?

Hal had that necessary leadership quality and he had the money on his side, which was probably the most important thing of all. Mercer Inc. was obviously, surprisingly, a well-run company and she had no doubt that they could successfully merge and assimilate the two firms.

If Mortimer threw his support behind Hal and the merger didn't pass, he was as good as finished at D'Arville. Despite the financial crisis, she and Chuck and her father controlled thirty percent of the voting shares. Certainly they had their supporters on the board. Chuck had come up with some pretty good numbers showing a light at the end of the tunnel. Which way would it go? This was too real for her. She preferred reading the quarterly reports at Starbucks with a nice latté. This was too close to the action.

Mortimer sat with Foster and D'Arvilles junior and senior at a white-clothed table at the front of the room. There was a lectern sitting on a side table to their left.

Burke Foster continued where he'd left off. "We'd like to proceed with some discussion before the vote. Who would like to go first?" He looked around the room.

Brian Meyer stood up and buttoned his suit jacket. "Mr. Chair, I'll speak on behalf of the bank."

Meyer clasped his hands behind his back and rocked slightly on his heels as he spoke.

Kate looked down at the floor as the banker talked. She sighed. One for Mercer, as expected. Meyer caught her eye several times and looked away quickly. Stuffed shirt.

"… unless the family is willing to inject some more capital into the business," Meyer said. "That's all I have. Thank-you."

"Thank-you, Mr. Meyer," said Foster. "Perhaps this would be a good time to address the issue of additional funds from the founders. Charles?"

Charles D'Arville stood, leaning his hand against the table for support. "Thank-you, Burke. Uh, yes. Additional funds. I can't help thinking that such a move is, uh, premature." He coughed and cleared his throat. "What are we really facing here that we haven't been through before? I think once you see the projections that Edward Mortimer and my son have put together, you will see that this is just a, uh, hiccup. My family are shareholders, too. With, uh, even more to lose. Potentially. And I firmly believe that we'll get through this stronger than ever. Thank-you."

Kate joined in the polite applause. Her father did not look well. He had a pale, pasty look about him, wiping his brow with an old handkerchief. By rights, he should be long retired by now. She couldn't help thinking that if Chuck had shown more potential, he'd already be there. If they could turn this thing around, how could the board support Chuck as successor to the President's chair? Maybe she would have to throw her own hat in the ring.

"All right, then. Thank-you, Charles." Foster looked over at Mortimer and Chuck. "Would you gentlemen like to go next?"

"Sure thing," said Chuck, looking impeccable in a shirt, tie and jacket. He looked over at Mortimer, who nodded and stood up. They walked to the lectern together and set up their papers.

"Thank-you, Mr. Foster," said Mortimer. "I would just like to echo the comments made by Charles D'Arville. We are all in this together and we all have a lot at stake here. I can honestly tell you that we have found a way through this. But I'll let you judge that for yourselves when you see the evidence. I'm going to let our VP of Sales take you through the sales projections."

Chuck smiled and patted him on the back as he approached the microphone. "Thanks, Eddie. I second that emotion, and I gotta tell you, I don't know what all the fuss is about, really. When myself, Eddie and Frankie, our VP Finance sat down yesterday to go over the figures, it rapidly became apparent that all we needed was to really tear it up at the Fall trade show in Windsor, like we always do, and we'd be back on solid footing. This company has been in business a long time, as my father noted, and we've come through worse than this and always managed to make our shareholders a buck or two." He laughed and looked around. Nobody else laughed. He looked back down at the papers. "So, okay. Tough crowd. Why don't I take you through the sales projections in your handouts?"

Everyone rustled their papers and shifted in their seats as they found the correct page and tried to follow along with Chuck's presentation. Kate ignored what Chuck was saying and watched the board members for any reactions. There wasn't much going on out there that she could see. Most eyes were cast down on their handouts. No nods of the head or grunts of disapproval. It was a hard crowd to read. She caught Mortimer's eye, also ignoring Chuck. She raised her eyebrows at him and he tried a smile.

"… with the best sales force in the business," said Chuck. "So on that note, I'll hand things back to Eddie. Thank-you." There was some scattered applause as he stepped aside to allow his co-presenter back to the mike.

"Thank-you, Chuck." Mortimer gripped the lectern with one hand on each side, looking out at the crowd for a second before he began. "What you have in your hands is a plan to turn this company around. If you somehow think that these sales targets are 'pie-in-the-sky,' then let me set your mind at ease. We achieved the same level of unit sales at this trade show in '08, and actually exceeded it in '06." He paused to let this sink in, looking out at his audience. "The emergency action plan we've outlined in those handouts, including our executives foregoing salary in the short-term and stretching payables and jumping on receivables in the next two weeks, will allow us to get through the trade show and satisfy the bank's requirements within 60 days.

"This company has had a long tradition of profitability that we're eager to get back to. While the Mercer offer may be a tempting way out of some, let's call it temporary difficulty, don't be fooled. D'Arville Industries still has good essentials, young talent coming up," he said, indicating Chuck. "And has been and will continue to be an industry leader for years. Don't fall for a short-term solution; there is more money to be made for our shareholders in the long term by sticking with us. Thank-you." There was stronger applause now as he and Chuck took their seats at the head table. Kate felt she had just heard the election speech of the next President of D'Arville Industries.

"All right, then," said Foster. "Are there any more presenters?" He looked across at Monty Wells, the CFO and Corporate Secretary, sitting in the front row.

"No," said Monty. "That's everyone on the agenda."

"Does anybody else have anything to add, then?" Foster looked around the room, as did Kate. There must be something else to say. The scales were too precariously balanced. She couldn't tell which way they would tip in this vote and it was killing her. Silence. Burke nodded. "All right, then. With respect to the Mercer offer, can I have all those in favor of presenting it to the shareholders?"

* * *

Hal and Owen were on their way back to the office, stuck in traffic waiting to turn left off Front Street. They were still on an emotional high, so they weren't even bothered by the delay.

"That was amazing," said Hal for the third time. "The feel of the adrenaline, the sense of half the room being hot against you and the other half hopeful that you have the answers they've been looking for. It was intoxicating."

"You knocked them dead," said Owen.

"Especially Chuck. He looked completely pissed off, but wouldn't catch my eye."

"Yes. He looked like a petulant child."

"And now the suspense is killing me."

"I know what you mean. It was amazingly difficult to stop myself from listening at the door to see which way it went."

Hal laughed. "You felt that, too?"

"Oh, yes. Edward Mortimer and I go back a long way, as well as a few others in that room. I would have *loved* to have heard what they had to say."

"You and me both." Hal tucked himself in behind a Toyota Camry going around the corner on the red light. "When do you think we're going to hear something?"

"I gave Jim Flesherton my cell phone number, and he promised to call me after the vote," said Owen, just as his cell phone rang. They looked at each other and laughed.

"Eerie," said Hal.

Owen pressed the button. "Owen Percy," he said. "Hi, Jim. How'd we do? Well, thanks, I appreciate that. But how did the vote go?"

Hal looked over at his face to gauge his reaction.

"I see. No, that's all right. Thanks for calling, Jim. Right. Bye." He pressed the end button and stared at the tiny device in his hand. He took the tip of his tie and wiped off the little display window.

"Well?" said Hal, looking over and finally catching his eye.

Owen shook his head.

Chapter Fifteen

"'Tis true that we are in great danger:
The greater therefore should our courage be."

- Act 4, Scene 1, Henry V

After dropping Owen at the office, Hal took a drive over to his mother's home. He pulled up in the driveway and turned off the ignition. The garage was a detached two-story coach house, set back on the lot. The house was in swanky Rosedale, not far from downtown. It wasn't the place he had grown up—his parents had moved here after he had gone away to university—but it was the last place he remembered as his father's. They came here after the funeral, and he had wondered how he could ever go back to the office again, just as he was doing now.

Henry Mercer had started in the business at the age of 19, selling for an older gentleman who was in poor health. Hal couldn't remember the man's first name, but the company was called "Watson's" something. When the man died two years later, Henry had to buy out the widow and run the company himself with only a high school accounting class as his business background. He changed the name to Mercer Incorporated and never looked back, growing the company bit-by-bit, adding new salespeople, contracting out warehouse space, and acquiring other small companies along the way.

128

Hal always wondered how he would have fared, given the same prospects. Instead, his lot had been to take over an already established company that came with high expectations. It wasn't as if he'd trained for it. He'd started at Upper Canada College as a day school student and, although he passed all of his classes, he'd been more interested in team sports, student council and the social committee. He never really understood what a big deal UCC was to other people until later, when they would whistle or raise their eyebrows when they heard what school he'd attended. At the time, he just assumed that all Schoolmasters blathered on about tradition and excellence and all that crap. Even though his university degree had the word "Commerce" attached to it, it was mostly the same experience as his high school years.

He got out of the car and walked up the cobblestone sidewalk to the front door. The gardeners had apparently been there recently, as everything was neatly raked or trimmed. The mailbox was overflowing, so he took out the handful of fliers, bills, and junk mail and sorted through it on the doorstep. Before he could knock, his mother opened the door.

"Oh, hello, dear," she said. "I thought I heard a car. Come in."

"Hi, Mom. Here's your mail."

She took the mail and put it on a side parlor table. "I'm sure it's all junk."

His mother looked smaller. She was average height with a beautiful auburn 'do that came with its own shade number. She was still wearing her reading glasses and a purple velour bathrobe. He obviously wasn't interrupting important plans.

"Yeah, probably junk." He walked in, took off his jacket and loosened his tie. He followed his mother into the kitchen at the back of the house.

"Would you like some coffee?" said his mother, moving automatically to the cupboard for a mug.

"Thanks," said Hal. He took a seat at the breakfast bar island in the center of the kitchen on a tall, padded stool. He looked out the window at the back garden as his mom filled the two mugs with coffee and then a little milk for him, just the way he liked it. She passed him his mug and leaned against the other side of the island counter, looking at him and waiting.

"What?" he said, sipping his coffee.

"Nothing. How are you today?"

"Fine." He picked at the Mercer logo on his mug, one of the old ones. Part of the M had worn off.

She smiled. "You just decided to drop by in the middle of a work day?"

"Sure." He smiled, too, and shook his head, laughing. "Oh, I don't know what I'm doing. You ever have one of those days?" He took a big slug of coffee.

"All the time, it seems."

"We're in the middle of a takeover. Or, it started out as a merger, and then… well, it's turned into a battle. I just made my big pitch to their board."

"And?"

He looked down into his mug. "They turned me down."

"Oh, well. You win some, you lose some. That's over, then, and you can get on with your life."

"That's the whole problem. It's not over. We have to keep working on them until they cave. It doesn't look like they will."

"Who says you have to keep working on them? Can't we survive without them?"

He shook his head. "It's pretty much do or die. The

market is very tough right now."

"That sounds very familiar to me." She touched her fingers to her forehead. "Now who could that remind me of?"

"Very funny, Mom. But Dad would've just got it done."

"Not always. It didn't always come so easy."

Hal waited for her to follow with a story to illustrate this. It didn't come. "He always made it look so easy." He drained the last of his coffee and looked out the window. "I had no idea what I was getting myself into. I don't even know how I got into it."

"Your father made you an offer."

"But why?" Hal got up and took his mug over to the sink. "Why did he choose me?"

"You're such a poor choice?"

"No, but you know what I mean. David was always the big achiever in the family. Science club, good grades, always interested in the family business. I was more of the social type."

She gave him a look over the top of her glasses. "And your grades reflected it, as I recall."

"Exactly. So why me?"

"We believed you were capable of more than just scratch golf and cocktail parties."

"We?"

"Of course. Your father always believed you had that… leadership quality, but he was frustrated with you. I gave him a nudge now and then, and finally made him talk to you."

He smiled. "Ah, so I have you to blame."

She came over and gave him a hug. "You went along with it, so you have only yourself to blame." She pulled back and straightened his tie. "And look how it's worked out. You are the success your father always believed you could be."

"Not yet, I'm not. What have I accomplished so far except not screwing up in a noticeable way?"

"I'm sure you have the staff eating out of your hand already."

He took a deep breath and let it out in a sigh. "It's hard to tell."

She took his arm and led him towards the back door. "Come out here with me and I'll show you the greenhouse I'm having built."

"Greenhouse?" He could feel the sense of urgency calming in him as he walked between the shrubs and garden statues, listening to his mom tell him her plans. Whatever the fates had in store for him, he felt he was safe from them here. He was wrong, of course. Their work went on elsewhere unabated.

Chapter Sixteen

"The sum of all our answer is but this:
We would not seek a battle as we are,
Nor, as we are, we say we will not shun it."

- Act 3, Scene 6, Henry V

On Wednesday morning, Hal was out on the golf
course, far away from the office. The course was St.
George's, a private club where Hal had a membership.
The fairways were green and well-tended and the rough
was strewn with leaves of various hues. There was a nice,
easy breeze coming from the southwest—a one-club wind,
if that. He was one under after four holes, and just sizing
up his drive on the par 5 fifth. He took a practice swing
from several feet back on the tee box, looking down the
fairway where he wanted his ball to land. He walked up
and addressed the ball. First his usual smooth takeaway,
and then a seemingly effortless downswing with a wicked
club head speed through impact that propelled the ball in
a slight drawing motion to the top of its arc and then
down into the middle of the fairway.

"Very nice," said his partner, Jaswinder Krishnakumar,
who went by "Jas" for short. He then stepped up and
pushed a ball and tee into the ground and stepped back
for a quick practice swing, which was a little rough. His
dark hair was styled just so and his serious, calculating

look was aimed at the fairway ahead. The Nike golf shirt and shorts looked as though they'd been freshly pressed and matched the Nike golf shoes perfectly. He was wearing Tiger Woods Sunday power red, but it wasn't helping his game. He was five over after four holes. Hal could see he played a lot and worked hard at it, but his slightly off swing mechanics said he had taken up the game late in life. Jas took a rip at the ball and propelled it up the fairway about two hundred yards, ten feet into the rough on the right.

At least he didn't curse and swear and carry on about it, thought Hal. They walked off the tee together, gathered their bags and headed off toward their next shots.

"This is a beautiful course," said Jas. "I only wish I could do it justice."

Hal brushed this comment aside. "You're doing fine. How long have you been playing?"

"Four years. I began playing with some fellow students in the second year of my MBA."

"Because everyone told you it was going to be an essential business skill, right?"

Jas laughed. "How did you know?"

"I've been there."

"But I was surprised by how intriguing the game is, how obsessive it becomes."

"It's an addiction."

"The way you hit the ball, you must have been playing a long time."

Hal nodded. "Ever since I was 10. My dad taught me to play."

"I wish I had started earlier," said Jas as he reached his ball, which was about half visible in the thick rough with a tree about six feet in front of it.

Hal watched as his partner selected a club and prepared

for his shot, brushing away a dead leaf and assessing his options. It was funny how the mention of his father sharpened his mind. His first thought was the usual chill that his father was gone, and the wish that he was still alive and able to advise him now. The second, following in close succession, was the resolve that he should get on with it and he would do fine.

Jas was an investment banker. This was their first meeting.

"You haven't got much green to work with," said Hal.

"No," said Jas. "I think I'm going to take my medicine, as they say, rather than try for a hero shot." He put back his five-wood, and selected a seven-iron instead.

"Very wise." Hal watched as he slashed through the grass with his iron, popping the ball out and across the fairway to the rough on the other side. "Hard luck," he said.

"Oh, well," said Jas, putting away his club and picking up the bag. "Maybe I won't be trapped behind a tree this time."

"How long have you been working in I-banking?"

"Almost three years."

"Wow. And what's the usual burnout period?"

He laughed. "Three years. But I love it."

"Are you married?" said Hal. He put down his golf bag to the right of his ball and looked greenward.

"No, I don't even have time for a girlfriend. It is all the time way too busy. But Toronto has so many fine prostitutes."

Hal looked at him. "Oh," he said, and nodded, pursing his lips. "So you're going to make the one mega deal and then get out, right?"

"Absolutely." Jas smiled and closed his eyes as if savoring the idea.

135

Hal's first thought was five-wood and attacking the green, but as the group ahead of them were still putting out, he went with a lay-up club instead. His four-iron left him an easy chip shot of about fifty yards. He picked up his bag and set off after Jas to help him look for his ball.

"I'm sure it came in right here somewhere," said Jas, walking around a sapling.

"I had it on line with this spruce right here," said Hal, walking past him towards the fairway bunker from the fourth hole. "Here it is." He pointed into the middle of a nasty patch of fescue.

Jas sighed and made his way over, pulling out a low iron again. Despite his careful swipe at the ball, he bladed it sharply and his ball came screaming out of the deep rough towards the green.

"Fore!" yelled Hal. The group on the green covered their heads and watched Jas's ball bounce by the front of the green and into the bunker. Hal waved their apologies.

"I'm so sorry," said Jas, shaking his head. "How embarrassing."

"Not your fault. You skulled it."

Jas picked up his bag and they began walking towards the green as the other group was leaving. Hal chipped to within ten feet and Jas made a decent sand recovery, leaving himself a fifteen-foot putt. Hal two-putted for par and Jas, clucking at himself the whole time, three-putted for a seven. The other group was just leaving the sixth tee as they walked up, so they selected their clubs and took a seat on the bench to wait.

"So," said Hal. "I understand you had a visit from Edward Mortimer this week."

"Yes," said Jas. He inspected his golf ball. "Bad numbers."

"I know."

"Rumors are starting to fly." Jas turned on the bench to face him. "Tell me... why do you want to acquire D'Arville?"

Hal looked him in the eye. "Market share. We want to add their customer base to our own before we introduce new products so that we eliminate some of our competition, as well as opening up new markets. We want to be the biggest. Their company still has good essentials, but the management isn't there anymore."

Jas nodded. "That's the word on the street. You have strong financials and no fires that I could see in the operating reports. I just hope their share value doesn't take a nose-dive before we can pull this off."

"Me, too."

"I also had a look at your annual report. P&L looked good, equity position good... we would have to work out some debt ratio covenants, and our bank would be sole signer on your Accounts Receivable."

"Not a problem."

"Good. So why don't you send me your prospectus? I need to know specifically how much you can finance internally, and details of any previous bond releases. This could all come together pretty quickly, I think."

"That's great," said Hal. "What makes you say that?"

"The entire D'Arville plan, as I understand it, hinges on this trade show you have coming up. If they don't go there and hit a 350-yard drive, shall we say, then I think we'll be putting their tombstone in the paper the following week."

Hal laughed. "Exactly what I was thinking."

"I think they're off the green," said Jas, pointing in that direction. "You're away."

Chapter Seventeen

"KATHERINE: *Alice, tu as été en Angleterre, et tu parles bien le langage.*
ALICE: *Un peu, madame.*"

- Act 3, Scene 4 - Henry V

"What do you think of this?" said Kate, holding up a blue corduroy top.

"Mmm," said Alice, shaking her head. "I don't see you as the corduroy type."

They were in the Hazelton Lanes shopping center in Yorkville at noon on a Wednesday, taking advantage of the October sales on Fall fashions. The mall was busy, as always, even though it was a workday, but nobody seemed to be in a hurry.

"How about this?" Alice held up a blouse in a soft yellow. Her long, blond hair fell over one shoulder as if offering a complementary hue for the garment. She pushed the thin frames of her eyeglasses up the bridge of her small nose with the thumb and middle finger of her other hand and looked at Kate, who was squinting at her.

"Is it for you?"

"No, for you." She held it up to Kate.

"This is how you see me?"

"What?"

"It looks like something an old lady would wear."

"You think?" Alice looked at the label, and put it back on the rack. "Mmm."

"There's nothing here. Let's go across to *Petra Karthaus*."

"What about some lunch first? I'm starving."

Kate looked at her watch. "Yeah, I guess. Where do you want to eat?"

They walked in the general direction of *Aquascutum*, Alice in the lead. "There's *Lettieri's*. Or the open courtyard place in the middle.

"We always end up there," said Kate.

Alice considered. "Yeah. What about that *Spice Room* place? They have a chutney bar."

"What are my other choices?"

"I think that's all there is, unless we walk over one block."

"The courtyard it is, then."

They selected a table and placed their orders. Alice got started on the fresh bread right away.

"Oh, my god," said Alice. "This bread is to die for."

Kate nodded and took a sip of her coffee.

"So tell me more about Hal," said Alice. "I can't believe you said no to him."

"It's a point of honor. He's trying to take over my dad's company."

"Who cares about that? Hello, he's hot."

Kate laughed. "You don't have to tell me. But I've been down that road before."

"And what? You caught him making out with some sorority chick? Oooooh, did you leave a note on his locker after gym class?"

"No, but you think it would've ended there?"

"He was a lot younger. And it was one weak moment at a stupid party. Do you still have feelings for him?"

Kate broke her eyes away from her friend's probing look.

"There you go. Listen, girl, he's rich, single, and gorgeous. I don't know what else you're looking for in a guy, but you'll probably be waiting a long time to get it."

"It's not that."

"Then what?"

"Once a player, always a player."

"Still?"

"Well, he says not. He said seeing me stirred something up in him."

"And you? Are you stirred up?"

Kate had to smile. "Like a daiquiri in a blender."

"So?"

"There's also the takeover. I saw him at the shareholder's meeting yesterday. That's when he asked me out the second time but—"

"What was he wearing?"

"Oh, just a dark suit, with this French blue shirt and matching tie."

"And is his hair still long and wavy?"

"No, it's pretty short now."

"But it looks great, right?"

"Oh, yeah." Kate paused with her fork in midair. "So where was I? Oh, right. He was giving a speech at our shareholder's meeting to get everybody to accept their share offer to buy up the company."

"Listen, he's offering a merger in more ways than one. Marry the guy, and it's all in the family either way."

"Don't go there. He's just so smug. I think I basically can't stand to see him get his way."

"He can have his way with me anytime."

Kate laughed. "That's the problem. Half of me feels that way, the other half is..."

"Stupid?"

"Stubborn."

Alice wiped her mouth. "What if he never asks you out again?"

Kate looked at her, and then looked out into the mall.

"You want him to ask you again, don't you?"

"Here's what I want. I want to help my family's company turn the corner and be setup for another twenty years of success and have the takeover be out of the question. Then I want him to ask me again just for me."

"Sounds great," said Alice. "How are you going to make it happen?"

"I know I can do it. I just don't know how, yet. I'll let you know."

* * *

Pete took Amy with him on Wednesday when he went to pick up his new comics for the week. He had a regular order with *The Silver Snail* on Yonge Street, and they walked over after work. It was a sunny Fall day, and they held hands like a real couple.

"Do you always go on a Wednesday?" said Amy.

"Oh, yeah. All the hardcore geeks come in on Wednesdays. It's the day the new stuff comes in. We're the 'can't wait until the weekend' crowd."

"So you're a 'hardcore geek?'"

"When it comes to comics I am. But it doesn't seem geeky to me."

"What does it seem like?"

"It seems cool."

"What is cool about it?"

"I love the artwork first and foremost, which is way cool, but I also love the collecting, the organizing, and the… nostalgia, I guess. It still gives me that feeling of excitement I got when I was a kid."

"But they're just comic books."

"Yeah. What we need is a highbrow name for the hobby like 'numismatist' or 'philatelist' to give it some respect."

"Oooh, philatelist. Can we try that tonight when we get home?"

Pete laughed. "Philatelist just means a stamp collector."

"Hmm, I see what you mean. Maybe we could make up a term. Cumicmatist?"

"That could be worse, actually. Here it is." He pointed up at the sign as they approached.

The store was located up a flight of stairs and occupied the second floor of the building. There was a café at the front of the store and rows and rows of shelves filled with toys, models, figurines, games, books, cards and, of course, comics. Pete walked to the order desk at the back to ask for the week's arrivals. Amy was looking around at all the different displays of eye-catching merchandise.

"Quite a lot of stuff, isn't it?" said Pete, as the clerk handed him his bag of comics.

"I had no idea there were this many different comic books," said Amy.

"You've never been in a comic store before?"

She shook her head. "Never."

"It's quite a place," he said, starting to walk back towards the front. "People think comics are only about superheroes, but there are as many genres here as there are in a regular bookstore."

"But there are a lot of superheroes."

"Yes. And it just so happens that's what I buy."

"Adolescent male power fantasies."

"Pardon?"

"Sorry, I take that back. Look at the boobs on this chick." Amy picked up a comic from the shelf as they were passing by. "These feature the entire range of adolescent male fantasies."

"Shh," said Pete. He took the comic she was offering him and put it back on the shelf. "Talk like that will get us booted out of here."

"Look at that poor shmuck," said Amy in a whisper, indicating an overweight, acne-ridden teenager with greasy hair who was staring at them. "He's probably never seen a girl in here before."

"No," said Pete. "There are girls in here from time to time."

"How many of them look like Catwoman?"

"Not many," said Pete. He put his comics down on the counter and took out his wallet. The total came to thirty-five dollars, and he gave them two twenties.

When they were outside again, Amy asked to see the bag. "How many comics did you buy?"

"Five," said Pete.

"For forty bucks?"

"Yeah, they're getting expensive, all right."

"You've got, what? Batman, Superman, Thor, Spider-Man, two Batmans." She picked through them one by one, looking at the covers. "So what are the stories like?"

Pete shrugged his shoulders. "Not great, really, most of them. They battle super villains, save the world, that sort of stuff."

They started walking back the way they'd come, towards the subway. Amy passed the bag of comics back to him.

"I don't get it," she said.

"I can't really explain it, either. I just like them."

"How long have you been buying them?"

"Ever since I was twelve. I had a couple of friends who were into comics, and that's how I got started. Reading comics is what first got me interested in drawing."

"I guess that makes sense. And your drawings are fantastic. Why don't you try to do that professionally? I've seen you do better stuff than some of those comics I saw in there."

"It's a tough field to break into."

"Have you ever tried?"

"Um, yeah." He stopped beside the entrance to the subway. "But, listen. Where do you want to eat tonight?"

"I don't know."

"Do you want to eat downtown, or up by your place?"

"Wanna get takeout and bring it back to my place?"

"Sure," he said, looking around. "What kind of takeout?"

"There's a Chinese place in that strip plaza up near me, if we get off one stop early. That way it'll still be hot."

Pete took her hand again as they walked down the steps to the subway entrance, and got on the northbound train.

As he scanned the waiting crowds on the platforms, face after face snapping into focus through the window and then whipping into blur, holding her hand in his lap, the thought occurred to him that things were going well. Having sex again was fantastic. But they were also having so much fun together. They liked eating out, going to movies, they had hung out on the weekend—just like he had with Rose. But this time it would be different. He would be "emotionally available." He was going to share his feelings with Amy. He wouldn't get stuck in a rut.

She didn't really talk about the future much and he didn't want her to feel any pressure. Maybe she was just having such a good time right now that it didn't occur to her. Even when she had to study for her courses he would go over and read a book or do some drawings. And he saw her at work every day. They were spending lots of time together, and not much time apart. It had to be going somewhere.

Although he tried to shake it off, he still felt the question hanging in the air. Have you ever tried? Had he? The short answer was yes. He had sent his drawing samples to DC and Marvel, the two big comics publishers, and to several others. He had even received a couple of style tests where he had to draw what was described or copy a drawing of one of their superheroes, but he was never able to just give them what they wanted. Always had to put his own stamp on things, like adding a cartoony flourish that appealed to him, but not, apparently, to the editors. Why was he too embarrassed to just tell her that?

He turned to look at her face and she smiled at him and then looked away, offering herself only in profile. She was so pretty, sometimes he would get a weird ache in his throat, like the beginning of a cold you see coming a few days away. But there was no physical reason for the pain. It made him think of it, but it wasn't exactly like the pain he had to swallow several times during the sad parts of movies.

After the Chinese food, and the rented movie, and the sex which kind of started up during the movie a little bit and then finished after the end credits, and the lying around for a while, he was on the subway again, heading back to his place for some sleep and clean clothes for the next day. Sitting in the last car and facing backwards, he could see each station receding into a small rectangle of light in the distance as they moved forward into the darkness, wheels rattling and screeching.

He flipped through one of his Batman comics, holding

the pages with deliberate care. Such clean lines. This imitation of motion. The line of a jaw such a simple, pure gesture. Style classic, iconic. Riddler, Robin, Nightwing, and Batman: a study in dark perfection. But always this feeling that he could do better. He would do better.

Chapter Eighteen

"Where have they this mettle?
Is not their climate foggy, raw, and dull,
On whom, as in despite, the sun looks pale,
Killing their fruit with frowns?"

- Act 3, Scene 5, Henry V

Kate positioned herself directly opposite Mortimer's desk so that she was the first person he noticed when he walked into his office Thursday morning at 9:00. Mortimer did a double take, stopped dead, then crossed to his chair, putting his briefcase down beside him. He was not quite frowning, but definitely not smiling either.

"I'm here to talk about the Mercer takeover situation," she said.

Mortimer raised his eyebrows and leaned forward slightly. "Go on."

"I know Chuck isn't worried about it, but I've been talking to Hal Mercer. I just wanted to come down and get your thoughts." She looked at his face for a clue as to how he was taking this visit from his boss's daughter, to whom she rarely spoke.

Mortimer nodded for a second. "I see. And what are your concerns?"

"That we should be taking this as a serious threat and not a joke. That Hal is shrewd, pretty sure of himself, and his speech was dynamite. That they may be smaller, but size isn't everything." She waited to see if this would provoke any amusement, but Mortimer's expression was uniformly grave.

He nodded again. "Yes, I share your concerns. I said as much to Charles after the board meeting."

"Thank God." She let out her breath. "I thought I was the only one. Every time I talk to Chuck about it, he just laughs it off."

"I'm not laughing. We all saw Hal talking to Teschke in the lobby before the meeting, and I'm sure he's not the only one they're talking to."

"So what can we do to convince Chuck and my father? Can we meet with them today? I think we should all be talking about how to defend our company. Just because the merger offer was voted down by the board doesn't mean the shareholders won't consider a purchase offer."

Mortimer sat back in his chair, nodding and looking at her with his hands folded in front of his face. His mostly white hair was combed over just so and probably set in place with Brylcream or some other relic of bygone days. But despite his best attempts at grooming and apparel, he had a weird thing on the end of his nose that reminded her of cartoon witches. She tried not to look as if she were staring at it.

"I agree," he said at last. He picked up the phone and pushed three numbers. "Good morning, Julia. Yes, I did. Go ahead. And would you please schedule a meeting for this morning with the senior staffers? Check their schedules, but make it as soon as possible. Yes. The boardroom will be fine. Excellent, thank-you." He hung up the phone. "We're on."

"Thank-you. I really appreciate this."

"I'm glad you came in today. Maybe together we can

make your father and brother listen."

"I hope so." She stood up. "I'll go and wait in the boardroom. Give me a buzz if there's anything you want to go over."

Kate left him to poke around in his briefcase and prepare for the meeting. She walked down the hall to the boardroom, pushed open the heavy glass door and switched on the lights. There was a pitcher of water and eight tall glasses on a sideboard, so she poured herself a glass and sat at the table. She took out a small purple notebook from her purse and started to review the last few entries.

About an hour or so later, after she had made more notes, Mortimer came in and sat beside her. Her father arrived with Chuck following closely behind.

"Katie?" said Chuck. "What are you doing here?"

She took a deep breath and restrained herself from contradicting him on her name. "I came to talk about the Mercer situation. Hi, Daddy." Her father gave her a kiss on the cheek.

"Is that what this meeting is about, Eddie?" Chuck sat beside his father, who occupied the head chair.

Mortimer took a similar deep breath before replying. "Yes."

"You're not actually worried about that pathetic speech he gave?" said Chuck.

"Let's wait until everybody's here," said Mortimer, as Brenda Whitney from HR walked in with Frank Stokes from Finance.

"Who're we waiting for?" said Chuck, looking around. "Oh, yeah. I guess Pepé's not here."

Pepé was Chuck's nickname for Orlando Bretagne, a seasoned marketing professional who was well respected in the business, but now had the misfortune to be working with her brother. She sat forward and said, "Yes, Chucky. He'll be coming along in a moment."

Chuck scowled at her, but Brenda and Edward Mortimer exchanged glances and shared a subtle smile. She gave her brother a grin. These meetings could be fun after all.

Orlando walked in, and Mortimer began.

"Thanks, everyone, for meeting on short notice. The agenda for the meeting is to come to grips with the takeover threat we are facing—"

"What threat?" said Chuck, looking around.

Mortimer glanced at Chuck and then completed his thought. "—from Mercer Incorporated and Hal Mercer. Thank-you Chuck. That's an excellent starting point, and where we've been on this issue for a while now. Why don't we capture some of this?" He walked over to the corner of the room and picked up a black marker and wrote on the front page of the flip chart as he talked. "Our first possibility here is that there is no threat, and we have nothing to worry about."

"The only possibility," said Chuck nodding his head and looking around the room for agreement. Nobody else nodded, and he folded his arms and sat back in his chair with a sigh.

"What are some other possibilities?" said Mortimer. He looked around the room but everybody remained silent on the issue. "Well, I guess our second possibility is that our competitor is making a lot of noise about taking us over and we should take it seriously and adopt some counter-measures." He wrote this on the flip chart.

"I agree with that option," said Kate. "I think we have to—"

He flashed her a quick glance and shook his head slightly. "Let's just capture all the possibilities first, Kate.

Then we'll get into some discussion."

"Sorry," said Kate. She made a note in her purple notebook.

"What's that, a grocery list?" said Chuck. Kate didn't even look up.

"A third possibility," said Mortimer. "Is that we are already in the advanced stages of a hostile takeover, some of our board of directors have been turned, and we should already be considering shark-repellent options. Poison pill, golden parachutes, etcetera."

There was silence in the room. They all seemed to be studying their hands or the papers they had in front of them. Except for Charles, who was looking at the flip chart with a frown. Mortimer slowly transcribed his third possibility, the squeaking of the marker the only sound in the room. When he finished, he put the cap back on the marker with an audible click and sat in his chair without saying anything.

"Shark-repellent." Chuck snorted. "What we need is guppy-repellent." Nobody said anything. "Come on… these guys are like mosquitoes buzzing around our heads. All we have to do is swat them. Don't ever forget that we're still running a profitable company with a huge future earnings potential. We weren't just blowing smoke with what we presented to the board."

Frank Stokes leaned in. "You're right that we're still posting profits on our quarterly reports, but we have to pay our bills with cash. A company dies from a lack of cash, not profit. It's possible to be both profitable and bankrupt."

Everyone exchanged glances at this unwelcome thought and observed an involuntary moment of silence, nobody wanting to follow that little commentary.

Kate looked at Mortimer, who nodded. She said, "I

don't know if we're all the way to the third possibility, but we definitely need to start taking this seriously. I have been talking to Hal Mercer on and off over the last week or so, and I know he is serious about this, and he believes he will be successful." She looked at Chuck now. "And the 'pathetic' speech you mentioned was actually very effective. What he offered sounded like a good deal. There were one or two people nodding their heads. And with the sales figures he posted for the last four quarters, I could see there was a little bit of doubt creeping into the room."

"Add to that," said Mortimer. "The fact that he openly spoke to Teschke and who knows what other board members at the meeting. I think we can all agree that this is becoming a problem. If we don't do something now, we may miss our chance altogether."

"What do you suggest, Edward?" said Charles.

Chuck looked at his father and shook his head.

Mortimer addressed himself to Charles. "Priority number one for us is to own the floor at that trade show. Everything we proposed to the board hinges on hitting our sales targets."

"All right, then," said Chuck, sitting forward again. "Let's bring ten times as many people as last year and really blow them out of the water. We'll spend some bucks on a fantastic booth, give away prizes, have girls in bikinis, whatever." He grinned and looked around to make sure that everybody was feeling the wonderfulness of his plan.

"With the exception of the part about bikinis," said Mortimer. "I would agree that that is a good starting point in our fight. We might be short on cash, but we're not short of people."

Charles nodded and looked from Mortimer to Chuck. "Excellent suggestion, Chuck."

"Can someone also talk to Teschke?" said Kate. "If they've turned some of our board, we have to start working on turning them back."

"Yes," said Mortimer. "Our second priority is certain board members that need to be dealt with."

"Hear, hear," said Chuck. "Forget about talking to him. We need to turf pesky Teschke out on his ass."

"Exactly," said Mortimer. "I will talk to a few of the others today and let them know where the chips are going to fall, and to make sure that they're on the right side of the line when they do. First things first, though. The show is less than a week away, so we have a lot of work ahead of us. Orlando, do we have signage for the booth and some giveaways in stock?"

"Yes, we have the signs from the Ottawa show, and we've got lots of the mugs and desk clocks. I'll see what else I can find."

"Excellent," said Mortimer.

Brenda Whitney spoke up. "Another thing we should look at, before we decide on the numbers we will have attending, is how many of our sales people have had the sales effectiveness training. Let's get our best people out there on the floor."

"Agreed," said Mortimer. "Can you get me those numbers, say, right after lunch today?"

"Sure," said Brenda.

"I think I'll go myself," said Chuck. "Make sure things run smoothly."

Mortimer didn't even hesitate. "Excellent. And I'll also be there. Together we can make a show of strength, fly the flag and make sure we carry the day."

"Good work, everybody," said Charles, standing up. "I see we have things well in hand, here, and there is, ah, clearly nothing to worry about. All this takeover business and so on. So, I think I'll be moving along, unless you need me for anything else, Edward?"

"No, thank-you, Charles. I'll come and talk to you later about the poison pill idea. I'm serious about that."

"Excellent." Charles D'Arville made his slow walk out the door and down the hallway. Kate watched him turn the corner and winced when he put his hand on the door frame. She thought of her talk with Chuck, and wondered why there was no evidence that her father was taking it easy and her brother was taking more responsibility. Of course, the substance of that concept was that Chuck would be more in control around here, and she found she couldn't support that idea, especially now.

Brenda Whitney and Orlando Bretagne also excused themselves, saying they would get to work and talk to Mortimer later that day. That left Chuck and Mortimer sitting across from each other at the boardroom table with her: a perfect diagram of the company's internal conflict. She thought of what things would be like if Edward Mortimer left the company. He was getting older. Could she honestly say that Hal wasn't a better choice than Chuck to run her family's company?

"I still say they're no threat," said Chuck. "But it will be fun to really kick their asses at the trade show. That alone should announce that we are still the big fish in this pond."

"We've got to be proactive, Chuck," said Edward. "We have to get to a point where we can tell ourselves we have nothing to worry about because of the steps we have taken. You can't just rest on your laurels in business and expect things to work out as they always have. Business just isn't like that anymore."

Kate watched Chuck's face as he went on the defensive. He had that sort of half smile about him that said he knew better and he was just humoring the person he was talking to. How did he come by such arrogance? She had seen the most recent financial report on the company, the gradual build-up of debt and the decline in sales. How could he just shrug that off? It had to worry him a little bit.

"I agree that grabbing a couple of their people could be called proactive," said Mortimer when Chuck had finished. "But that's one move in a battle that's going to require many."

"Bring it on," said Chuck. "I'm ready for whatever golf boy can dish out."

"Yes, good," said Mortimer. "Well, Kate. Thank-you for dropping in today and provoking a valuable discussion." He looked at his watch. "I see it's almost lunchtime. Well, early lunch. Why don't the three of us discuss this over lunch in the executive lounge?"

"Sure," said Kate. "I have no plans."

"I'm starved," said Chuck. "What's on the menu today?"

"I believe it was the beef today," said Mortimer, getting up and pushing in his chair.

"That sounds heavy," said Kate. She and Chuck followed Mortimer out the door. "Will there be any other options?"

"Of course," said Chuck. "Just tell Henri what you want and he'll whip it up. One of the perks, baby."

One of the perks, right. Kate thought about what that must cost every month to have a chef on the payroll and the cost of the space and it fit with what Hal had said about them. Their high expense ratio was one of the things dragging them down. If this kind of thing leaked out to the *Financial Journal*, it wouldn't look too good. She actually knew a reporter there, she realized. Erik Markovich was a friend from university. She stopped dead in her tracks outside the door to the lounge, Chuck bumping into her.

"I've got to go," she said.

Chapter Nineteen

"What a wretched and peevish fellow is this King
Of England, to mope with his fat-brained followers
So far out of his knowledge."

- Act 3, Scene 7, Henry V

"Well, hello, gorgeous," said Erik Markovich as he
stood to pull out her chair. "Your phone call was an
unexpected pleasure."

"Hello, yourself," said Kate, smiling. They exchanged
cheek kisses and she allowed him to take her coat before
sitting down. Her bright, casual attire was in the minority
this lunch hour at the Benihana restaurant on the lower
floor of the Royal York hotel. The crowd here was mostly
dark suits and expense account lunches since it was very
close to the financial district, which included Erik's office
at the newspaper. The smell of seared meats, sesame oil
and rich smoky teriyaki sauces cooking in the open really
got to their palates and made everything on the menu look
great. They ordered their lunches amid the buzz of stock
prices and mergers and acquisitions. Japanese chefs
prepared the food at some tables as their audience mostly
ignored them and carried on talking business.

"So you've done very well for yourself," said Kate. "I
always enjoy your column."

"Well, thank-you," he said, smiling. "It's a living."

He had short dark hair with a slightly receding hairline, but no comb over. Dark suit with a blue oxford button down and navy patterned tie. Rather dapper, actually.

"How long has it been since we've seen each other?" she said.

"Since convocation, I think. I took off that summer to backpack across Europe and I worked in Ottawa after that."

"Seriously? That long?" She tried to look amazed, but she knew that their very thin friendship at university wouldn't have lasted had they lived two blocks apart. "And were you in journalism right from the start?"

"Sure, including getting coffee and picking up sandwiches." He laughed. "There's a real apprenticeship program working for a newspaper. But I wrote an obituary or two in my first year."

"Well, you stuck with it and it paid off. You obviously love writing and having a job you love is a precious thing."

"Sure," said Erik, taking a sip of his Sapporo beer. "But what about you? What have you been up to since university?"

"Oh, this and that," she said. She looked at her small cup of sake. "I've done some traveling here and there."

"Uh-huh. And you probably married Hal Mercer and have 2.5 children and happily ever after, am I right? Diapers and nannies, summer place in the Muskokas?"

"No. Hal and I broke up right before grad."

"You're kidding me. I thought you guys were a lock. I totally had the hots for you back then and that guy was always standing in the way."

He glanced down at her ring finger and she looked away and tried to pretend she hadn't noticed.

"So," he continued, smoothing a hand over his thinning

hair. "Never married. Not seeing anyone, either?"

"No, uh, nobody. But it's funny you mention Hal Mercer. I just saw him this week for the first time since we broke up."

Erik frowned. "Oh?"

"Yes. His father died earlier this year and he has taken over the company. But things aren't going very well. Staff morale is very low and there is some unrest among the executives. He has already had two key defections where execs have come over to my father's company." She looked at him for a reaction. He didn't say anything for a moment.

"Are we on the record, here?" he said, looking at her as if afraid of the answer.

"Absolutely," she said, holding his eyes steadily.

"Damn," he said, sighing. "I was hoping I had a chance. All right, what have you got?" He took out a notebook and pen and waited for her, some of the hopeful look gone from his eyes.

She looked down at her napkin and smiled. "Tom Grey and Ken Walker came over to our side and I've... heard some things."

"Such as?"

"Since his father died, the staff has been convinced that the company is going down the tubes. Hal has been resorting to desperate 'team-building' clichés like paint ball war games to build morale."

"Uh-huh," said Erik, looking bored. He hadn't written anything in the notepad.

Their lunches arrived and Erik put his notepad to one side and began eating. Kate picked at her salmon teriyaki and tried to think where to go next. He watched her face and chewed silently. She hesitated and then plunged ahead.

"The rumor is he is looking for financing to satisfy his payroll."

Erik thought for a second. "I've never heard that about Mercer."

"It never would have happened with his father at the helm. But you know Hal—he's not serious about anything. You think he would take a job seriously?"

"That's true, he was the party guy, never the studious type."

"He's a very inexperienced CEO at a minimum and, get this, he recently asked us for a merger to bail his company out."

"Are you kidding?" Erik put down his fork and began making some notes. "What were the terms of the deal?

"I can't disclose specifics, but it would have seen our executive taking over the operations in the short term and full integration in the long term."

"Wow," said Erik, eyes widening. "What a turnaround for Mercer. They've always been a solid company."

"Of course they were. But Hal views this as a kind of golden parachute for himself. He probably just wants to get his money out and ride off into the sunset. When I visited him this week, he actually said to me he always thought of himself as the guy 'most likely never to work a day in his life.'"

Erik looked at her, pen poised above the notepad. "Can I use that?"

"Absolutely," she said, smiling. She picked up her fork and began cutting into her salmon.

* * *

"Erik, you old hack, how are you?" said Hal when he got the call.

"Fine, Hal. How've you been?"

"Never better, my friend."

"I was so sorry to hear about your father. I should've called."

"Thanks. I'm sorry, too. There are times I really feel like I could use his advice."

"So things aren't going too well?" said Erik.

"No, things are fine. It's just that the old man was a legend, right?"

"Well, don't worry about that. Nobody thinks any the less of you because you don't measure up. I hear you've been looking for financing."

Hal paused. Had Erik heard that he met with the bank to talk about financing the D'Arville takeover? How could that be? "Are we on the record?"

"Just having a conversation. But I might use some of this in a piece about your company. Transfer of power, etc."

Hal thought for a moment. "No comment, then."

"Okay, no problem. So you must be missing Grey and Walker about now, am I right? Their experience would've been quite an asset to you."

Holy shit. What was going on? He took a second to choose his words.

"What's the matter, Hal? Nothing to say about two of your key executives defecting to the competition?"

"We wish them well in their new endeavors."

"Okay. No comment again. Are there any other changes coming down the pipes?"

"No. It's business as usual."

"No talk of a marriage of convenience with D'Arville?"

"Marriage of what?" Hal looked down at his phone as if

there would be an explanation on the display screen. "Are you screwing me here, Erik?"

"No, no. Just two old friends having a conversation."

"Well, that's great. But I'm really busy right now."

"So, just to confirm, you're saying there were no merger talks with D'Arville?"

"Good-bye, Erik," said Hal, and he hung up the phone. He sat for a moment trying to figure it all out. Then he got up and walked down the hall to see Owen. His door was open, so Hal knocked twice on the door frame and sat in front of his desk.

"Yes, sir," said Owen, not looking up from what he was working on. "What can I do for you?"

The smooth mahogany desk and credenza, the potted plant in the corner that he always watered himself, the many degrees on the wall, all this stored knowledge on the shelves and in the files—it made Hal more comfortable just knowing he had him on his side. Owen finally looked up.

"I just got a weird phone call from a guy at the Financial Journal," said Hal.

"Uh oh," said Owen.

Chapter Twenty

"Would I were in an alehouse in London! I would
Give all my fame for a pot of ale, and safety."

- Act 3, Scene 2, Henry V

Rather than distract her attention from another night
class, Pete waited for Amy in a nearby Starbucks. Lattés
and butterscotch scones helped to pass the time, as well as
his habitual doodling. He had started work on some
characters for a new project he'd been thinking about for
some time. They were initial sketches for a new superhero
concept, just working on a handful of photocopier paper
he had grabbed from the office. He was developing some
Toronto-inspired backgrounds in a cartoony-realistic style.
Greektown, the business district, old City Hall, and
Chinatown had already found their way into one layout
or another, and the story was beginning to come together,
too.

The place wasn't busy, just a few people sitting at tables
with laptops or iPads, and the odd 9-to-5er coming in for a
coffee to take home on the subway. There were some high
school kids hanging around outside the front window,
some teetering on skateboards, all nursing Frappuccinos,
the "gateway drug" used to hook kids on addictive
stimulants. They didn't have Frappuccino when he was in
high school; they'd had to rely on good old-fashioned

Coca-Cola for their caffeine high.

He watched them for a while, noticing and then beginning a few vague sketches of their "cool" clothing: army fatigues, canvas bags, black and blue denim, leather, all emblazoned with the names of various bands and their logos and symbols, as if the music they listened to asserted their identity. Things hadn't changed much since his high school days. It was strange the way teens through the decades clung to music and musicians, their cliques, apparel and even hairstyles based on musical preference. Unless they were jock types, in which case the same things could be said of their sport.

He had never been like either of those types. He didn't belong to any particular clique, didn't dress a particular way. Wasn't a school nerd with top marks or chess club whiz; didn't join the band or play any sports. He and his friends mostly kept a low profile, going to movies and reading comics, sometimes playing role-playing games. Would Comics Geek cover it? Or probably just geek, period, in some people's eyes. High school had been something he survived.

After he graduated, his love of drawing had led him to the Fine Arts program at Georgian College. He had spent three years there arguing with his teachers about his "cartoony" painting style, his "cartoony" sculpture style, everything too much influenced by comic books, which were considered derivative and lowbrow. So his marks weren't the greatest, but the courses had given him the grounding in anatomy, shadow, and perspective that all the great ones had.

Just as he was finishing a rough sketch of a punker kid balancing on a skateboard, he saw Randy coming in the front door, his trench coat incongruous with his wrinkled chinos and striped cotton button down coming untucked at the waist. He put in his order at the cash, paid and then circled around to the pick-up counter, surveying the room. Pete waved him over.

"Mr. Malden," he said as placed his coffee on the table and took off his trench coat, draping it over a nearby empty chair. "A pleasure." He sat opposite Pete. "I'm not used to seeing you in here."

Pete put down his pen. "No, I don't come in here that much. I'm waiting for Amy. She's at her night class just up the street."

"Oh, yes. How is that going with you two?" He took a sip of his coffee.

"Things are going great. It's been a little over a week, and we've already been out a few times."

"Good, good. I must admit you're very discreet around the office."

"Yeah."

"Well, I'm happy for you both."

"How about you?" said Pete. "Seeing anybody?"

"No, not me." He sighed, looked at the rim of his coffee cup and then at Pete. "It seems I am doomed to a life of bachelorhood." He smiled his resignation and took another sip of his drink.

"I'm sure you'll meet somebody." Pete sipped his latté, which had gone cold.

"Yes," said Randy, raising his eyebrows while staring at Pete's drawings. "What have we here? Some cityscapes. Ah, and one of the ruffians from outside. I like the hairstyle."

Pete turned some of the pages Randy's way. "Just some doodles," he said.

Randy flipped through some of the pages. "These are excellent. Have you ever thought about doing this for a living?"

"Sure, but there's a chance I might enjoy myself if I did that. Weren't you saying the other day that we were born to a life of drudgery and hard labor?"

"Oh, quite right. I had forgotten about that. Carry on, then."

"Is that what you really think?"

"About the social hierarchy, and birth defining destiny to a large degree?" Randy sat forward with his arms folded on the table in front of him. "Absolutely. For all the rags to riches stories that are so widely reported, the actual number is statistically insignificant. For the great majority of society, the class you're born to is the one in which you will remain."

"That's not exactly the version of the American Dream I heard."

"No, it isn't. I really can't do anything about that."

Pete tapped his pen on the table and shook his head. "If that's true, then where does ambition come from? Why are all these people trying so hard to get ahead in the world? The subway full of them every morning, the sidewalks chock-a-block every evening? Their—"

"That's not ambition," said Randy. "That's just status quo. That's food on the table, roof over their heads—pure survival. Today's white-collar office worker is yesterday's field hand. They just moved the site of our labor."

"So, is it genetic, then? Or social?"

"Maybe a bit of both. They're doing studies right now on genetics and success." He snorted. "Genetics and choice of breakfast cereal, too, god knows, but there may be something to it. It could be that there actually is something genetic that gives people a simultaneous spark of self-confidence, intelligence, and, um, drive, let's say, that makes them born for success. And a move up the social ladder. I'd like to believe it's possible, but the historian in me says probably not."

Pete nodded. "I always knew there was a reason I lacked ambition. I have historical context." He looked off into the distance, lips pursed with a look of Zen-like reflection.

Randy laughed. "That's a good term for it. I've got lots of that myself. But seriously, you wouldn't have to beat the odds and rise above your position in the social order to draw for a living. And it is something you are clearly qualified to do, and love to do. Have you ever given it a go?"

"Kind of. Yeah. It hasn't really worked out." He nodded and gathered up his drawings, tapping them down at the corners so they were neatly aligned.

"Well, best of luck. Keep at it." He sipped the last of his coffee. "For now, you are no doubt deliriously happy with your position at Mercer, Inc., as am I."

"Oh, yes. Deliriously."

"I thought so. Alas, tomorrow is Friday, and our week will be over. How to last until Monday. Well, I should go." Randy stood up and picked up his coat.

"See you tomorrow," said Pete. He pulled a fresh sheet of paper from the bottom of his pile and moved it to the top.

"Say hello to Amy for me."

"I will."

With a wave and a nod, Randy made his way over to the front door, putting on his coat as he walked. Pete watched him as he went out the door and out of sight. He continued drawing.

Chapter Twenty-One

"Would it were day! Alas, poor Harry of England!
He longs not for the dawning as we do."

- Act 3, Scene 7, Henry V

The *Journal* article dropped like a bomb on Friday morning. Mortimer read it on his iPad over breakfast and couldn't get the smile off his face. His orange juice just couldn't have tasted any better.

Mercer Inc. in trouble… executives on the move… staff morale low… merger mayhem… Playboy President… prepping for sale to highest bidder… writing on the wall…

Thank God it's Friday! He could just imagine the anguish over in the Mercer camp. It looked good on them. It was just a taste of what he'd been going through. But how did this article come to be? Did it just drop down from heaven? He scanned it again. Yes, it was the fourth time, but it wasn't getting old. Markovitch mentioned "a source close to the inexperienced CEO." Could it be a Mercer insider? Would Owen Percy… no.

Kate.

Yes, it had to be. No wonder she left before lunch the day before. He dialed her number.

"Hello, Edward," she said immediately when she picked up.

"Hello, Kate. Beautiful day, isn't it?"

"Yes, it is. You're reading the article, I take it?"

"It's the best issue I've ever read. I assume we have you to thank for this?"

"You're welcome."

He laughed. "You really play hardball, don't you?"

"It's my family's company. I had to do something. The question is, do you think it will be enough?"

"It will put them back on their heels, that's for sure. It should make it difficult for him to find backers, or make them nervous if he already has some lined up. It's a big win for us."

"As in 'we won the battle, but not the war?'"

"Well, yes, but how do you win a war? Keep winning the battles."

"But money is still tight for us. And Daddy didn't agree to an injection of new capital."

"Yes, that's true. We are close to the edge right now."

"So what has to happen at the trade show for us to get some breathing room?"

"We have to hit our targets."

"And will we?"

"We've hit that level before."

"But that was a few years ago. What if we only hit 90% of our goal?"

"We'll be able to limp along like a wounded duck and hope we hit our targets for next quarter and maybe it won't fall apart."

There was a pause at her end and he heard her breathing, could imagine the mental calculations that were going on.

"What if we hit, say, 50% of our targets? Or just did the same as last year?" she said at last.

"We'll be having a very difficult conversation. Probably with Hal Mercer."

"And he won't be in a very good mood after this."

"No, not at all. But don't worry. I think this article is just the shot in the arm we need. It will give us some momentum going into the trade show and you can rest assured that Chuck and I have taken every possible measure to ensure our success. We are pulling out all the stops."

"That's good. We've got to win this thing."

* * *

Pete walked into the office to find Arthur and Amy crowding around Randy's desk, trying to look at his computer screen. He put down his bag by his desk and tried to see over their shoulders what they were looking at.

"So what do you think of your mission statement and job security now?" Randy said to Amy.

"Hmm. This really looks bad. I never thought we were in so much trouble."

"See what I told you about mergers being trouble? Let the right-sizing begin!" said Randy. He had a smug look, almost like he was enjoying the situation. Pete scanned his screen.

"At least I've been working on my resumé," said Arthur.

"Very wise," said Randy, nodding. He was starting to get to Pete with his elder statesman routine, like he saw this entire thing coming and was so above it all.

"And how's your resumé, Randy?" Pete asked. He walked to his desk and smiled at Amy.

"As sad and useless as ever, I'm afraid." Randy

switched his browser window to their sales system and looked around over the top of the cubicle walls as if worried he'd be seen. "Just like Mercer Inc."

* * *

Hal was so glad the week was over. First his failure at the D'Arville board meeting and now this fucking pack of lies in the *Financial Journal*. He had already fielded about fifteen phone calls and heard from his managers that rumors were spreading all over the place internally. What timing—right before he needed everybody focused on success at the trade show.

Of course, the real surprise was that the blow had come from Kate. It was sneaky and underhanded, yes, but well played, he had to admit. He had thought his main adversary was Chuck and had let his guard down when Kate came to see him. Huge mistake, obviously.

On the golf course, some players blow up after a couple of early mistakes and the round would go to hell. They lose their focus. For Hal, early mistakes would always sharpen his concentration for the later holes. He never wrote off a round because of an early double bogey or ball in the water. Some of his best rounds came after a big number on the first or second hole.

There was still time to turn this thing around. And he wouldn't be making any more mistakes.

* * *

Her phone buzzed and Kate picked it up out of her purse to see who was calling. It was a text from Chuck: *Go K! U rck. Golf boy ded in wtr. Luv my sstr!* She smiled and texted back: *Ur wlcm. Kick ass @ trd show.*

Could this be enough? She knew that Chuck and Edward would do everything they could to win the day at the trade show and they'd had big successes there before, but what about after that? How would they get out of debt and then not fall back into it? They needed leadership and a plan for the future.

She wondered what Hal was going through and felt a twinge of guilt. Erik was easily lead, but she had lied to him a bit. As Alice had said, *all's fair in love and war*. It was just getting harder to figure out which was which.

Chapter Twenty-Two

"Fortune is Bardolph's foe, and frowns on him;
For he hath stolen a pax, and hanged must 'a be—
A damned death!"

- Act 3, Scene 6, Henry V

After a busy weekend of worrying over details for the trade show, Hal made it his business Monday to make sure that all those details would be taken care of before they left for Windsor the following day. It was already the 23rd of October. When he took a moment to realize that the trade show was in just two days, he could hardly believe that everything had happened so quickly. But he had a simultaneous feeling of impatience, as if things were moving too slow and too fast at the same time.

Owen's staff had arranged hotel rooms for them at the Hilton Windsor next to the Cleary International Center, where the trade show was to take place. The booth had been arranged and would travel with them Tuesday for setup. They had plenty of product pamphlets and demos. They had their best and most experienced people lined up for the sales floor. With any luck, this idea of having laptop network access on the sales floor would be unique, and truly set them apart.

He met with his VPs. He met with the supervisors. Did a floor walk to boost morale on the front lines. And all this before lunch. He was back in his office when Fluellen dropped by unannounced.

"Hi, Hal," he said after knocking. "Sorry to barge in, but Margaret wasn't there and I just need a minute."

Fluellen walked in clutching a file and took a seat.

"This isn't a last minute problem to do with the trade show, is it?" said Hal.

Fluellen hesitated. "Not exactly."

"Go on, then."

"Well, you know that IT installed that new spy software two weeks ago?"

"Yes." Hal glanced down at the file Fluellen was holding.

"Right, well, we've been keeping tabs on everyone since, and we've caught our first abuser." He paused. "It's, uh, Randy Bardolph."

Hal didn't say anything.

"And since you, you know, used to be... I mean, you worked with him when you were on the floor. I know you guys were friends, so I wanted to consult with you before I did anything."

Hal sat back in his chair and looked at the ceiling. "How long is he spending surfing the net every day?"

"Almost three hours."

Hal looked back at Fluellen in shock. "Three hours?"

"Yes. Some days higher. It makes me sick, frankly, with all the attitude he gives me."

Hal shook his head in disbelief.

Fluellen went on. "Time is money, and I consider goofing off on company time to be the same thing as stealing money from the company."

Hal caught his eyes and stared him down. "I wouldn't go that far. If that's the case, I'm sure I've been guilty of it myself in the past."

Fluellen looked down at the file. "I didn't mean to say…"

"All right." Hal motioned with his hand and then began drumming his fingers on the desk. "Are we sure these sites weren't work-related?"

"Yes, of course. I have the list right here." He opened the file in front of him. "Nothing pornographic, but lots of historical sites, on line gaming sites… and Google." He passed the sheet over to Hal, who opened it and scanned the top sheet.

"Jesus Christ." Hal looked up at Fluellen. "The second worst offender is spending less than an hour a day."

Fluellen nodded.

He looked down at the list of Internet sites, admiring the way the repeated www's made a zigzag pattern down the left hand side, his eyes blurring slightly. Hal thought of the times he and Pete and Randy had hung out in the lunchroom or the coffee place downstairs. Thursday nights at the pub. It seemed they were laughing all the time back then. He sighed. It felt like he hadn't had a really good laugh since he stopped working the floor with the two of them.

"So we've found our example, then?" he said at last.

"I think so."

"Okay. Write it up and I'll sign it." Hal passed him back his file. "When do you plan to do it?"

"Right away," said Fluellen, putting his papers back in order.

"Today?"

"Yes."

"Won't that have an impact on the morale of your unit? Maybe it would be better to wait until after the trade show."

"I know what you're saying, but believe me, getting rid

of Bardolph will be the best thing ever for the morale of the unit. His negative attitude is my main problem right now."

Hal nodded. "All right, I trust your judgment."

"Thank-you."

"Just make sure you tell him explicitly why he's being fired. The grapevine will do our work for us. The entire staff will hear about it by the end of the day."

"Yes, sir."

"I'd also like to see the numbers a month from now to see how the usage pattern has been affected."

"Of course." Fluellen made for the door. "I'll be back in ten minutes with the sheet. Will you be here?"

"I'll wait for you," said Hal.

Within five minutes he was back with the sheet for Hal's signature and it was done.

The first thing that crossed his mind when the door closed after Fluellen was Randy's apartment. Randy had a gorgeous place near Yorkville with a pretty high rent. He always liked living slightly beyond his means, he was fond of saying. Hal hoped that his famous stock portfolio had been going gangbusters lately, because he was going to need it. What if he had to move because of the piece of paper Hal just signed? What if he had to get some grungy little bedsit in the student area? That wasn't Randy. But this wasn't Hal, either. He wasn't the kind of person who fired people. Why did the business world make an asshole of everyone? Or a martinet?

It wasn't like they were at war and people's lives were at stake. Just livelihoods. This was his company now. Why didn't he just laugh it off and disconnect Randy's Internet? Put a reprimand in his file. Now that would be something they would have laughed at in the cube. Randy would have some way of explaining it in the context of the

Roman military command model or Peloponnesian war council which would have been hilarious, and they would all have gone for coffee.

But it wasn't really his company. He had to answer to the shareholders and protect their interests along with his own. Nobody forced him to take on this role. It was his own choice. Tough decisions were part of the role.

Fuck. Just the thought of the Inside Sales Group meetings without Randy made him cringe. He had to get out of the office for a while.

Owen agreed to have lunch with him and they went to the deli up the block. Smoked meat and mustard for Hal and Black Forest ham and Swiss for Owen. They took a seat near the back.

"Nothing like a classy wax paper wrapper," said Owen.

"You love it," said Hal. "And you know that my aunt would kill me if she found out I was letting you eat that."

"It's all true."

"So don't complain."

They both took jaw-stretching bites of their sandwiches and munched in silent appreciation. For a while, they just ate without talking.

"So what's bugging you?" said Owen at last.

"What do you mean?"

"You haven't asked me to go for lunch in a long time."

"I normally eat in my office, that's all."

"I know." Owen just chewed and looked at him.

"Okay. I had to fire a guy today."

"Is that all?" Owen wiped his lips with a paper napkin.

"Yeah. But I approved it myself, and it was a guy I used to work with. Randy."

"Bardolph? The smartass I get all the complaints about?"

"Yeah." Hal took a sip of his drink and nodded, looking

out into the street.

"He made his own bed. You've got nothing to feel guilty about."

"I know."

"So don't."

Hal nodded and looked back at his uncle. "There are days I wish I never got into this thing, that's all."

"We all have them."

"I guess." He took another bite of his sandwich.

"Listen," said Owen. "I forgot to tell you, I just heard today that Simon Teschke was ousted from the D'Arville board at a vote today."

Hal swallowed. "What?"

"Another casualty."

"All for talking to me?"

"Don't worry about it. We'll bring him back in when this is all over."

"Well, yeah, but…"

"His kids aren't going hungry, believe me."

Hal shook his head and had the last sip of his drink.

Owen crumpled his wax paper wrapper and napkin. "Are you ready to get back at it? We do leave tomorrow for the trade show, you know."

"You don't have to tell me. I couldn't sleep all weekend for worrying about it."

They made their way back to the office and parted ways after the elevator—back to business. Hal walked down the hall to his office, looking in at his busy staff, nodding at people along the way. When he rounded the corner near the staff room, he almost bumped into Pete coming the other way.

"Hal, thank God," said Pete, stepping back. "I was just looking for you. You've got to do something about Randy. Fluellen's trying to fire him for using the Internet." Pete paused and Hal broke eye contact. "What?"

Hal said nothing and looked back up at him.

"You knew about this," said Pete, staring at him. He stood up a little straighter. "You fucking knew. You okayed this?"

"Pete, listen…"

"So that's how it is now. You've got your nice office and screw your old friends."

"This isn't about me and Randy. I love Randy, he's a great guy. But he's not great for morale and he doesn't work hard."

"You know he always got his work done. He was just faster than anyone else at it. That shouldn't be a reason to fire him."

"That's just it. He's too smart for this stuff, anyway."

"Is that what you're telling me, or yourself?" Pete crossed his arms across his chest. "Does that make me just dumb enough to work here?"

"Come on. You know he'll find something better. It'll probably be the push he needed. He'll be happier, and we'll get some young keener in here for you guys to abuse."

"That should have been Randy's decision." Pete shook his head and walked past him. Hal let him go. Not even looking over his shoulder, he walked the rest of the way up the hall, into his office, loosened his tie so he could breathe easily and lay down on his couch.

He was so tired.

When he opened his eyes again, there was a split second when he thought he was in his dad's office. His heart started up with a thud and he looked at his watch. He'd only dozed off for about ten minutes or so. He shook his head and sat up, looking around him. The office seemed calmer now, the air having lost its edge of urgency, and he did up his top button and tie again.

He didn't blame Pete for what he'd said. His loyalty to his friend did him credit. But this much he knew: he had done what he had to and Pete's job depended on him doing the right thing. If that meant that Randy had to go, then so be it. There were tough decisions to be made and all their jobs depended on his ability to make them. What was best for the company was best for everyone. And he wasn't *Just Hal* like he used to be. *Just Hal* was their buddy and he wasn't here to make friends anymore. He was Hal Mercer, and this is what he did now.

He crossed the floor to his desk. He touched his finger to his laptop touch pad to see what was next on his schedule.

* * *

Pete sat looking at Randy's empty chair and squeezing a stress ball with the Mercer logo over and over again. His co-workers all seemed to have their heads down. He guessed they were worried there might be more firings to come. Pete Malden didn't care. He didn't even like this job.

His father had called and asked him out for lunch Saturday. He even came down to the Danforth area to meet him. He had seen the article in the Financial Journal and was worried that the company was in trouble and Pete's job might be in jeopardy. Aren't jobs always in jeopardy? That's what Randy said, anyway. He'd have to text him later and see how he was doing. Probably in shock right now. All because of that backstabbing little shit in the phony front office, fuck him and the silver-spoon-mouthed horse he rode in on, equestrian lessons be damned. What about a code of honor? What about loyalty and friendship?

It was Dad who got him the job in the first place. He was a friend of Owen Percy's or was it a business associate? He gave him a call when Pete finished college and had no job prospects. At the time, he had thought it was a really nice thing, his dad looking out for him like that. He had been about twelve years old when his parents had divorced, right about the time he had started reading comics, a comforting escape from some lonely times. His father had supported the habit and was always buying him a few here and there on their weekend visits together. He had another family now, a young son. Pete didn't see his half-brother much.

It was a nice lunch. He told his father about Amy, how great things were going. He told him about his dream of drawing full time. Dad had tried to sound encouraging, but Pete could tell it wasn't a plan in which he had much faith. When they talked about work and the market changes their industry was facing, Pete found it hard to work up any enthusiasm for the topic. That conversation seemed unreal somehow in light of recent events.

Randy fired. Hal's true colors. This job meant nothing to him now. Three squares and a roof, that's all. He looked down at the Mercer logo stress ball in his hand and saw that his fingernails had gouged holes in the surface. He worked his finger into the soft inside, tore the ball in half and then threw it into his garbage can, the fill sand spilling on the carpet around his chair.

Chapter Twenty-Three

"From camp to camp, through the foul womb of night,
The hum of either army stilly sounds,
That the fixed sentinels almost receive
The secret whispers of each other's watch."

- *Act 4, Chorus, Henry V*

Due to a cancellation, Edward Mortimer had been able to double the size of their original booth to a magnificent 80 feet by 10 feet, the largest booth in the show. Ten monitors would play the D'Arville corporate video. They would have product demos on two sides of the booth, prizes, giveaways, and several closing stations for finalizing the orders. They were confident that they would rule the show.

Checking the directory for the whereabouts of the Mercer booth on the floor plan, he took a break from the Tuesday morning setup. The Cleary International Center was an enormous convention facility that faced the south bank of the Detroit River, as if prepared to repel attackers coming by water. From the front, mirrored glass was separated by what looked like concrete stilts propping up the front of the building. At each end was a rectangular brick and concrete turret topped with a lighted glass pyramid. It looked like some architect's post-modern equivalent of a medieval castle. Across the river, the many skyscrapers of the Motown Metropolis sprawled along the riverbank, anchored at the east end by the huge GM towers.

The trade show was taking place in the enormous Canadian Club room, which encompassed the entire second floor. Wholesalers and manufacturers from all over the US and Canada would be showing off their wares in booths ranging from a hundred or so square feet on up. And the buyers, the key to all of this and the focus of everyone's attention, would be descending on the center tomorrow. There would be such wooing, such wining and dining, and so many sales.

Mortimer smiled. He had never actually been to this show—he'd only seen the receipts that came back at the end. He wondered why they'd never thought to do this, and had to hand it to Chuck for coming up with the idea. He just hoped that the extra push would win them the sales they needed to make their forecasts come true.

The site of the Mercer booth was empty and, as he had expected, much smaller than their own. He guessed that with so little to set up, they didn't need to get there until the afternoon. Pathetic, really, this third-rate upstart who thought he could take over D'Arville, an industry giant. The buyers would show them who ruled the roost around here. Their former market share would come back, and he could start working on his Presidency bid. Not that there was much work to do in surpassing the hapless D'Arville heir, but one thing at a time.

Making his way back towards their own booth, he tried to cross each corridor, row and alleyway to see what other competitors and even unrelated vendors were doing. It always paid to have lots of ideas that worked. When he returned, their booth was just starting to take shape.

"Come on, let's get it in gear," Chuck said to one of the

delivery guys who didn't even work for them. "I want to go have lunch sometime soon."

"How's it going?" said Mortimer.

"Slow. Where do we get these guys? They must be union. I've never seen anybody move so goddamn slow."

"I'm sure they are, but don't worry about it. It'll all get done. We're one of the first ones here."

"And a good thing, too. Otherwise we'd've been up all night."

"Why don't you go take a walk around? Check out the Mercer booth. It's tiny."

Chuck broke into a big grin. "Really? This I've got to see."

"It's down to the right there and all the way to the back wall, in F217."

"We're really going to smoke their asses, aren't we?"

"Definitely," said Mortimer, giving him a pat on the back to send him on his way.

As Chuck walked down their corridor, turning his head this way and that, still with that big grin, he reminded Mortimer of a little boy looking for a cat to kick or a sleeping dog he could poke with a stick. The thought of him leading any company was frightening. Mortimer turned to the staff and delivery guys.

"Let's take five, everybody. Coffee and donuts are on me: for all your hard work." Everybody immediately dropped what they were doing, and followed him to the cafeteria. They all ordered their beverages and pastries and then pushed a few tables together and sat around them.

There was silence at first as people sipped their drinks or munched their donuts, but then people started talking and Mortimer heard what he wanted to hear.

"The hotel looked very nice, Mr. Mortimer," said Holly

from Sales.

"Yes, the Radisson is an excellent chain," said Mortimer. "Nothing but the best for our troops. But call me Edward, everyone." Some people nodded.

"Cool, Edward," said one of the guys from the delivery company. "So, what's with that Chuck guy? Somebody piss in his cornflakes, or is he always like that?"

Everyone looked at Mortimer with held breath to see what he'd say. "He's pretty much always like that," he said, laughing. Everyone broke into laughter with him. There was no question, this was unanimous.

"Usually he's worse," said Holly. "You should see him around the office."

"Yeah," said Phil from Holly's team. "He's always been great for morale." He looked at Mortimer.

"We're stuck with him," said Mortimer, nodding. "His name is on the door, after all."

"His grandfather's name is on the door," said Phil. "On him it looks like a hand-me-down shirt."

Edward nodded again. An anonymous staff survey should do the trick. Show the board how little support there was for the little brat. His own record should do the rest.

"Shh," said Holly. "Here he comes."

Chuck had entered the cafeteria and was looking all around him, finally seeing them and walking their way. "Where's my coffee?" he said as he approached their table.

"It's on me, Chuck," said Edward, standing up. "What do you take?"

"Nothing, forget it. I just saw the Mercer team arriving." He looked around at all the smiling faces looking his way and pushed his chair back in, looking back at Edward. "I'm going to go get lunch back at the hotel. Why don't you call me on my cell when everything is ready?"

"No problem," said Edward with a smile of his own. "Have a good lunch."

Chuck nodded for a second, had a last look around the table, and walked back out the way he'd come in. Everybody laughed and talked about him some more. Edward shook his head and rolled his eyes at the appropriate times, and sipped his coffee, occasionally glancing at the exit sign that had been above Chuck's head as he left.

* * *

Hal was the first to arrive at the Cleary Center. He took an orienting walk around the next day's field of battle as preparations were still being made. He noted the D'Arville logo and the huge booth, wandered by a few other competitors, and stopped one section away from their booth. There were two of their people already setting up. They must have been new since he didn't recognize them. He made his way back to the delivery entrance and found the guys from the moving company just opening up the truck.

"Hi, there," he said to the guy with the clipboard, who was taking off his jacket. He hung it on the handle of the freight door along with his *AAA Movers hat*. "You guys are here for Mercer Inc., right?"

"That's right." He looked at Hal's jeans and t-shirt. "You with Mercer?"

"I'm here to help."

"That's great. Just grab any one of those boxes." He

started walking around to the front of the truck. "Ernie will be back in a sec, so just leave the booth stuff for us."

"Okay." Hal put on the guy's hat and his AAA Movers jacket, which said Al in a circular red patch over his heart. He picked up a couple of boxes and made his way down to their site. He nodded to the new guys as he approached. "Hi, there. Are you guys with Mercer?"

"Yeah. You one of the moving guys?"

"I'm here to help." He put down the boxes and stood up.

The taller of the two had a look at his patch. "Al? I'm Rick Williams and this is Jeremy Bates."

Hal shook hands with each of them. "Hi, Rick. Hi, Jeremy. I'm here for setup as well as unloading. Let me get another box and then I'll give you a hand with some of this stuff."

"Sure." Williams yawned and tested how heavy the new boxes felt.

Hal walked back to the truck and put the hat and jacket back where he'd found them. He picked up another box and made his way back to the booth site. Williams and Bates were talking as he approached.

"Things are pretty bad. Did you hear about that article in the *Journal*?"

"Hasn't everybody? It just goes to show you that management really doesn't give two shits about us. If we're lucky, D'Arville will let us keep our jobs when they take over. Are they here?"

"Yeah, they are," said Williams. "Wait till you see how big their booth is."

"Fuck."

"They are going to slaughter us." Williams opened a box of brochures. "Hey, Al. You wanna help me sort these brochures?"

"Sure thing," said Hal.

"Just put them in three piles over on that table."

Bates began cutting open the boxes that Hal had just set down. "It's going to be a total David and Goliath smackdown."

"Totally." Williams nodded and then shook his head.

"Who's going to slaughter you?" said Hal as he made his neat piles of brochures.

"Oh," said Williams. "D'Arville. The enemy."

"And you said their booth was huge?"

"Fucking enormous. I can't wait to see how many people they need to work that thing."

"So D'Arville is the Goliath and you're the, uh, you're David?"

"Yeah," said Bates. He looked at Williams, who shrugged his shoulders. They both looked back at Hal.

"But it was David who beat Goliath," said Hal. "Not the other way around."

"Oh, yeah," said Bates. He squinted. "But that was a lucky shot. Goliath would have won if it was best of three falls." He smacked his fist into his palm.

"Or if it was WWE RAW," said Williams, pointing a finger at Bates. "He would've come back the following week for a cage match."

"So you're saying they're going to, what, have better sales than you?"

Williams snorted. "Yeah. That's pretty obvious."

"Because they have a bigger booth?" said Hal.

"They're just bigger, better, stronger, faster." Williams began setting up some three-dimensional signs.

"Why does that matter?" said Hal. "If they're a bigger company anyway, wouldn't they be expected to have more sales?"

Bates chimed in, "Yes, but our company is in bad shape

and D'Arville is poised to take us over."

"And then it will be pink slips for everybody at Mercer," said Williams.

"So you guys are defeated before you even start?"

"Yeah," said Bates, without looking up.

Hal finished stacking his brochures and broke down the box. "So why bother even setting all this stuff up? Why not just go home now?"

"Can't," said Williams. "The big boss is coming today. Hal Mercer. He's the one trying to merge with D'Arville."

"Hal Mercer is the owner?"

"CEO," said Bates. He began to stock the signs with the brochures that Hal had separated. "Why don't you grab some of the order forms out of that box, Al? Sort them into two piles and then staple one of each together."

Hal heaved the box up onto the table and began sorting. "So your CEO is going to be here, he wants to merge with Goliath, and you think this idea, what, sucks?"

"I guess so," said Williams. "Who gives a shit, really?"

"Not you?"

"Not Hal Mercer, either."

"What?" said Hal. "How do you mean?"

"He doesn't give a shit about us," said Williams. He seemed to have stopped working now, and was just sitting reading through one of their brochures.

"How do you know that?" said Hal, watching Williams's face.

"He's already fired one of our most senior guys." Williams began folding the brochure like an airplane.

Hal had an immediate pang, as this made him think of Randy.

"What did the guy do?" said Hal, stapling faster.

"I don't know," Bates said. "He surfed the net or

something."

"Yeah," said Williams. "Might as well fire us all."

"Yikes," said Hal, nodding his head. "So maybe this merger would be a good thing."

Williams looked thoughtful for a moment. "Nope. Then he *can* fire us all."

"Think of the cost savings," said Bates, pointing a finger up in the air.

"Yep. Time to bust out the old resumé," Williams said and threw his brochure plane, which swooped in a slow arc into the next booth. "Oops. Sorry." The plane came swooping back.

Hal caught the plane in his left hand. The Mercer logo was emblazoned on one perfectly symmetrical wing. "I'm glad I won't be affected by all this."

"Yeah, you're lucky to work for AAA," said Williams, standing up. "Say, are you guys hiring?"

"I'll ask around." Hal threw the plane back to Williams. It hit his chest and bounced to the floor.

Chapter Twenty-Four

"The King's a bawcock, and a heart of gold,
A lad of life, an imp of fame;
Of parents good, of fist most valiant."

- Act 4, Scene 1, Henry V

Fucking Hal. Screw friendship. Screw what's right. Mr. Corporate bigwig now, writing people off with one stroke of his mighty pen.

Pete looked up at the ceiling of his hotel room, stretched out on top of the bed by himself. What was he even doing here? It's not like they needed help with the booth, which was all set up when he and Amy had arrived. They just stood around with Bates and Williams talking about Randy being fired, which put him in a great mood for dinner.

"Those guys don't give a rat's ass about Randy," Pete said to Amy once they were seated at a restaurant a few blocks from the hotel. "They're just worried about their own hides."

"Maybe they were," said Amy.

"Are you?" said Pete, stirring his soup.

"Well, not really. They said it was because he surfed the net all day."

"But he did great work, too. What else should we be judged on?"

"Three hours a day on the Internet is a start."

"But don't you think that that spy software or whatever is a complete invasion of privacy?" He tasted the soup, scalding his tongue. He put down his spoon and reached for the ice water.

"I don't think we have a right to that kind of privacy when we're being paid to work. They have a right to know how we spend our time."

"I guess so, but what about a warning?"

"Randy used that up a long time ago."

"But that's my point, so did Hal. He was every bit as much of a lazy ass as Randy when he worked the floor with us. But because his name is on the door, he gets away with it."

Amy just nodded, eating her salad and giving him a raised-eyebrow look that said he was crazy.

"Well, that's bullshit if you ask me. Hal probably just stepped on Randy to convince his new cronies in upper management that he wasn't one of us anymore—that he's one of them, now."

She wiped her mouth with her napkin. "Do you think Randy was happy working at Mercer?"

"What?" He found the *non sequitur* annoying, and stirred his soup some more.

"Do you think he liked his job?"

"I don't know. No. I don't either. But that's not the point…"

"Well, I think it kind of is. I think someone who enjoyed their job wouldn't spend that much time pushing his luck and talking back to management."

Pete looked at her and said nothing.

"Hal just gave Randy what he'd been asking for for a long time. I don't think he would've wanted to do it, based on what you've told me."

Pete sighed and shook his head. "I guess that's why they call it the rat race. The rats always win."

"That's not what I was saying. Were you even listening to me?"

"Yeah, I heard you. I know what you're saying, but it doesn't change the fact that it really burns me what they did to Randy, that's all."

She rolled her eyes. "I get that."

The waiter removed their dishes, his soup almost untouched. Another person brought their main courses right away afterward. Pete could tell she was kind of pissed at him, but he couldn't seem to help himself.

"Let's talk about something else," he said.

"That would be nice," she said with a big fake smile.

"But one thing before we do. I don't think I can work for god-damned Hal Mercer anymore. I'm going to look for a new job."

She gave him a look. "What is that going to solve?"

"It'll show him that what he did is not okay. If that's the kind of ship he's running, then I want no part of it." Pete jabbed his fork into a carrot disk and thrust it into his mouth, biting down hard.

"Peter, Peter." She shook her head and smiled at him. "What I'm trying to tell you is that what he did wasn't totally out of line—he had every provocation, and I can't see any other manager acting any differently. You can't throw away a good job because of a disagreement with the CEO. If that is the standard you're using to judge them, you'd probably hate any CEO you worked under."

Pete chewed and swallowed some more carrot. "You may be right. Yeah, that's probably right. But I'll take them on one at a time. The reason they get away with it is because nobody takes a stand."

"You're not getting it," said Amy, winding her pasta

around her fork and emphasizing her point with the bulbous wound-up end. "Hal did nothing wrong. Randy was in the wrong and he paid the price. There is no stand to take here. I don't know how much clearer I can be."

Pete shook his head and cut into his chicken. "So, you want to catch a flick tonight?" And smiled his own fake smile before popping a bite of chicken into his mouth.

Idiot. He rolled over on the polyester floral bedspread and pulled out a sad little flat pillow for his head. The net result of that conversation was that he was now lying here by himself and Amy was acting all weird. He should've known when she ate the raw onions in her salad that sex was out of the question for the night. Maybe he was out of luck from the start.

After the movie, they walked back to the hotel, past late night clubs and strip bars, live music bursting out onto the street under neon beer signs. That was when Amy said the weird thing. He jokingly asked her if she wanted to go check out the band as they passed a particularly loud bar.

"That would have been a nice change," she said.

"What do you mean?"

"Nothing."

"No, what?"

"Nothing. It's just that all we ever do is see movies." She folded her arms across her stomach.

Alert! Alert! Danger signal. Proceed with caution. He put his arm around her, in case she was cold. "Honey, why didn't you say something? We can do other things."

"I know we can. We just don't."

"I thought you liked movies."

"I do like movies, but I like other things, too."

"That's cool. Well, we live in one of the most happening cities in the world. There are always festivals, and live music and whatnot going on. Let's check out a NOW

Magazine for this weekend."

She nodded. "Sure. Great."

He rubbed her shoulder. "Let's get you back to that hotel room. You seem cold. Are you cold?"

"I'm fine."

If there was one thing he'd learned in life, it was that when a woman said she was fine, she was anything but fine. She was, in fact, the opposite. Unfortunately, he had not yet learned how to undo the situation. He walked beside her in worried silence.

As they approached the front doors of the Hilton, a thought occurred to him.

"I guess we better go back to our separate rooms first, and then I'll sneak down to yours about ten minutes later."

"Um, I don't think so. Not tonight."

"What do you mean?"

"We've got an early start tomorrow."

"But it's only ten o'clock."

"Not tonight, okay? Tomorrow is very important for me. I've got a chance to really impress some of the higher ups. I don't want to waste this opportunity. I need my rest."

He grabbed her hand, with his other arm still across her shoulders. "It doesn't have to be about..." He looked around, and then whispered, "... sex. We could just hang for a while. Watch some TV, or whatever."

"Not tonight," she said with a hand squeeze to seal the deal. "I'll see you in the morning. Let's have breakfast together."

He looked into her pretty eyes, and everything looked okay there. He could see what she was saying and guessed he had to be understanding.

"Okay," he said at last. "Let's do that."

They arrived at her hotel room door, and he looked up and down the hall and then kissed her. "Goodnight, lover."

"Goodnight," she said, looking into his eyes, and then kissing him again.

And here he was, alone in his hotel room, not knowing what the hell was going on with anything. What did it mean that she was fine? And why could she not see what he was talking about when it came to Hal? He'd had the same fantasy about punching Hal in the hallway that day about a dozen times since they'd met. He so wanted to quit. Although she did have a point about him not liking any CEO he worked under. He could see that the business world was full of rat bastards, and there was no escaping that conclusion. Chief rat bastard Hal Mercer. Heartless corporate assassin. Smug son of a mangy cur.

It was money that was the problem. He needed it to live, but didn't feel he cared about it beyond that. All the ways they tried to tie you to a life you didn't want were connected to money. The whole system was geared towards making you spin like a hamster in a wheel, faster and faster. Your reward for all that effort? A bigger wheel. The business world in a nutshell.

That was when the plan first started coming to him.

Chapter Twenty-Five

"What infinite heart's ease
Must kings neglect that private men enjoy!"

- Act 4, Scene 1, Henry V

Once Owen Percy had retired to his room for the
evening, Hal went back down to the hotel lobby and sat
by himself in the bar. The River Runner Lounge was a
fairly nondescript little hotel bar with a pool table and a
big screen TV. There had been a half-hearted, corporate
chain designer's nod to a nautical theme sometime in the
past.

He was too agitated to sleep. The overall mood seemed
to be low, and it was starting to wear on him. Some kind
of general malaise had overcome the staff despite the
several attempts he had made to boost morale.

The bar was empty but for Hal and a young couple over
at a corner table. Rick, the bartender, was drying the last
load of glasses that had gone through the dishwasher
down at Hal's end of the bar. He dried each glass till it
squeaked and then slid it base-first, upside down into slots
above the bar.

"That is an amazing invention, Rick," said Hal. He
indicated the slots. "Where would you have room for all
of those glasses if not for that?"

"Exactly," said Rick.

"Admirable in its simplicity."

Rick shrugged. "Works for me."

"Probably busy tonight with all these trade show stooges?"

"Yeah, we had a pretty fair crowd."

"I figured," said Hal, nodding. "That's why we're here."

"Where's your company from?"

"Toronto."

"The Big Smoke. Buying or selling?"

"Selling." He raised his glass to Rick. "And lots of it, I hope." He took a sip of his scotch.

"Are you the only one here from your company?"

"No, we've got a whole team here."

"And they left you down here by yourself? Cruel bunch."

"I'm here because I can't sleep. You see, I'm the CEO, and of course they all blame the boss for everything. When it comes right down to it, they're all sleeping soundly while I'm up worrying."

"Uh-huh."

"I can tell you, I wish I were one of them right now. Just to be one of the sales staffers again, without a care in the world. People always think the top job is such a big deal, but what it amounts to is a whole lot more stress and a nicer office."

"I hear you." Rick switched to drying highball glasses and stacking them on the bar in front of him.

"I'll take another one of these, Rick." He drained the glass and set it down.

He rinsed out the glass in his sink and dried it inside and out before pouring the new shot. "There you are, sir."

Hal raised the glass, rolling the amber liquid this way and that and watching the bar lights play through the cut glass. He took a sip and placed it on the smooth counter by his elbow.

"So, it sounds like you're on the hot seat," said Rick.

"You've got that right. There's a lot riding on the outcome of this trade show. I've got a lot of balls in the air right now, and not much control, ultimately, over where they land. But if I can just keep the momentum going through tomorrow, it'll all come together."

"That's all right, then."

"Yes, it would be, all things considered. But the staff, the bloody staff, the crybabies and whiners, the sleeping beauties, the naysayers… the staff isn't convinced we can pull it off." He closed his eyes and ran his hand up over his forehead and through his hair.

Rick looked at him. "Well?"

Hal looked up. "Well what?"

"Can you? Pull it off?"

"I don't know." He took a sip of his scotch. "I mean, yes, of course. But I've got to get these people switched on. Got to get them believing we can do it, first of all. Then that they're not going to be fired. And last, get them out there and doing it. But how?"

Rick stacked the last highball glass and flipped the towel over his shoulder. He leaned against the bar. "Pardon me for saying it, sir, but maybe they're whiners because they're worried about making the rent and feeding their kids if it doesn't work out."

"You're right. Plus I know what they're thinking. I used to be one of them. We used to make fun of the senior management constantly. Couple guys I used to work with, we thought the whole thing was a big joke for the most part. Now I see what my f—, I mean the previous CEO, was going through."

Rick nodded. "I know what you mean. It's like here; the

last bar manager we had in here was one of those business school types. Nothing but org charts and flow charts and whatnot, and we didn't give him the respect, you know what I mean?"

"Sure."

"Guys were quitting, and nobody was happy. So the upper man, that's what we call the upper management, they moved him to a different division, and they promoted one of our own to bar manager. Now we get along really well, because he knows how things operate around here, because he used to do the job."

"Of course."

"So the way I see it, you've got an advantage, having done their job before. They'll listen to you."

"You think so?"

"Sure. Just don't give them any of the business talk, right? Talk to them the way they talk to each other."

"That might just work. I like it. Gather them early and talk this thing up. Assuage their fears."

"Exactly. But don't use words like 'assuage,' right?"

Hal laughed. "Right." He took another sip of his drink and nodded as he held the scotch in his mouth for a moment and then swallowed. He stared out the door of the lounge into the lobby, and then nodded again. "I think this might just work, Rick."

"Without a doubt."

"That's what I want. I want them to have no doubt that we can do this, and no doubt that we will all be the better for it."

"Well, you convinced me."

"You want a job?"

"I've got one, thanks. But good luck out there tomorrow."

"Thanks a lot, Rick. This really helped." Hal offered his

hand and Rick shook it. "I'm going to sleep like a baby, now." He drained the last of his drink.

"Yes, sir. One more before you hit the hay?"

"No thanks. I'd better get back to the room and get some shut-eye, or I'm going to be no use to anybody tomorrow. I'll be up early as it is." He got up off his stool and put a $100 bill on the bar. "Thanks for the advice."

Rick picked up the bill and called after him. "Sir, there's no need for—"

"It was worth every penny, believe me." Hal waved over his shoulder.

"Okay. Goodnight."

"Goodnight."

Chapter Twenty-Six

"There is not work enough for all our hands,
Scarce blood enough in all their sickly veins
To give each naked curtle-axe a stain
That our French gallants shall today draw out,
And sheathe for lack of sport. Let us but blow on them,
The vapour of our valour will o'erturn them."

- Act 4, Scene 2, Henry V

The Riverview Restaurant at the Radisson was very bright early in the morning, the many windows allowing light in on all sides. The tables were elegant in simple white cloth.

Mortimer was already finished his breakfast and reading the paper by the time Chuck struggled down in the morning. He was wearing slacks and a dress shirt with no tie, and Mortimer sighed and shook his head. Chuck looked around the restaurant, blinking and blinking as if his lashes could brush aside the bright light. His scan of the tables finally turned up Edward Mortimer, and he walked over to join him.

"Morning, Eddie." He plopped down in a chair across from him, signaling the waitress for coffee.

"Good morning, Chuck," said Mortimer, putting down his paper. "The mushroom omelet was excellent, if you're looking for some breakfast fare."

"No, just coffee."

"Late night?"

"Oh, yeah. You wouldn't believe how many peeler bars they've got in this town."

"I'm sorry, peeler bars?"

"You know, strippers, beer, loud music, lap dances."

"You weren't arrested, I take it?"

"Almost." Chuck laughed and rubbed his eyes. "I had a couple of the guys out from Wholesale West. Bought them a few pops, showed them around, and let me tell you, guys from Utah really like to party when they're away from home. Oh, thanks." He accepted his coffee from the waitress and took a long sip. He smiled and watched her walking away from the table.

"So, are you ready for a busy day?" said Mortimer.

"Oh, yeah. I'm going to be busier than a one-legged man at an ass-kicking contest." Chuck laughed and pounded the table, making the cutlery clink.

Mortimer smiled. "That you are."

A cell phone started up with a muffled bleating and Chuck retrieved it from his pants pockets and pressed a button. "Go for Chuck," he said into the tiny device, giving Mortimer the 'just a second' finger. "Dude! S'up? ... No way. ... Last night? ... Shut up! ... OK, Friday, then. ... All right, man. ... Yeah, later." He pressed another button and shook his head, smiling. "That guy, he kills me."

"Mmm." Mortimer managed to raise his eyebrows.

"So where is everybody?" said Chuck, looking around.

"I believe they were all meeting at 'The Golden Griddle' for a buffet breakfast of some sort."

"Oh, man. Why wasn't I invited?"

"Maybe they weren't at the same strip bars that you were."

"Ha-ha."

"Anyway, it's probably best that they spend some time together without management around. They'll build their camaraderie and provide each other additional momentum for today."

"I see what you're saying. So I guess it's just you and me."

"Yes." Mortimer flicked a speck of dust off the cuff of his suit jacket, and then looked at his watch. "I'm getting antsy to get going myself."

"Me too. We are going to totally rule out there today."

"That is an absolute certainty. I almost feel some pity for Hal Mercer, his sorry crew and their tiny little booth. We are going to steamroll right over them."

"We're going to kick his country club ass all the way back to Hackensack."

"Yes," said Mortimer, laughing in spite of himself. "If ever an ass needed to be kicked, it is Hal's. I would have liked to kick it myself at that board meeting, the smug little…"

"Go, Eddie!" Chuck held up his hand for a high five, and Mortimer looked at him strangely for a moment and then held up a flat palm and Chuck slapped it. "Woohoo," he said, and several other diners looked their way.

Mortimer cleared his throat and sat back chuckling. "One thing is for sure. Buyers are going to be all over us out there."

"Oh, yeah. Like white on rice."

"Um, yes. With our multi-media presentation, modular closing stations, and product demos, we are going to rule, as you said."

"Now that's what I like to hear. I want to personally walk up to golf boy afterward and twist the knife a little bit. Just to see him squirm."

"Yes, that would be… exquisite."

"What are the odds that we could turn the tables on him? Take over his stupid little company?"

Mortimer looked at the table for a moment, moving the salt shaker into perfect alignment with the pepper. "Well, we'd have to improve our cash position and get rid of some debt. The *Journal* article should help us line up some backers. Thank-you, Kate. It's not out of the question. That would be a very long-term goal. But it would be a sweet victory."

"Would it ever. And I'm going to be the one to hand him his walking papers if we do, believe me."

"We'll do it together." He offered his hand and Chuck shook it to seal the bargain. "It will be our pleasure."

"You got that right."

"So, are you really not going to get anything to eat?"

"Nah. Maybe I'll grab a donut over at the Cleary or something. I just need the coffee to wake up right now." He drained his cup and signaled the waitress again.

She came over with a full pot. "More coffee, sir?"

"Yes, indeed," he peered at her name badge, "Melanie. That is some good coffee."

"I'm glad you like it. Can I get you anything to eat this morning?"

"No, thanks. Just need the java."

"Will that be everything then, gentlemen? Just the one bill?"

"Thank-you, yes," said Mortimer, getting out his wallet as she walked away.

Chuck leaned over. "She is totally hot. Ouch." He shook his hand as if his fingertips had been burnt.

Mortimer looked at him. "Well, you're unmarried. Why don't you ask her to lunch or something?"

"Are you kidding me? A serving wench from Windsor?

Don't make me laugh." He laughed, but it sounded a bit forced.

Mortimer smiled. "No, I suppose not. You probably have lots of girlfriends back in Toronto."

"No way. I don't like to be tied down." He sniffed and wiped his lips with his napkin. "Can we go?"

"Yes, let's. I'll just leave her a fifty. With the money we're going to make today, it doesn't even matter."

"That's right, Eddie. Between myself and you, we are going to take down Hal Mercer. He'll be back on the golf course full time by next spring."

"Let's go make it happen."

Chapter Twenty-Seven

"We few, we happy few, we band of brothers:
For he today that sheds his blood with me
Shall be my brother; be he ne'er so vile,
This day shall gentle his condition..."

- Act 4, Scene 3, Henry V

They started early. Hal had Owen Percy talk to the hospitality manager at the Hilton about opening up a meeting room for them. It didn't need to be set up for anything; just an open space where they could all eat together and he could talk to them.

"I want everyone in that room in matching company shirts, all eating the same thing and hearing the same message," he said to Owen when he phoned his room shortly after 6:00 that morning. "I want that energy in the room so they really hear me."

Owen prepared the room and contacted the staff about the impromptu meeting while Hal prepared what he was going to say. By 7:30, they were to be gathered there in their red golf shirts with the Mercer logo over their hearts. The room was a large rectangle with a screen at the front. It was empty but for the chairs stacked near the walls and some tables folded up and standing on their sides near the door.

Hal walked in around 7:35 in his own red company

shirt. Amy and Pete were there together, along with Fluellen, Arthur, Bates and Williams, Sarah McMorris and John Gower, and a couple of other marketing and sales people, numbering about twelve in total. They were all eating the muffins and drinking the coffee that had been set up at Owen's request and talking amongst themselves, glancing around between bites and waiting. Hal grabbed a coffee and a muffin and went over to say good morning to Owen. Rick Williams, who was standing nearby, came over to say hello.

"Morning, Al. I didn't expect to see you here today. Are you staying for the whole thing?"

Hal looked at him for a moment, lost in thought. "Oh, hi, Rick. Yeah, I'm staying to help out."

"That's cool. Let me know if you need a hand with anything."

"I will." Hal shook his hand and patted him on the shoulder as he walked back towards Jeremy Bates and Arthur.

"What was that all about?" said Owen.

"New guy," said Hal. He took a bite of his muffin and wiped some crumbs off his mouth with the napkin. "How's everything? Any problems?"

"No," said Owen. "Even the coffee's pretty good."

"Okay, I'm just going to go around and say good morning to everyone and then we'll begin."

He began walking around the small group, greeting everyone by name, saying his good mornings, how are yous, and introducing himself where required. He even confessed his identity to Rick Williams and Jeremy Bates, who looked a little pale, but managed to laugh about it. Arthur gave them a look that said they were crazy. When Hal reached them, Pete gave him the cold shoulder but his friend Amy was very warm and positive. He made a mental note to work on Pete back at the office, explain himself again. He walked to the front of the room and called for silence.

"All right, everybody. Thanks again for getting up a little early and joining me for breakfast. There's more coffee and lots of muffins for those who are hungry. I just wanted to say a few things before we went out there today. We all saw the D'Arville booth, and the huge crowd of their staff setting up. We're all probably feeling a little outnumbered. Am I right?" He looked around the room and several pairs of eyes looked down at the floor rather than meet his.

"That's okay. It's only natural. Let's acknowledge it right here and now. They are a larger company than we are, and they have a larger, better-looking booth. They outnumber us, let's say, three to one probably. All right? Everybody agrees with that?" People nodded despite themselves and Hal looked around for dissenters. "Yes? Good. Because I don't want anyone to think we're going to have it easy out there, or that it's going to be a cakewalk or anything.

"Yes, our booth is smaller. Yes, we're a small team. But if we could call back to the office right now and get a hundred more people out here right away, I wouldn't do it. Not because I'm a martyr or anything. It's because we're going to win this thing and we don't need to share any of that glory. We're going to be the better team today. There's more than enough people in this room to share in our success, we won't need even one more person to muscle in on that action." Several people laughed, and then covered their mouths.

"That's right, I said we're going to win. And the reason I know that is because of something else I said: I said that we're a team. The better team. I have worked on the front lines with many of you here today. We have worked together. We have learned teamwork together, fighting side by side, each person willing to take a paint bullet for a teammate." A few people laughed and exchanged glances. "They don't have that kind of teamwork, I can guarantee it. I can guarantee that Chuck D'Arville doesn't know the name of even one of his co-workers out there today.

"So, yes, we're a small group. But you are my people, and I'll tell you this: we're going to take this company for a ride. We're going to take it to the next level, and we're going to do it today. We will share the credit amongst our 'small group.' We will be legends back at the office!" Everybody just stood there looking at him.

"How can I be so sure? Well, for starters, we have great people and we actually listen to them. Thanks to Amy Quick's suggestion, we are going to be connected to the network to give on the spot inventory answers to our customers." Fluellen started clapping and everyone joined in. Sarah McMorris patted her on the back. "That's right. Thank-you, Amy. Sometimes all it takes is a good idea to turn the tables. We're going to go out there and own the floor. Once we beat them on the sales floor, we're going to take them over—that's right, we're not merging anymore. We're going to buy them out and make our company the industry leader we deserve to be. We can all be proud to say that we were there on October 25th and we got this thing done together. That we were part of the team that took Mercer Inc. to the top."

"Woo-hoo," shouted Jeremy Bates, swinging his arms around. "Go Haa-al, it's your birthday." Everybody laughed, including Hal, shaking his head. It struck the perfect note.

Hal pointed at Bates. "You're damn right it is. It's everybody's birthday today, and I'll give you this promise, not as a gift, but what you all deserve. Everyone in this room is part of the long-term picture at Mercer Inc. In fact, all of you are key to our continued success. Because good people are the ultimate resource a company can have, I give you my personal guarantee, here, today, that there will be no jobs lost from Mercer staff after the takeover."

Pete snorted. "Except for Randy." Several people frowned, and those immediately beside him moved a step or two away. Fluellen glared at him.

"Absolutely except for Randy," said Hal. "He made his choice a long time ago and never joined the team. Never did the work, if you want the truth. Except for anyone who isn't serious about our success. Does anybody here really believe Randy was anything but a slacker who got what he deserved?"

Hal looked Pete in the eye for a moment until Pete looked away and sighed. He changed gears. "Randy was the exception in our office. We have a group of really great, smart people who work hard. I want each and every one of us to have opportunities to learn, to grow, and to continue to be a part of a team. It's teamwork that got us where we are now. It's teamwork that's going to sustain us in the years to come. The size of the team doesn't matter."

Hal looked around at all of the nodding heads and smiling faces, his eyes falling on Jeremy Bates. "So, Jeremy. What are we going to do out there today?"

"We're going to go out there and kick some ass," he said, pounding his fist into his palm. There was more laughter, some jostling around between Williams and Bates.

"You got it," said Hal. "So let's stop talking about it and get over there and get it done."

Hal walked across the room without looking back, the first one through the door with everybody behind him.

Chapter Twenty-Eight

"Mort Dieu! Ma vie! All is confounded, all!
Reproach and everlasting shame
Sits mocking in our plumes. *O méchante fortune!"*

- Act 4, Scene 5, Henry V

Colin Mayer had flown into Detroit Tuesday night. He
rented a car and drove across the bridge to Windsor. The
Radisson hotel was full of the usual crowd of sales reps,
buyers and other charlatans all yukking it up together.
Alone this year due to the budget cuts that had halved his
company's travel budget, he passed a quiet dinner, then
watched some TV and checked his e-mail before turning
in.

In the morning, he had a quick breakfast and then hit
the Cleary Center just as the trade show opened. He kept
up a pretty brisk pace for the first hour, hitting the booths
that he had planned to hit, placing orders at some and
gathering information at others. Then he browsed for a
bit, said hello to a few of the other buyers that he
inevitably met up with at these things. Mostly he wanted
to hurry and catch the early flight that afternoon.

He became aware of the huge D'Arville booth two rows
from it, like a frat party you could hear going on three
houses away, with monitors blaring and people milling
around everywhere. Since he usually stopped at their

booth, he turned in and had a look around. They had product demo tables and tons of their staff wandering around with brochures. Most of the people he could see around him seemed to be D'Arville employees. They were sitting in pairs behind little oval shaped desks, so he approached one of these.

"Hi, there, Holly," he said, reading her name tag and then turning to her partner. "And, Phil. Hi, Phil." He shook hands with both of them. "I'm Colin from GWG."

"Hi, Colin," said Holly. Phil nodded.

"How are you guys doing today? Making lots of sales?"

Holly looked at Phil and shrugged. "I guess so. It's been pretty busy around here."

"You guys sure have a lot of people here." Colin looked around the booth, and then up at the monitor suspended from the pole above his head. The synchronized sound of all the monitors was a kind of background babble that wouldn't quite recede into white noise.

"Yeah," said Holly. "Almost my whole department is here."

"That's good," said Colin. "How's the company been doing?"

"Pretty good," said Phil.

"Any new products coming out?"

Phil and Holly exchanged glances. "I don't know. You could ask Mr. Mortimer or Chuck over there." Phil pointed across the booth at two men standing together and talking to a man in a three-piece suit. "They're VPs."

"Okay," said Colin. "I'll do that. So what kind of time frame are we talking about for delivery?"

Holly checked the back of her brochure as if the answer was printed there. "Well, I guess as soon as we take the paperwork back to the office, the warehouse will start shipping the orders."

"Good. Okay." Colin nodded and looked over at Phil, who was now studying the back of a brochure, and then back at Holly. "But are we talking days, weeks, months, what?"

Holly laughed. "Not months. I don't know, probably days. You'd have to check with the Orders Desk. Is that number on there, Phil?"

Phil looked up from his brochure. "What? No. It's on the back of the order sheet."

Holly flipped over the top page of her clipboard. "Oh, yeah. There it is." She pointed it out to Colin upside down and smiled.

"Good. Well," he said, getting up. "Thanks a lot for your help."

"No problem," said Holly and Phil nodded in agreement.

"I'll have to think some more about it and let you know."

"We'll be here," she said. She watched him and he smiled and waved to her as he left the booth. He was glad to leave the wonder twins and the hundred TVs behind him. GWG generally placed an order with D'Arville, but he figured he'd come back later and talk to somebody else. Might as well just check out the competition quickly before he did.

The first thing he saw of the Mercer booth was the line-up. There were four people waiting to talk to a girl who was working on a laptop computer at a small desk. The booth was small and simple, with no room for TVs or elaborate demonstrations. They just had a few tables set up with brochures and order forms and were calmly going about their business. He decided to get in line and see what they had to offer. There were three other people with laptops so he wasn't waiting long.

"Hi, there," said the girl. "I'm Amy Quick."

"Colin Mayer," he said, shaking her hand and taking the chair opposite her.

"Where are you from, Colin?" said Amy.

"GWG in Atlanta," he said.

"Wow, that's a long way," she said. "I hope you didn't have to fly in this morning."

"No, last night. What about you?"

"We're just down from Toronto, so it's no big deal for us."

"That's great. Looks like things are going well for you."

"They sure are. It's been like this since we opened."

"So the company is doing well overall?" he said, taking a brochure from the table.

"Yes, we've hit all our sales targets this year and our stock value is up."

He looked at her. "Really?"

"Yes," said Amy, fingers poised above the keyboard.

"Any new products coming out?"

She relaxed her hands. "I've heard about at least two new things coming down the pipe. We're very strong on R&D, so I'm sure we'll have some stuff for you this time next year."

"Is that a fact? And what kind of delivery terms?"

"Let me check for you," said Amy, typing a code into her computer. "What are you looking for?"

He looked back at his brochure. "Let's say I was going to order… 1000 of these," he said, pointing to an item midway down the right hand fold.

Amy typed something and then clicked her mouse button. "Okay, it'll just be a second." She smiled at him and looked back at her screen. "Here we go. Okay, we've got them in stock, and current shipping time to the States is, let's see, um… four business days, so you'd have it by next Wednesday at the latest. We could expedite that if you needed."

Colin just sat there for a second in stunned silence. "Are you online with the company through that thing?"

Amy nodded. "Yeah, we're all connected wirelessly to our network back at the office through the Wi-Fi here. And we've automated the shipping and inventory systems. It was my idea," she said proudly.

"That's amazing," he said, shaking his head. "Our industry always seems so far behind the times, but really, everybody should be able to do something so simple as check inventory in real time."

"Did you want me to process the order?" said Amy.

Colin thought about the question for a moment, looking down at the brochure he was still holding. "Yes," he said finally. "I guess I do."

* * *

By 11:00 a.m. the Mercer booth was looking like the trading floor of the TSE, with people calling out questions over others' shoulders and lineups at both sides of the booth. People from other booths were coming over to see what all the ruckus was about, this small booth that was a flurry of activity from the get-go. Hal broke away at one point and gave some money to Bates to go and get donuts for the people who were waiting and they positioned several boxes at each side to keep people busy while they stood in line for their turn.

The laptops were humming as they processed orders from Alberta, B.C., Quebec, and all over Ontario, as well as many from Michigan, Pennsylvania, Indiana, and even

Kentucky and California. There were new orders from existing accounts, as well as many new accounts just finding out about them for the first time. There were overseas reps dropping by who came over just because of the buzz, and Sarah McMorris had her hands full with requests for additional trade show appearances and supplies of brochures and product information.

Things slowed down during the lunch hour so people could get off their feet for a few minutes and grab a bite to eat. Hal and Owen Percy were able to take some time away from the sales floor with a member of a Japanese trade consortium who wanted to meet with them in Osaka. They took him for lunch back at the hotel and made the necessary arrangements. Business cards and pleasantries were exchanged, and then they hurried back to the floor to pitch in again.

Representatives from their few competitors in the show, including Edward Mortimer from D'Arville, must have gotten wind of the Mercer phenomenon, because Hal would occasionally see them milling around an aisle or two away and glaring at their busy booth with furtive jealousy and rage.

But his people didn't have time to notice such small triumphs, as busy as they were with taking the orders.

* * *

Holly and Phil were sitting behind the D'Arville product demo booth, playing hangman on the back of an order sheet. Mortimer had to restrain himself from taking out his frustration on them. In fact, there were more people idle in their booth than there were people with something to do. He had been sending ten at a time for long coffee breaks, just so they didn't all look completely ridiculous standing around with nothing to do.

It had been slow all morning, with the odd regular customer dropping by their huge, empty booth to chat, an occasional prospect stopping to watch their video, listen to a product demo, or say they were "just browsing." They stuck with it, handing out brochures to passersby and trying to keep the staff motivated. By about 11:00, they had written up a few orders, but realized that things were far off their expectations and something must be wrong. It was Bill from Emstar who finally told him.

He dropped by to say hello but didn't put in an order. Considering his firm was a ten-year customer, this was odd. When he actually turned to leave, Mortimer had to stop him.

"Whoa, Bill. We haven't written up your order, yet. You're not coming down with the old-timer's disease, are you?" He chuckled.

"No, no," he said, laughing at the joke. "Yeah, I'm going to look around some, okay? I'll come back later."

"You're not shopping around on us, are you?" Mortimer nudged him with his elbow.

"No, I've just got to look at all the options, okay?" He paused and looked uncomfortable. "There's a lot of competition this year, Edward."

Mortimer waited for him to look him in the eye. "Who is it?"

"Oh, it's not…"

"Level with me, Bill. I've known you for a long time."

"Yeah, I owe you that much. This isn't coming from Bill from Emstar, though, okay? This is from me to you."

"Understood."

He looked around as if to see who might be listening. "I

already ordered from Mercer. They guaranteed delivery and they…"

"What?"

"They shaved a point for me because it was a large order. Sorry to be the bearer."

"No, that's all right. We're doing great today, anyway. Don't worry about us." Mortimer nodded and patted his shoulder.

"Well, that's great. Good luck with the rest of the show, okay?"

"Thanks, Bill. See you."

Of course, he had to go and see it for himself, telling everybody else he was just going for a coffee. He walked down to the end of the row of booths across from the Mercer station. He got a cold feeling behind his eyes when he saw the crowds of buyers. The upstart was the main attraction. They were killing them.

Chuck left at lunchtime, saying he thought the situation was "under control." Coward. Driving back to Daddy so he didn't have to take the blame. By around two o'clock and 20% of budget achieved, he realized that they had lost. The irony of it all was that he had been right about Mercer being a serious threat, but now he was going to go down for it just like Chuck and his short-sighted father.

But it was too late now. Preparations would have to be made, board members contacted. It would probably fall to him to capitulate. He dreaded that more than unemployment. He wondered if he could just get in his car like Chuck and drive away from this whole mess. Go home and not even call the office. Take Marjorie up to the cottage for a week and let them talk to his voice mail.

At two-thirty he made the call to Charles D'Arville.

Chapter Twenty-Nine

"KING HENRY: I tell thee truly, Herald,
I know not if the day be ours or no;
For yet a many of your horsemen peer
And gallop o'er the field."

- Act 4, Scene 7, Henry V

Hal came back to the booth with a flat of coffees and lots of sugar and cream after a short walk around 3:00 p.m., set it down on the back counter of their booth, and went to find Owen Percy, who was just finishing up with a customer.

"Can I have a word with you when you're finished there, Owen? No rush."

"Certainly," he said.

Hal nodded and returned to his coffees to get one for himself before they were all gone. Pete was just taking a coffee when he approached.

"You take yours black, I believe," he said. Pete glowered at him and said nothing. Hal picked up a creamer for his own cup. "Don't you think it's time you got over this?"

"I'm sure you're over it," said Pete.

"Is that what you think?" He poured in his cream and stirred. "Look, I wish that Randy hadn't made it necessary. But he did, and I did what I had to do."

"You sure did."

"And I didn't appreciate your comment this morning. It had nothing to do with what I was saying. But I'm willing to overlook it. I know where you're coming from."

"Oh, great. So you're not going to fire me, then?"

Hal sighed. Fluellen was watching them from across the booth. He lowered his voice. "I'm not going to fire anyone I don't have to."

"Oh, well, then. I'd better watch myself." Pete gave him that same look he had the day Randy had been fired, and walked away, just as Owen came over.

"Is that guy still giving you a hard time?" said Owen. He chose a coffee from the tray.

"I think he's still a little bitter," said Hal. He took a sip of his coffee.

"Little prick. I couldn't believe he said that. You had more restraint than I would have, let me tell you." They looked over at Pete who was reading one of their brochures in the corner.

"Yeah, well, we've been friends a long time." Hal shook his head. "Forget about him. I wanted to tell you about D'Arville."

"Oh, right. How are they doing? Did we leave them any sales?"

"Not much, by the looks of it. Their booth looks like an enormous ghost town."

"It looks good on them."

"Totally. It was hilarious to see all those TVs babbling away about their cutting edge technology and nobody watching. Their huge staff is just standing around with nothing to do for the most part."

"I would've loved to have seen the look on Chuck's face."

Hal nodded agreement. "Me, too. But I didn't see him

there."

"Too bad. I don't think he'd be making golf ball jokes today because they have definitely taken a hit here. How big, we'll have to wait and see. Our booth is humming along like a well-oiled machine. I think it's safe to say we've carried the day, here, Hal."

"I guess so." He smiled.

"And now I can tell you… your father would have been proud of you today."

"Thanks. Wasn't that amazing the way these guys came through for us? I'm so proud of them." Hal looked around the booth and couldn't stop smiling.

"Yes, and I meant to tell you. Amy Quick over there wrote up the Hanson account today."

"Are you kidding me? I didn't even see them."

"They came up cold and stood in line with everyone else."

"No!"

"Yes. She wrote up the orders for their whole chain. I don't think she even realizes what a coup that is. She's been great today. I've been watching her."

"Everybody's been great. These laptops were a great idea."

Owen nodded and walked back over to the far side of the booth where Amy was deep in conversation with a buyer.

Hal wondered what he was feeling, apart from sore feet. He was smiling and nodding, waving at people, and enjoying the feeling of victory, but he was strangely unsettled by the whole experience. The thought of Kate came back to him. What was she going to think of this? Her father's company was almost in ruins. Maybe it was guilt parked in his stomach. Although she had taken that shot at him in the paper out of nowhere. That stung.

There must be something to the fact that he kept thinking about her. The whole thing was unusual for him. It had been a long, long time since a woman turned him down for a date. Then for him to ask her again, knowing that rejection was likely… it was like he couldn't stop himself. She got to him somehow. The old feelings were back. The shock of her smile and those eyes, so intent on his, non-verbal information passing between them, giving him the jelly knees. He felt a connection there.

Maybe it hadn't been such a good idea to take time off from women to concentrate on his career. Was he just horny, or was this love?

Hal wiped his lips with a paper napkin to keep himself from laughing. He noticed Ed Mortimer from D'Arville walking toward him. *This should be good.*

Mortimer walked right up to Hal and shook his hand. "Hi, Hal," he said. "I just wanted to come over and congratulate you on a great day. You and your team did very well for yourselves."

"Thank-you," said Hal. "I appreciate that, Edward. You know Owen Percy, of course."

Mortimer shook his hand. "Of course, Owen. We saw each other at the board meeting."

"Yes," said Owen. "How are you doing?" He then completed the introductions and Mortimer shook hands and exchanged pleasantries with Fluellen and Sarah before turning back to Hal.

"So, I'm sure you know this was quite an unexpected result for us. We're still in a state of shock, I think."

Hal looked down the aisle. "We? I don't see Chuck around anywhere."

"Yes," said Mortimer, clasping his hands behind his back and glancing down at his shoes. "He was called back to the office."

Hal smiled. "That's too bad. I would've liked to have said hello."

"I'll pass along your regards. I spoke to his father, however…"

"Oh, yes," said Owen. "How is Charles?"

"Doing very well. He has asked me to request a meeting with you. In view of today's, ah, outcome."

Yes! We've got the bastards on the run, thought Hal. He had a huge grin on his face and he had to restrain himself from giving Owen a thump on the back.

"I'd be happy to," said Hal. "Will this be another board meeting?"

"We can put four people in a room with you who control almost two-thirds of the voting shares. We'll be in a position to strike a deal."

"Excellent. Where and when did you want to meet?"

"Let's say our boardroom at 9:00 a.m. Friday. I'm going to have John Burgundy sit in on the meeting, as long as you have no objections. John is the CEO of one of our suppliers, and I would propose he could act as an arbitrator, if necessary."

"Yes, I know John. He was a friend of my father's."

"Oh, of course." Mortimer nodded.

"No, I have no objections to that. Owen, you can make it on Friday?"

"Yes," said Owen, smiling.

"Excellent," said Hal. He extended his hand. "We'll see you Friday, then."

"Thank-you," said Mortimer, looking down at Hal's hand. He shook it and left.

Hal, Owen, Sarah, and Fluellen watched him depart and looked around at each other with huge smiles on their faces. Fluellen walked around behind the three of them so he was facing away from the staff.

"So, are we going to get pissed drunk now, or what?" said Fluellen, putting his arms around Owen and Hal's shoulders. They just looked at each other and laughed.

Chapter Thirty

"The Mayor and all his brethren in best sort,
Like to the senators of th'antique Rome,
With the plebeians swarming at their heels,
Go forth and fetch their conquering Caesar in…"

- Act 5, Chorus, Henry V

At the office the next morning, Hal was hailed as the slayer of dragons, the young warrior victorious and toast of the Senior Management Team. There were various meetings all morning to re-jig the share offers, prepare for the summit meeting the following day, and generally wrap their heads around what the acquisition would mean to the organization at every level.

Back in his office at lunchtime, Hal's head was spinning with figures. There were only so many spreadsheets that one person could look at in a day before he went loopy. He didn't know how Archie managed it. When he arrived in the morning, Archie was the first person to come up and congratulate him. It was beautiful. He was just walking up the hall to his office when Archie poked his head out of his office.

"Good morning, Hal," he said. "I hear we have reason to celebrate." He patted him on the back and gave him a big, fake smile.

"Hi, Archie. Yeah, we did pretty well out there in the

trenches. I'm really proud of our guys."

"Well, this is what happens when you think outside the box. You put this thing on the fast track from the start, with a results-driven game plan and a proactive mindset, and at the end of the day, it's gravy for everyone. Kudos to you."

"Well, thanks, Archie. I appreciate that."

"I just wanted to touch base with you this morning so you don't feel like you're out of the loop. After you called yesterday, I set up a finance meeting for this morning so we can go over the numbers for the buyout."

"Yes, I saw that."

He looked at him with wide eyes. "You did?"

"Yes, I logged in last night with my laptop when I got home. I arranged another couple of meetings as well, but I worked around yours."

Archie frowned. "Can I be set up to work from home?"

Hal smiled. "Walk with me, Archie. I'd like to put this stuff down at my desk," he said, indicating his briefcase and coffee.

"Of course, I'm sorry."

They walked in the direction of his office. "I don't see any reason why we couldn't get you set up to log in from home. Especially when you're going to be so busy over the next little while. I'll set it up with Julie today and get her to send over the connection link and a password for you." Hal put down his briefcase as he entered his office and gave him a pat on the back. "You are going to be my right hand on this takeover and I'll need you at the meeting tomorrow at D'Arville."

"Of course," said Archie, wringing his hands together in the doorway with a pained expression. "I won't let you down. Oh, and I also included the board chair on the list of invites for today."

Hal smiled. "I talked to him myself last night."

"Of course you did." He looked around the room in a distracted fashion. "Okay, well, I see everything is under control here. I'll just go, ah, gather my things and see you at the meeting."

It made Hal laugh all over again just thinking about the scene that morning. Poor Archie and his failed presidency bid. He'd have to wait a long time now. Hal looked at his watch and wondered about lunch, but didn't really feel hungry. That same restless feeling from yesterday was invading his thoughts today. Despite all the accolades and pats on the back, the one person's opinion that seemed to matter most to him was still unknown. But how to get a hold of her?

He looked up "D'Arville" in the phone book—there weren't many. There were three C. D'Arville's in the Toronto listings, but what if they were unlisted? There was one in Forest Hill that seemed most likely. He dialed it and prepared to apologize for a wrong number if necessary.

"Hello?"

"May I speak with Kate, please?"

"Just a moment."

Well, they had a Kate, anyway. Good start.

"Hello?"

It was her. "Hi, Kate. It's Hal."

"Oh."

Not a good start. "How's it going?"

"Fine."

Not fine. "I just wanted to call to see how you were feeling. About everything."

"Well, Hal, how do you expect I'm feeling?"

"Yeah, I know. I'm just, I just want to reassure you that this is for the best for everyone. I'm going to take our two companies to the top. I don't want any more bloodshed over this. I want to make a deal that's fair for all parties."

"That's nice."

"I want to get your input on it. How about dinner tonight to talk it over before the meeting tomorrow?"

She was silent. He waited.

"Kate? How about it?"

"If that's the only reason you want to have dinner with me, then forget it."

"No, that's not… Kate? Kate? Damn."

He looked at the receiver in his hand. What was he doing wrong? This used to be so easy. He leaned over, lay his forehead on the edge of his desk and looked down at the floor. The desk's smooth, lacquered wood was lovely and cool. He closed his eyes and rolled his head back and forth to spread the coolness. He took a deep breath and exhaled. The phone started making a beeping noise in his lap. He put it back in its cradle and sat up straight in his chair.

A few minutes later he walked down the hall to his uncle's office and knocked on the door frame. Owen was at his desk thumb typing on his BlackBerry. He looked up at the sound.

"Owen?"

"Yes, Hal?"

"Let's take no prisoners tomorrow, okay?"

Owen sat back in his chair and looked at Hal for a beat. "Sure. What makes you say that?"

"Let's just get it done."

Chapter Thirty-One

"Ha, art thou bedlam? Dost thou thirst, base Troyan,
To have me fold up Parca's fatal web?"

- Act 5, Scene 1, Henry V

Amy was acting weird. She had been quiet in the rental car all the way back to Toronto from Windsor, and then just dropped him off, saying she was tired. When Pete arrived at work the next morning, she wasn't there. Arthur said she had been called in to a meeting. Since when did she have meetings that the rest of the group didn't?

As he put the finishing touches on his drawing, he thought back to their dinner on Tuesday night. She was probably still pissed at him. He had to tone it down a little about Hal. There was no way she was going to be able to understand how he felt about that asshole. She was more of a serious career go-getter so she didn't need his negativity about the company bringing her down. Maybe it would be better when they didn't work at the same place anymore and weren't seeing each other all the time, like normal couples.

He had been working on the drawing for some time. It was the one Amy had wanted of him as Superman. It had actually been quite a challenge. He wasn't used to doing self-portraits, and it was hard to be objective about his facial characteristics. What he ended up with was what he would look like wearing Superman's actual gear: the sleeves too long for him, the shoulders drooping, his knees knocking, and the spandex baggy all over. He was holding out a bunch of green kryptonite roses, and the caption read, "For the one who makes me weak."

He loved the whole look of the drawing, actually. It had nice clean lines and a great vulnerability about it that had been difficult to achieve. The whole concept of Superman also made more sense if he didn't look all muscled up. As Kal-el, a humanoid from another planet, he enjoyed superior strength due to his proximity to their yellow sun and ability to defy gravity. He didn't come to earth and join a gym to start pumping iron. The idea was that he looked like a regular guy, like Clark Kent, but had super powers because of where he was from. From Joe Shuster to the artists on the current titles, they were all way off track with his bulked-up image.

When he looked up, Fluellen was standing right beside him and he hadn't even noticed. Unholy mother-loving piles of green shit from the planet Krypton, he was losing his touch. He pushed the drawing aside and turned around.

Fluellen raised his eyebrows and then gave him a patient smile. "Good morning, Malden. When you have a second to tear yourself away from all that important art you're working on, I'd appree-see-ate a moment of your time."

"Sorry about that," he said. "Just something I worked on last night. Finishing touches, you know." Lame.

"I don't want to interrupt."

"No, I'm fine. Now's good."

"All right, then. My office?"

"Sure."

Fluellen led the way out of the cubicle, down the hallway and over to his office. He held the door for Pete, who sat in the chair opposite his desk. Fluellen closed the door behind them. Never a good sign, but this time, Pete didn't care. He had a plan.

Fluellen sat at his desk, pushed the *Do Not Disturb* button on his phone, and leaned back in his chair, cradling his head in his hands. "So, Malden."

"Yes, Fluellen." Pete looked him dead in the eye.

His boss looked at him for a moment, scratching his chin, and then continued. "That was quite a little show you put on at the Cleary on Wednesday. Mr. Bad Attitude. I know it's been a tough week for you. I know you're still bitter about Bardolph being fired, but when you mouth off to the CEO, how do you think that makes me look?"

Pete shrugged his shoulders.

"Not good. Hal seems to have a soft spot for you because you two go way back. He cut you some slack and I'm willing to do the same. We've also worked together a long time and I've never had a problem with your work or your attitude before."

As his boss was talking, Pete became fascinated with a little string of yellowish spit or something that would attach itself from his front teeth to his bottom lip, stretching, breaking and then reattaching. It wouldn't quit. Stretch and break, attach and stretch. If he had to draw Fluellen right now, he'd draw him as Sgt. Rock, who always had that weird piece of skin attaching his top and bottom lips. He'd have him frothing at the mouth a little bit, scrub brush hair, and heavy, overbearing red eyebrows, connected in the middle.

The thing he liked most about Sgt. Rock was that he was always willing to do whatever it took to save his unit.

Take a bullet, dive on a grenade, and even die for them if necessary. The art style was a little more cluttered than he liked, which was part of that dirty, ragged "Dogs of War" feel.

He remembered the British war comics his father had given him from his childhood and how different they were from the American ones. The British soldiers would be facing the worst conditions imaginable, but would still have their top buttons done up and their uniforms spotless. They also respected the chain of command, whereas Sgt. Rock and his boys were always going against orders, because they knew better than "the brass" sitting in their comfy chairs behind the lines.

It's funny that you never see war comics these days, he thought. There were no regular war titles on the racks at the Silver Snail. What did that say about today's comic buyers? That they were more escapist, and didn't like reading gritty, realistic stories of combat? Now it was all superheroes. An escape from reality.

Fluellen was still talking. Blah, blah, blah, something about his first job out of university when he came to Canada. The spit was still hanging in there, still with the same elasticity. Stretch, snap, stick, stretch, snap. What a truly disgusting thing. Didn't this guy brush his teeth in the morning?

"So anyway," he said, sitting forward. "You look a little burnt out. Take some time off, think things over, and come back committed and refreshed, or don't come back at all. Your choice."

Not fired? "Oh, yeah," said Pete. "I guess that would be all right." He looked down at his hands, not knowing what to say. "Can I let you know tomorrow?" Was that really Fluellen talking? What he was saying sounded... nice.

"Sure, that would be fine. We're going to be busy as hell around here, but I think you need to pull yourself together and make some decisions. We'll all pitch in and do some extra work. Everybody is still really fired up about the merger."

"Except me, right?"

"Exactly. I need you back at 100%."

"Okay, I'll give it some thought tonight. So next week would be fine? To take off?"

"Fine and dandy." Fluellen stood. "I hope you decide to stick with us. Things are just starting to get interesting around here."

Pete stood and opened the door. "Yeah." He looked at him for a moment and nodded. "Thanks, uh, Bill. For this." He held out his hand and Fluellen shook it.

"Ah, go on, now. I want you back and playing bingo at our meetings again. Back to your old self."

Pete nodded and walked back to his desk. There was still no sign of Amy, which left only Arthur. The Super Pete drawing sat beside his keyboard. He picked it up and looked it over one last time before slipping it into her briefcase. She would find it later.

Pete left for the elevators, street level, fresh air, and some coffee. The momentum of the plan was fueling his resolve. It was a beautiful thing in his mind and the pieces were falling together like a video playing in reverse with the shards of a broken mirror reassembling. Perfection.

Chapter Thirty-Two

"O fair Katherine, if you will love me soundly
With your French heart, I will be glad to hear you
Confess it brokenly with your English tongue."

- Act 5, Scene 2, Henry V

Friday morning, Hal, Owen and Archie decided not to drive to the D'Arville office. They walked up Bay Street instead so they could savor the moment. It was Hal's idea. He had looked forward to this day for so long that he didn't want to rush anything. They walked along three abreast with their briefcases and sunglasses, passing all the young executives on their way to work, the office workers with their business suits and sneakers, and the homeless people finding their places on the sidewalk and getting ready for another day in the big city.

Amid all the mirrored buildings, the TSE, the National Club—the hub of the Canadian business world—Hal felt as though he finally belonged. He wasn't a fish out of water anymore. Sure, his father had built the company with his hard work and sharp mind. There were those who always thought that the son had had it easy and wouldn't amount to much. This had been his challenge to overcome.

But he really felt like he'd accomplished something here, taken the company a step beyond what his father had

236

anticipated. It was Hal's vision that had brought them to this point, and his ability to make others believe it was possible. There was a thrill to this beyond anything he had ever experienced on any golf course. He breathed deeply and tried to take it all in. It helped steady his heart, which was setting a blistering pace. Calm was what he needed — calm and focus.

They entered the lobby of the absurdly busy office tower at 8:55am and caught the first elevator to the 26th floor. Hal looked at Owen, who seemed absolutely calm and gave him a smile and a wink, and at Archie, who was a bit pale and humming as he watched the numbers light up above the door. The doors opened and they stepped off the elevator.

"Welcome, gentlemen," said Edward Mortimer, shaking hands with each of them in turn.

"Thank-you, Edward," said Hal.

Mortimer nodded. "Mm-hmm. Well, they're all waiting for us. It's right down the hall here, if you'll follow me."

Hal brought up the rear, marveling at the opulence of the décor, the smooth mahogany, the rich leathers and smoked glass everywhere. It was no wonder they were in debt if this is what they spent on their offices. There was even a rumor that they employed a chef for the executive lounge. He wondered where that was and had a look down each hallway as they passed.

When they reached the boardroom, Mortimer opened the door and ushered them in, Archie and Owen in the lead, saying hello to Charles D'Arville and the rest of his team. Just as he was about to enter the doorway, he saw her. All he saw was her profile and a shock of her brown hair, but he knew it was her. He paused. She was sitting in a chair in a little waiting area down the hall.

"Hal?" Owen held the door for him. "Are you coming?"

"Just give me a minute." She looked up at him, and then looked away. He looked back at Owen. "Why don't you guys go ahead and get started, and I'll join you shortly."

"Go ahead?" Owen looked at him and gave him a half shrug.

Hal stepped in and whispered. "You guys know the plan of attack. I just need five minutes."

"All right," he said, nodding. Owen closed the door and, as Hal walked down the hall, he heard him behind the door saying, "We're just going to go ahead."

When he got to the doorway, he hesitated, trying to think what he was going to say to her. Without looking up, Kate said, "You come to gloat?"

"What? No." He gripped the back of a chair by the door, a few chairs away from her.

"What, then?" She looked up at him. "Congratulations, you won. Get in there and make it official."

He looked back at her. "That's why I came here."

"Well, what are you waiting for?"

"I saw someone more important to me that I had to talk to first."

"Uh-huh." She sighed and rested her head on her hand. "What's to talk about?"

"You. I've been thinking about you ever since our phone call yesterday and I had to clear something up."

She blinked her eyes several times slowly, looking bored.

"I was an idiot. Sometimes I can't believe the things that come out of my mouth. What I should've said was that I want to take you out and talk about anything but the merger. I just want to see you, Kate. Not 'Kate D'Arville Industries.' I don't care about that other stuff."

She looked at him for a moment. "I see. And why

should I trust this rather abrupt about-face?"

He came around and sat in the chair nearest the door, one chair closer to Kate, who was sitting against the side wall. "I can see why you wouldn't. I've been so caught up in this whole thing that I haven't been making much sense. I wish you had nothing to do with this. I wish I had met you by chance and we had a drink, got caught up, and weren't so immersed in... all this."

She forced a tight-lipped grimace. "Well, that's life, isn't it?"

"Yeah, I guess it is." He looked down at his shoes, and shook his head. "Look, I'm sorry for the way I've handled this. I think at times I needed a friend, and I really wanted you to be there for me, although I totally understand why you couldn't. I've missed what we had together. Since I screwed things up with you, I've never met a woman with the same connection we had. Where the physical chemistry is all there but she... you, are someone who is a friend. Someone I like and respect."

Her face softened somewhat, and she gave him a smile with something behind it. "Oh, flattery, eh? Trying to break through my defenses?"

"Whatever works," he said, smiling. He stood and she held his eyes as he moved over to the seat next to her and sat again. He picked up her hand in his and held it between their chairs. "Kate, will you let me take you out so we can get to know each other again? I want to show you that I can be a better person than you know."

She continued holding his gaze without saying anything, with just that hint of a smile again.

"Well?" he said after a few moments of silence.

"I don't know," she said. She smiled and looked out the window.

"Well, do any of your neighbors know? I'll ask them. I'll

talk to your mother, get your father's blessing… whatever it takes. Just say you'll go out with me. Just that one thing."

"Oh, I guess so. You've been so persistent."

He breathed deeply. "Well, you're worth it."

"Would it have been a record for you if I said 'no' for a fourth time?"

"I hate to tell you this, but it was a record the first time."

They both laughed at this and leaned forward, so he took that opportunity to kiss her on the lips. She didn't resist, but came up smiling, looking into his eyes. "What was that for?"

"For saying yes," he said. The sound of a door opening behind him caused him to look over his shoulder. "Here comes your father." They both stood.

"Here you are, Hal," he said. "We were wondering where you'd gotten to."

"Hello, Mr. D'Arville," he said before he could stop himself. He felt himself blush. "I was out here talking to your beautiful daughter." He looked at her and smiled.

"Well, you were in good company, then. I just wanted to tell you that what you and your people have proposed today is eminently fair, given the circumstances."

"Thank-you," said Hal. "We want to make this work."

"I left it to the sharks in there to hammer out the details, but it has my stamp of approval."

"Are you leaving, Daddy?" said Kate.

"Yes, I am. You know that hammock in the backyard?"

"Yes."

"I really haven't given it the attention it deserves. My work is done here. I'm taking the rest of the day off."

She put a hand on his arm and kissed his cheek. "I think that sounds like a fabulous idea."

Charles D'Arville began walking away, and then

240

turned back. "Will I see you later on for dinner, honey?"

"Nope," she said, looking up at Hal. "I've got a date."

Chapter Thirty-Three

"There is one goat for you. (He strikes him)
Will you be so good, scauld knave, as eat it?"

- Act 5, Scene 1, Henry V

Pete and Amy had lunch together for the last time on Friday. He sat there in his desk across the cubicle with his back to her that same afternoon, knowing that it was utterly true. She hadn't said that, of course, but he was getting good at recognizing the signs.

Things had started out okay, but seemed to go off track sometime after she told him her news. He hadn't had a chance to talk to her alone Thursday afternoon at work after his conversation with Fluellen and her meeting in the morning. When he called her Thursday night after her class, there was no answer. When she arrived at work on Friday morning he asked her out to lunch. She said she didn't have much time, so he agreed to a food court lunch.

When noon finally rolled around and they grabbed their things and headed out, he had already felt awkwardness in the silence of the elevator, the way she just watched the numbers lighting up one by one as they descended to below street level. They walked the underground walkway to the food court under a nearby office tower, not talking much, just surveying the daily specials posted by the various establishments around the perimeter. They each decided on a different restaurant. Pete watched her fidget with her purse while her plate was being filled and then they met up again when they had their food.

"Is this one okay?" he said, indicating a table that was identical to perhaps a hundred others in a grid formation. She failed to see the humor in it.

"Sure, this one's fine." She set down her Teriyaki Chicken and rice.

He put down his Big Beef burrito and they sat down. "You know," he said. "Burrito is Spanish for 'little donkey.'"

"Really?" she said, mixing up the food on her plate.

"It makes you wonder about the meat they put in here."

She smiled and had a mouthful of chicken.

He started cutting up his food with the little plastic utensils. "So, I didn't see much of you yesterday."

"Oh, I know. Isn't it crazy busy right now?"

He shrugged. "I guess. I also called you last night but there was no answer." He picked up a forkful of little donkey and blew on it.

"I was at my mum's. I had exciting news." She looked at him, waiting for him to ask.

"What news?" he said.

"Are you ready for this?"

He nodded and continued chewing.

"You know that meeting I had yesterday morning? It was with Owen Percy." She sat there, beaming at him. "VP Owen Percy?"

He nodded.

"He was very impressed with my performance at the trade show, and they are offering me a newly-created position. I'm going to be a 'Section Leader.' It's a kind of sales supervisor."

"That's great," he said. "That's just what you were

hoping for. I guess all that extra sleep paid off, eh?"

She tilted her head and gave him a sarcastic slitting of the eyes. "Yes, it did. So I'm going to be supervising an inside sales team after the takeover goes through. There's going to be three supervisors, and we'll all be working under Fluellen. Isn't that fantastic?"

"Yeah! Congratulations, honey," he said, putting his hand over hers and smiling in what he hoped would be a genuine way. She smiled back, hung in there for a second and then pulled her hand away to pick up her cup for a sip of Coke. He would remember this gesture quite clearly later.

"As a matter of fact, I have some news of my own," said Pete.

"What's that?"

"I'm quitting Mercer."

She stopped, her fork hovering in the air. "When?"

"When? Actually, today is my last day."

She just looked at him. "What? How?"

"I'm taking my last two weeks as vacation and I gave my notice to Fluellen today."

"Well, that's... great, I guess. You must have something really great lined up." She gazed off into the distance, and then her eyes snapped back onto his. "Oh, let me guess. You got a job as an artist on a comic book!"

He shook his head. "No, I'm just looking for a job that will pay the bills. Whatever, I don't care."

Her mouth hung open a bit while her eyes flicked back and forth, looking into his as if in search of a punch line. "But, okay. Isn't that a bit risky?"

"Yeah, it'll be all right. I just can't do the Mercer thing anymore."

"But you're going to try to get a job as an artist."

"No." He stirred his refried beans.

"But why not? You're so good. You'd be a great comic book artist."

"I just do the doodling for fun. If I tried to do it for money, it wouldn't be fun anymore."

She sat up straighter, and then leaned forward. "Why do you think that?"

"It would just be different. Like sex is different for a prostitute, I imagine. Not fun."

"But you're good. And what's wrong with being paid for what you're good at?"

"It's the commerce of it. It would be tainted somehow. It would change it into something… commercial. And there would be limitations, and demands, and I'd have a supervisor, and there'd be some other CEO with his focus groups and nine reasons why I should draw it his way instead of mine, and then that would be my work. My job. And what would I do for fun?"

They sat there for a moment just looking at each other, and Pete felt a distance come between them. She looked away, and down at her plate, and then back at his face, and there was something different in the way she looked at him. At that moment, he wondered if he could just forget the plan and get a nice safe job and move in with her and make her happy. Make him happy.

"Well, as long as you're happy," she said, digging into her Chicken Teriyaki with her fork. It was too late.

He tried to go on as if nothing had happened. "So, what do you want to do tonight?"

"Oh, I've got to study tonight."

"On a Friday?"

"Yeah. All weekend, actually. Owen is sending me on a first time manager's course all next week. I have to do all my night class work on the weekend to keep up."

"So I won't see you at all next week?"

"Yeah, no. I'll try to call you. Or e-mail you."

"Okay," he said, nodding now. Realizing how far it had gone.

"So when do you start looking?" She wiped her lips with her napkin and put it on top of her plate.

"Right away, I guess." He laughed. He watched her reapply her lipstick in a little mirror, and knew he wasn't even going to be able to kiss her now. The image of her eyes when he kissed her outside her hotel room in Windsor came to him as he realized that that had been their last kiss. Then the image of Super Pete with the kryptonite flowers came back to him, and he could feel his cheeks flush.

They made some small talk as he finished eating. He couldn't even remember what they talked about. Her new job, maybe. He gave up on eating when his throat became too dry to swallow. They gathered their trays, dumped the garbage into the nearby can, and walked back to the office in all the lunch hour rush, more small talk, and the realization that she was really, actually, when you thought about it, choosing Hal over him. The feeling burned in his dry throat and at the corners of his eyes. And turned to rage. One more thing that Hal Mercer had taken from him.

* * *

Kate was looking through her closet while talking to Alice on the phone. She couldn't remember ever having bought these clothes and didn't know how they had ended up in her home.

"You were right," said Kate. "It was like I was waiting

to breathe again. Now that it's over, I'm almost relieved."

"I won't even say I told you so," said Alice.

"He's different now. So sure of himself, but in a less cocky, more grounded way."

"You guys are so good together. It was totally meant to be."

Kate crooked the phone under her chin and pulled a shirt out of the closet and held it up to herself, looking in the mirror. She sighed and put it back. "Well, let's see how it goes first."

"Oh, come on," said Alice. "He's good looking and successful and you still love him. That's a good start."

Kate smiled and felt a warm kind of giddy feeling flutter inside her chest. "Yes, it is. Oh, I don't know why I was so against the idea of a date with him. I think part of my resistance to the merger was my resistance to Hal. The thought of him coming into the picture was like him asking to come back into my life, which was scary on all levels."

"I would gladly take a little of that scary in my life right now."

"With the way my relationships have gone over the last five years, I was starting to feel like I was in the Bermuda triangle of my 30's."

"Some of us still are."

And right now, Kate thought. *She was in the Bermuda triangle of her closet, where all the sharp outfits had disappeared into the void.*

"It'll happen for you, girl. What about that guy at the gym?"

"Still nothing but flirting. He's probably married, anyway."

"Oh, come on. That was one guy." Kate gave up and lay down on her bed.

"It's not that hard to leave a wedding ring in your locker."

"I guess not. Too bad it isn't summer. At least then you could look for tan lines. Ugh. Why do I have nothing to wear?"

"Oooh, emergency shopping trip? Do we have time?"

Kate looked at her watch. "Sure, he's not picking me up until 8:00."

"I'll be there in ten minutes."

Chapter Thirty-Four

"All hell shall stir for this."

- Act 5, Scene 1, Henry V

"Pistol" Pete Malden, erstwhile corporate young gun, prepared to leave the building that Friday night. He cleaned out his desk, taking down all his cartoons and drawings, clearing out all personal effects, the pencils and pens that he liked, and deleting all his e-mail. He wanted to leave with no trace of his having been there.

In the hours after he and Amy returned from lunch, he sat at his desk and stared straight ahead, doing nothing. He hadn't talked to her, or anyone else. He sat. He stewed. His eyes were black coals of hatred, ready to spark into flame like the eyes of the Human Torch.

It was there in the flames that the plan had been formed, so it was right that it would be carried out in the same way. He stuffed everything into his knapsack and looked around the office. All the wasted effort he had put in here, the friendships betrayed or come to nothing, and all the money someone else made off the sweat of his labor. And that kind of "someone" existed on every floor of this building, and every other building in town; someones just like Hal, a colony of rat bastards, profiteers in white-collar sweatshops.

The plan was simple. They could keep their car leases,

their consumer credit, their cutting edge electronics, their package vacations, their once-in-a-lifetime offers. They could keep their wonderful mortgages, where you thought you were buying a house, but really the bank was buying you. Fuck them, they could keep it all. What they were selling, he wasn't buying. That was part one.

Part two was that he would no longer serve a system in which he didn't believe. His drawing was sacred, and he would use as its defense the only arms he would allow himself: a simple life, subsistence wage, and cunning. This was his only recourse. He knew there would be sacrifices. He'd sell his car and get a smaller apartment within walking distance from work. He'd have to get his movies from the library instead of going to the cineplexes; buy fewer comics, fewer dinners out; keep it simple and watch out for the pitfalls of the system. The temptations of excess. Hell, he'd sell his comics if he had to. And someday, if he had a piece of sequential art he was completely happy with, and he felt he'd made no compromises and the time was right, he would share it with the world. On his terms. The new job and the new discipline would give him the chance to really refine his work.

The cubicle looked even smaller than usual. He walked out trying not to look around at Randy's empty desk or Arthur's things, or worse, Amy's. He walked across the floor, passing row upon row of empty cubicles, dozens of computers and fax machines, photocopiers and other signs of industry and exploitation. He continued down the back hall past the executive wing towards the back door. Hal was still in his office. Good.

After he left the building, he got into a cab. He knew exactly which store carried what he wanted. He had just Googled it an hour ago. Thank God he had already quit or he might be fired for using the Internet! Fuck you fuck you fuck you fuck you. The guy at the store was really good. Helped him get what he would need. Got the automatic instead of the manual. Faster repeat. That would be ideal.

The poetic quality of this final gesture was too good. It gave him a swimmy head. Here was he, embracing the purity and the whatsit of Art and staunchly, resoundingly rejecting the perversity and infamy of the world of commerce. This final act the punctuation at the end of what could have been a life sentence.

And then he would be free! Early parole for good behavior. For being a true believer. Then it was all ivory towers for him. The unassailable world of creative… he hoped that ivory was a color and not a material in that sense. Sheesh. Bad karma elephant soul haunting he did not need.

In the cab on the way back to Mercer, he felt like The Punisher: armed to the teeth and ready to make the guilty pay. How cool was that? He paid the driver and walked across the sidewalk and through the lobby of the Mercer building as if nothing could be wrong with the world. Nodding to the security guard as he passed, he entered the elevator as if it had been waiting just for him.

* * *

The security guard grabbed for the phone as soon as the weird guy with the bulky coat had passed him and entered the elevator.

"Hello, 911? I'm calling from… yes, that's right. The east tower. A man with a gun just got on the elevator. Yes,

I could see it sticking out from under his coat. He's just getting off at the, um, fifteenth floor. Okay, I'll monitor the exits. Hurry."

* * *

As Friday afternoon stretched into closing time and then into early evening, Hal still couldn't tear himself away from work. He stood in his corner office, looking out his window at the dark city. He cast his mind out like feelers in every direction, trying to imagine all of the people out there that were connected to him. He imagined the homeward routes of all his employees plotted out on the city like a giant map with him in the middle, thin red lines spreading out in all directions. Then all of the employees in their homes were dots on the map, with smaller blue lines stretching out to each member of their family. All those red and blue lines spread out like cracks in glass shattering in slow motion, the red like blood flowing through their veins, imperceptible beneath the skin, visible only in his mind, in actuality leaving no trace on the city. All those people were out there in the dark at that moment, eating their dinners, watching their TVs, out at the movies, and a hundred other unknowable things— all dependent on him for their livelihoods.

Add to those numbers the many employees from D'Arville with whom he would soon be connected, all the shareholders known and unknown who invested their money and trust in his ability to lead and the images made his mind go blank. He felt the overwhelming, unutterably awesome pressure of this responsibility at the same time as he savored the beauty of it.

How to explain this new certainty, this feeling of destiny? Maybe it came with the surges of adrenalin over the last week and this successful D'Arville conquest. Something dormant in his nature had been awakened: his ability to lead. What he now understood was that leaders are born, not taught. All the MBAs in the world couldn't make you a leader. You either were one or you weren't.

His father had had it. Looking back, he now saw the essence of a leader in him, the ability to both deal with the pressure and inspire his people as if everything were easy. He had passed that on to his son like a king would his crown. And, as in the time of kings, he had prepared his son for the life that would choose him.

He could see it all now. Everything comes together as it should. Part of that vision was the work that remained to be done with the company. D'Arville would be absorbed, and then they would survey the landscape for another acquisition. They would be the biggest and the best. All the logistics of that transition and growth didn't frighten him at all. It would be done. The first priority was getting the D'Arville people to buy into the Mercer corporate culture. That was his specialty, of course, but maybe he could also appoint Mortimer as a VP in charge of the transition, to ease the pain of Chuck's departure. He smiled at his reflection in the window.

Checking his watch, he turned back to his desk and began to turn off his laptop and put stray pages into their folders. He'd said he would pick up Kate at 8:00. The sound of the elevator told him the cleaning people were here early, but the office was otherwise empty this late on a Friday. He would slip out the back door. He gathered his laptop and a couple of files into his briefcase and—

"Hey, ass-wipe. Trying to figure out who to fire next?"

Hal turned to see Pete in the doorway of his office. He

was wearing a bulky coat and knapsack, hair askew. Hal frowned at this.

"Pete. What's going on?" He put his briefcase on his desk and rested a hand on top of it. There was something strange about the way Pete stood there, blocking the doorway.

"I came for my severance package," he said.

"Yes, I heard. I'm really sorry we—"

"Save it. You got everything you wanted, didn't you? So don't pretend you give a crap about it. Got your merger in the end. Oh, Golden Leader! Everything's coming up roses for our boy, Hal."

"Couldn't have done it without—"

"And you took Amy away from me."

"I what now?"

"You turned her head with your glittery corporate ladder. Your promises of future promotions. But it's just a matter of time till we all outlive our usefulness, isn't it? And then we get the boot from one of your lackeys."

"Pete, you're being ridiculous. Why don't you take the weekend to think it over and we'll meet for lunch on Monday to talk things out. Nothing's been done here that can't be undone."

"Let me guess. There is no 'I' in T.E.A.M.? We've all got to pull together or we'll fall apart?"

Hal crossed his arms and spread his feet, looking down at the ground. "Look, this is bullshit. I know you're still upset about Randy and apparently you've broken up with Amy, but—"

"Don't worry, I can always get a job delivering the snail mail now that I've gone Postal! Get it? Postal?" He laughed until there were tears streaming down his face and Hal just stood there looking at him. When the laughter stopped, the tears kept coming.

"It's all gone to shit, now. Hasn't it?" said Pete. Then he reached under his coat and pulled out a gun.

Hal's eyes widened and his heart jumped in his chest. "Pete, whatever you're thinking here, you've gotta—"

"It's time for your final lesson in teamwork, Hal."

"We used to be good friends. I'm sorry for whatever I did to hurt you." Hal was backing up behind his desk and keeping an eye on the gun in Pete's hands as he adjusted his grip on the stock. The sound of the elevator doors opening distracted Pete for a second and it was then that Hal recognized the gun that was pointing at him.

"Police! Drop your weapon!" The shout came from down the hall to Pete's right. He looked in that direction and then back at Hal, the tears still standing out in his eyes.

"Looks like your luck holds, Golden Boy," he said, locking eyes with Hal. "As usual. Everything Hal wants, Hal gets. And I can't even... well, fuck it. Don't know how you were able to call them, but it doesn't matter."

"Pete," said Hal. "This isn't—"

The voice came from the hall again. "Drop it! There's no way out of here. Let's put the gun down and talk about it."

"No, don't, it's—" shouted Hal as he started towards the door.

"I'm all done talking!" Pete shouted as he raised the gun and took aim at Hal.

"No, don't shoot him," screamed Hal. "It's just a—"

Two gunshots sounded from the hall and then the silenced *Phut!* of Pete's weapon as he slumped over onto the floor. Hal felt a sudden impact slamming into his shoulder as he surged forward trying to catch Pete, but he was too late. There was a hollow clunk as Pete's head hit the wall behind him and the police were running down the hall towards them and Hal was on his knees. He picked Pete up by his jacket and rolled him over onto his back, seeing the blood rushing out of his side and his eyes rolling back, looking at nothing. The gun fell out of Pete's hands and hit the floor, the brightly-colored paint balls spilling across the carpet.

Hal straddled Pete's body in mute horror, their faces inches apart. He held him by his collar and he watched as the life in his friend's eyes went still, the police tugging at his arm and all the sound had gone out of the room.

Epilogue

"Thus far, with rough and all-unable pen,
Our bending author hath pursued the story,
In little room confining mighty men,
Mangling by starts the full course of their glory."

- Epilogue, Henry V

Hal sat on a concrete bench in front of a fountain. The downtown office lunch crowd streamed in and out of the small park in which he sat. It was noon on a Thursday in very early Spring where the feeling of warmth in the air could be erased by a cold wind in half a second and then nestle around you again a few minutes later when you'd forgotten all about it. He didn't mind the cold after being in the office all morning. He draped his trench coat over one leg and sat there with his tie loosened and one button open on his shirt. He waited for Kate.

He thought about his desk and all the things he had in progress and all the work that never seemed to get done. The merger was complete and the two offices combined. Once they were able to sublet the old D'Arville office their cash flow was going to really improve. But it hadn't come easy. He had met with every employee of both firms in small groups to get their opinions on core values and purpose. They talked about building a great company and what that would look like. They told him honestly what the current problems were at Mercer or D'Arville. It was a myriad of these and other meetings and org charts and employee surveys. This afternoon was no different: SMT Ops meeting and he was supposed to stop in to see the Sales Team Leaders in their meeting.

Amy Quick was one of the standouts among the supervisors. She had such smarts and enthusiasm. That made him think of Pete and the sound of those shots and the blood and the stillness in his eyes and he had to take a deep breath and clear his mind. Push all thoughts of the office out. Let it all just fall away. It had been almost six months and it was getting easier to do this, which brought its own pain.

He saw there were a few birds in one of the nearby trees. He couldn't yet see any buds on the branches, but he knew they had to be coming out soon. Given some more encouragement by the warm air, buds and flowers and more birds had to be on their way. One of the items on the top of his list for the new house was a nice garden in which he could sit out in the evening. It didn't feel right having Kate over at the condo, which was more of a bachelor pad. Now that they were getting serious, he'd begun to have some very domestic thoughts.

Then he saw her coming in from the street and his whole body seemed to warm up in an instant. Kate was so beautiful that he instantly felt the physical quality of the word breathtaking. She was wearing her favorite black leather coat and slacks and looked so Toronto. She smiled when she saw him and then glanced down at the concrete as she turned and walked towards him, catching and holding his eyes as she approached. He stood up and kissed and hugged her and they walked across the square together in the direction of the restaurant, her telling him about her day and him just listening, holding her hand.

All these little shared things were so valuable to him. He felt the comfort of her presence and pulled her closer, wanting the good feeling to penetrate him completely.

Discussion Points for Book Groups

Chapter 2 – The Archbishop of Canterbury is scheming with the Bishop of Ely. Enter the King. *Once Were Friends* is a scene by scene modernization of Shakespeare's *Henry V*, which you probably guessed from all the quotations from that play. I've added some new, original scenes, but in essence the whole play is recreated here. First and foremost, I wanted to write a novel that would be an entertaining read even for someone unfamiliar with the source material. At the same time, I felt that understanding the connection of the plot and the characters to the original play would enrich the reader's experience. For this reason, I made the subtext a part of the fun for myself and the reader, keeping the characters' names the same wherever possible. I enjoyed the symmetry of turning the "Archbishop of Canterbury" into "Archie Bishop," and took pleasure in portraying this avaricious religious leader from the play as the scheming VP of Finance in the novel.

Chapter 2 – "D'Arville" – I wanted to retain the French vs. English conflict of the play, but kept tripping over the contradiction of portraying the "French" people who owned this rival company as speaking unaccented English. Then the answer came to me: The Huguenots! I knew someone in high school who told me the story of his seemingly British family with this exact French-sounding name. I also liked the sound of the word "D'Arville," and its connection to "dark" or "Darth," which is a great onomatopoeia for the name of the novel's antagonist.

Chapter 2 – "A dozen golf balls" – These were tennis balls in the play, but their insult is the same: Chuck (the Dauphin) is saying that Hal (Henry) is a feckless goof-off and no threat to him.

Chapter 1 – Paint ball – I was at a friend's bachelor party years ago, figuring out what paint ball is all about while trying to keep my gun from jamming and not get shot, when I saw a big troop from a local office marching by for a team-building exercise. It seemed weirdly appropriate that they were relying on an inherently war-like activity to better prepare themselves for their inherently ruthless and combative roles in the corporate world. The entire concept of the novel came to me in that instant, right down to the Shakespearean framework and the theme of business as metaphor for war. It is impossible to miss the parallels between the language ("chain of command," "front lines," and "rising through the ranks," etc.), the attitudes and the hierarchies of both war and business, and I had fun with this throughout.

Chapter 1 – Names like "Pistol" and "Mistress Quickly" were more of a challenge to work into a contemporary story. Thanks to the paint ball, I had an excuse for a nickname like "Pistol Pete" and came up with Amy "Quick" as the best alternative. Most of the other names stayed the same, although I took "Hal" from Henry IV, Parts I and II, the scene of his wilder days, to which I hearken back in the book as well.

Chapter 4 – "We've got the big trade show coming up

in Windsor on the 25th." – October 25th is St. Crispin's Day, the anniversary of the original Battle of Agincourt where the English beat the French to assert Henry's claim to the French throne. This is somewhat bathetically represented as an industry trade show in the novel. Obviously, we haven't any shortage of real wars in the 21st century, but most of the hostile takeovers happen in the boardrooms these days.

Chapter 7 – The action shifts here from a Friday to a Monday. As this is a novel "about" business and the workplace, weekends aren't depicted. The only action taking place on a Saturday is the official company team-building exercise at the paint ball arena.

Chapter 12 – I skip "Chapter Eleven" for the same reason. In the business world, those words are extremely bad luck and a form of death for the corporation.

Chapter 21 – The firing of Randy – In the original version, Randy was hanged for stealing, but this seemed a bit harsh in a modern workplace context. The equivalent of death for an employee is termination, a kind of working death. Fluellen actually makes the point that wasting company time is like stealing.

Chapter 24 – "What infinite heart's ease must kings neglect that private men enjoy!" *Act IV, Scene 1* – It's not easy being King. It was difficult to conceive of a soliloquy in a contemporary context as anything other than a dude talking to himself. The idea of the sympathetic bartender as a sounding board may be a hoary cliché in movies and television, but it felt more dynamic than simply reporting on Hal's internal monologue would have.

Chapter 31 – Hal described as "young warrior victorious" – This is my name, loosely (Mark derives from Mars, the Roman god of war). It's not an inside joke because I'm sharing it with you now.

About the Author

Happily married since 1992 and a father since 2003, Mark has been a writer for as long as he can remember. He was born in Toronto and grew up in London, Ontario. He was the first winner of the *Lillian Kroll Prize for Creative Writing* at Western University, where he also completed a degree in English Literature. The manuscript for *Once Were Friends* was long-listed in *The Writers' Studio 1st Book Competition*. Mark has published novels, poetry, short fiction, feature articles, comic strips and book reviews in various media.

He lives in London with his wife and daughter, those to whom all his work and play is dedicated.

Connect with Mark at his website -
http://markvictoryoung.com/

Also from *Hanton House* by Mark Victor Young
Risk - a Novel

They're the most unlikely detectives.

Martin is a 38-year-old virgin marked for greatness by the insurance gods. In his professional life, he is paid to assess risk, but in his personal life he plays it safe. Experience has shown him that lonely is better than brokenhearted.

George is a wannabe architect with white man's dreadlocks. He risks his neck on the streets of Toronto every day as a bike courier, but his job is unchallenging and he chooses apathy over the risk of failure at what he really wants to do.

When George tags along with Martin to investigate the scene of his latest claim, they stumble upon a burglary in process. Now they are being hunted by an unknown adversary who will stop at nothing to get what he's after, forcing Martin and George into a dangerous game of cat and mouse in which they must risk everything.

Sample First Chapter

Martin Porchnik could see Jason from Claims approaching the Underwriting area with a yellow file in his hand and a big smirk on his face. A chill went through Martin, as it always did. A yellow file meant a property claim to be paid, and although he would ask not for whom the bell tolled, he still prayed it didn't toll for he.

"Good afternoon, 'Underwear' department. Whose day can I ruin today?" said Jason. "Anybody have a file for Ultimate Diecasting?"

Martin grimaced. He knew that name. Of all the shit files that landed in his lap, that one stuck out in his memory as one of the shittiest.

"Heads are going to roll over this one," said Jason, looking around with an evil grin.

"Not one of mine," said Darlene.

"It's not me," called Dave from his cubicle at the back.

"It's me," said Martin. Everybody looked at him and he shrugged his shoulders. What're ya gonna do?

"Is this the kind of crap you're writing down here?" Jason parked his bulk next to Martin's desk, leaning his elbow on the upper shelf. "No wonder I'm so busy paying out the big bucks. I need a dec page, underwriter boy."

He was what might be called a *big galoot*. Tallish and stocky going on fat with dark curly hair and thick eyebrows that looked angry or at least sarcastic all the time and a kind of goatee that made him look devilish.

"I haven't even issued the policy, yet," Martin said, looking away from Jason's dark eyes and back down at the yellow file that spelled possible doom. Did he have to enjoy it so much?

"Well, what's the hold up? Let's get it in gear. Do I have to come down here and crack the whip on you people?"

"It just came in last week." He dug through his pile of bound submissions waiting to be entered into the computer.

"Well, that didn't take long. What have you got for me, so I know how much I have to pay out here? Or did you want me to just give them a blank check?"

"We have a copy of their last year's dec page from the prior carrier. We bound coverage on the same basis." Well, he hadn't, but his boss had. The decs, or policy declarations, which were a listing of the coverages and wordings included, had just landed in his lap, in fact. And right away he had to hand them over to Jason so he could pay the first claim. Delightful.

"Gee, thanks. I guess it's something to go by. I'll make a copy, then."

"Can you leave me the claim file?"

"Sure. Read it and weep." Jason passed him the file and then walked away to the mail room to make his photocopy.

"Believe me, there will be tears," said Martin. He opened the file with a small feeling of self-satisfaction that he hoped wouldn't show on his face. He wasn't the one who had put them on the risk, so the blame wouldn't fully fall to him, come to that. It gave him a little get-out-of-jail-free card, but it was something he had to pretend he didn't think.

Underwriters spend most of every day considering risk. They read submissions of potential "risks," which in his department were businesses they were asked to insure. They had to assess the likelihood of having to pay out money because of some misadventure that might befall each. This would be some kind of lawsuit or a fire or a flood, etc. If you included famine, you would have almost all four horsemen of the Apocalypse. War is excluded. Underwriters choose which businesses to insure and how much money to charge so that, on average, a certain class of business would make money for the company.

The general principle of insurance is that the premiums of the many pay for the losses of the few. So they wrote up business for a whole lot of machine shops across Canada and only a few, like Ultimate Diecasting, would have a claim, and it should all even out and whatever was left over minus expenses was profit. If Martin did his job right.

So that is most of what underwriters do: consider which risks to get and which ones to keep by renewing. The rest of what they do all day is worry that the risks they have selected will have a big claim and they will be hauled onto the mat to answer for it. Consider risk and worry for a living. Nice work if you can get it. Martin shook his head and tried to concentrate on the claim report.

The date of loss was Sunday, so it had been the previous night. It was a professional hit. The line to the alarm monitoring station had been cut and the bars had been taken out along with the window, which was removed in one piece from the frame. The place was a mess and the only things missing were plans and blueprints from a current job. There would be a payout under "Valuable Papers" and a Business Interruption loss while the plans were reassembled. They would have to pay to have the line repaired and the window replaced. Nothing else stolen or destroyed. That didn't sound right.

This one had disaster written all over it from the start. He remembered when the phone call had come in from the broker, only a week ago, and it hadn't passed the sniff test from the start.

"Hi, Martin. Listen, I've got a piece of new business for you. It's a machine shop. Do you think you could do it for four thousand bucks?"

"Let me take a look at it. Put some details on paper and fax it over."

"Can't you just quote me over the phone?"

"Well, what do they make?"

"Just various metal products."

"It makes a difference to what we would charge. And I'll also need construction and protection details on the building to determine the property rate."

"It's HCB, steel deck roof, of course. What else? I'm a busy man, Martin. I don't have time to get into all this detail."

"I can't quote over the phone. I'll need something in writing. Including receipts. Do they sell to the U.S.?"

"What do you think? Everybody sells to the U.S. This is just a little risk, I don't see the big deal."

"Sales to the U.S. increases our exposure. You'd better send something over."

"I'll get back to you."

Unbelievable, was his first thought when he had hung up the phone. What do we even need underwriters for if that's the way we're going to deal in insurance? It's not about the size of the building they occupy, or the number of people they have working for them, their level of training and qualification, or who they sell their products to, or how much they sell, or how much equipment they have and what it costs to replace it, would a key piece of equipment shut down the whole shop while it was being repaired, or whether they deal in cash or credit, or how long a fire would put them out of business, or ten or fifty other things that Jed Johansen wouldn't think to ask... it's about a few thousand bucks and a quick sale. Granted, 99% of brokers were diligent and professional and trustworthy, but it was the ones like Jed Johansen that you had to watch or else you ended up in situations like the one he was currently facing.

Jed never did send in a full quote submission, he just went over Martin's head and spoke to Gerry. "Gerry" was short for Geraldine, his supervisor. She preferred the diminutive, as she didn't live in the Victorian age. She was tall and confident and blond, and Martin found her easier to deal with than his previous boss. She had an intelligent face and sharp eyes. She was impatient all the time, but kind. From looking at the pictures on the desk of her husband and kids, he imagined she was one of those busy moms who were great with their kids, efficient at work and able to keep the whole world spinning on the end of a stick.

"I just got off the phone with one of the Johansen brothers, I forget which," Gerry had said when she dropped by his desk not twenty minutes after the first phone call came through. "I bound that risk, the machine shop, for $5000. He's faxing over last year's dec page."

"Oh," he had said hesitantly. This was very bad form, indeed. Without a written submission, there were no declarations or representations from the broker upon which to rely, and as they say, a verbal contract isn't worth the paper it's printed on, ha-ha.

"I know," said Gerry. "You're not happy about it."

Martin shrugged but looked steadily at her. "Not really. I don't like him bypassing me to get to you. You can't be doing all the quotes in the department."

"I know. It was an accommodation. This is a growth year, and we have got to take it where we can get it. Besides, we can get it inspected and take care of any problems then."

"When it will be too late to get more premium if we need it."

"It'll be fine, Martin. Besides, we're $5K to the good, instead of nothing, and I want to switch the Johansens on so they'll start sending us more business."

"I understand."

Five thousand dollars? They knew nothing about security, products, contracts, warranties... it would have to be inspected, thought Martin, just as the fax had been dropped off in his IN box.

It was out in Scarberia, their nickname for Scarborough, the north east part of Toronto. It was in a moderately high crime area, big limits on tools and computers, which were the first to go. This was terrible. The Total Insured Value, or TIV, was over $4 million: the company's money on the line for who knows what. And now a claim, proving him right about his fears.

"Here's your so-called dec page back." Jason loomed by his desk again. "Can I have my file back, or were you going to take it home with you?"

"It's all yours. Why do you think thieves would break into a place like that and not steal any tools or computers? Things with a quick turn around. Those are usually the first to go, and yet these thieves ignored them."

"What do you think, oh brainy one?"

"I think they knew what they were looking for. All they took was highly specialized diagrams, plans, and design specs. What petty thief takes that?"

"Okay, so what?"

"It sounds suspicious, that's all. I think you should be careful with this one. It's bothered me since we wrote it."

"Well, thanks for the advice. I'm glad you know so much about how to do my job, because you obviously didn't know how to do yours."

"Hey, it was just a suggestion."

"I'll take it under advisement," said Jason over his shoulder.

When the adjuster had left, Martin quickly composed a fax form and fired it off to the broker: *Urgent. Insist that the insured upgrades security system to provide ULC-approved Line Security Level III protection, to prevent a recurrence of this kind of loss. Please advise ASAP how the insured intends to proceed. Our file is in abeyance pending your reply.* Then he walked over and knocked on Gerry's door.

"I know what you're going to say. I heard about it."

"I'm not going to say anything. I'm just wondering about this loss. It sounds suspicious to me. No tools or computers stolen. I still don't think we've got the whole story here, and that could mean non-disclosure. In which case we could VOID the policy *ab initio*."

"Marty. Get a grip. Bad losses happen to good underwriters. It's not your fault, and I know that. Leave the investigation to the Claims Department."

"Okay. I faxed the broker to get the line security in there or else face the hammer."

"That's all we can do. Now blow it off. You've had bigger losses than this. Besides, it builds character."

"It builds my stress level is what it does."

Leaving Gerry to her managing, he returned to his cube feeling dissatisfied. It was a mystery, that was for sure. But if he were reading this mystery in one of his detective novels, he would've put it down by now. Too boring. Something about this was not right, but it wasn't really his place to intrude. Let the Claims Department do their work. They were thorough, Jason's bluster notwithstanding. If there was something to find, they'd find it. Time to shake this off with a little caloric input.

He sat in the lunchroom quietly munching his sandwich. People came and went, mostly going back to eat at their desks, or going out for lunch. Martin was a fixture in the lunchroom: same time, same lunch, everyday. Lunch was about giving his mind a break. No magazines or TV, no conversation, no stimuli. It wasn't a Zen thing: be the sandwich, one hand clapping, or whatever. It just felt good to decompress and not think about anything, if he could manage it. Concentrate on the flavor of the sandwich and the chocolate bar.

It was the chocolate bars that gave him the spare tire, he felt, but he couldn't stop. They were an addiction. He was about 5'10", pudgy, especially around the gut. The old hairline was slowly retreating on him. At 38 years old, this was right on schedule, par for the genetic course. Thanks, Grandpa. But it didn't help that the media was always bombarding women with images of the ideal male, an ideal he couldn't live up to. Calvin Klein underwear ads had set his self-esteem back a pace, he could admit it now.

He poured another cup of coffee and went back to the cube. He tried to get back into the flow of things, but the stupid loss kept bugging him and he ended up just staring off into space for long periods of time, just trying to crack the code of this puzzle. That was how George, the bicycle courier who did their head office mail run every day found him, lost in thought at his desk.

"Hey, buddy," he said, picking up the name plate on his desk and flipping it over in his hand, tapping it on the desk. "Where's my envelope?"

"Hey, go easy on the name plate."

"Sorry about that. I don't want to break the last link to your sense of identity."

"Don't worry, my name's sewn into the backs of all my shirts."

"There you go. You'll be fine."

"All right, just let me collect it up." Martin got up out of his chair, glad for something else to think about and a chance to shoot the breeze with George. He had been doing the pick-ups at their office for a few years now and he and Martin had been out for drinks a couple of times after work. He was a good guy, despite his scary appearance. Tall, sunglasses, white man's dreadlocks, tattoos, pierced this and that... he wasn't like Martin's insurance friends, but that's what he liked about him. He was different.

"No rush. I'm ahead of schedule today," said George.

George came with him into the mail room, and talked to him as he gathered up all the envelopes, memos, and various other correspondence, packaged and weighed it all, and wrote out the receiving slip.

"So, rough day, or just hungry?" said George.

"It's been one of those days. Started out okay, but it all went quickly downhill this afternoon."

"Sounds like a pretty normal Monday."

"Yeah, I guess. Well, here it is. Signed, sealed, and now just to be delivered."

"Thanks. We going for drinks tonight, Marty?"

"Not tonight, but maybe some night this week."

"Just say the word." George put on his sunglasses as Martin walked him out through the office and over to the main door.

"Bye, George," called Janice.

"Bye." The door closed behind him.

"Whew, he's cute," said Janice. "Do you know if he's single?"

"Um, yes. I mean, yes, I do know he lives with his girlfriend."

"Too bad. Such a hottie! He can deliver my package

anytime."

Janice was a bit of a hottie herself, in that secretary way. Single secretaries exude this air of availability and eagerness, like bridesmaids. She was no supermodel, which Martin didn't mind. That type of woman intimidated Martin, anyway. They always looked so severe, so hard, with angry-looking cheek bones. He always imagined them as martial arts experts, capable of knocking his block off if he so much as looked at them.

No, she was solidly built, pretty, and seemed fun to be around. Shoulder length blond hair-product hair, small features, fair-sized bust and hips. Looking very fertile. In her early 30's, he guessed. But she would probably say no. Look at him. Why would she go out with him? He wasn't much to look at. And even if they did go out once or twice, something would happen and the whole thing would go to hell and it would hurt like the last time he got involved with someone. Then he wouldn't be able to look her in the eye at work the next morning. Always have to pretend to check out the paint job on the walls as he walked by her desk. And face the shame of a failed office romance. It wasn't worth it.

Quietly back across the office, shy glance around, wishing he could turn himself invisible, wanting to escape people's notice and make it back to the safety of his little cube without anyone confronting him. Feeling strangely persecuted, as if everyone were against him. Couldn't seem to face anything or anyone right now.

For further details or to purchase a copy of *Risk*, please visit http://markvictoryoung.com/risk/.

Praise for Mark Victor Young's writing:

"Solid writing with great dialogue and interesting characters!" – Bruce Elgin

"This is the type of book I go to when I want to unwind and forget the world." – Lucy Butler

"That voice makes us curious and keeps us reading." – Cynthia Dagnal-Myron

"A novel which moves along very nicely and captures my attention." – Ann Elizabeth Carson, author of *We all become stories*

Coming soon from Mark Victor Young
Award-winning author of *Risk*

Awkward Stages - *A book of short stories* - A girl and boy discover the difference between "Best Friends" and just friends. The summer before university is the catalyst for some strange longings. A woman wrestles with a difficult insurance claim which resonates with an event from her past. An aging writer gives a career-spanning interview with an unintended revelation. These and other great characters inhabit this collection of short stories which celebrate all of life's stages.

Praise for the stories:

"There are so many good things in this story it's hard to pick one. All I can say is I wish I had written it." - Charles Pinch

"Thanks for this potent kick of nostalgia. How important those days were to the adults we've become. Call that 'The High School Theory.'" - Beverly Akerman, author of *The Meaning of Children*

A note on Copyright and Licensing

from doing anything the license permits.

Notices:

You do not have to comply with the license for elements of the material in the public domain or where your use is permitted by an applicable exception or limitation.

No warranties are given. The license may not give you all of the permissions necessary for your intended use. For example, other rights such as publicity, privacy, or moral rights may limit how you use the material.

For any reuse or distribution, you must make clear to others the license terms of this work. The best way to do this is with a link: http://markvictoryoung.com/

Any of the above conditions can be waived if you get permission.

Full legal text available here: http://markvictoryoung.com/cc-by-nc-nd-4-0/

More info about Creative Commons here: http://creativecommons.org

www.ingramcontent.com/pod-product-compliance
Lightning Source LLC
Chambersburg PA
CBHW071124170626
46809CB00002B/487